THE MYSTERY OF THE ROSE
THE RETURN OF THE PRINCE

SUKH D. H. KHOKHAR

Book Reviews...

"Reading your book was a mystical and wonderful experience. It is the type of book you could read repeatedly and enjoy it even more. Your book is truly extraordinary. There is no doubt that your book has a potential of becoming a bestseller. One can tell the labor, dedication, and passion the author put in writing it. I'm honored to be one of the first few people who have seen your masterpiece."
— Shannon Tyler - Publishing Consultant/Writer

"A powerful story, fascinating background, and a great book!"
— Marcia Carroll – Thompson Precambrian Art Centre, MB

"Deeply engaging and totally riveting tale."
— Lila Amrita - Ashcroft, British Columbia

First published in India 2012 by Frog Books
An imprint of Leadstart Publishing Pvt Ltd
1 Level, Trade Centre
Bandra Kurla Complex
Bandra (East) Mumbai 400 051 India
Telephone: +91-22-40700804
Fax: +91-22-40700800
Email: info@leadstartcorp.com
www.leadstartcorp.com / www.frogbooks.net

Sales Office:
Unit: 122 / Building B/2
First Floor, Near Wadala RTO
Wadala (East) Mumbai 400 037 India
Phone: +91-22-24046887

US Office:
Axis Corp, 7845 E Oakbrook Circle
Madison, WI 53717 USA

Copyright © Sukh D. H. Khokhar

All rights reserved. No part of this publication may be reproduced, stored in or introduced into a retrieval system, or transmitted, in any form, or by any means (electronic, mechanical, photocopying, recording or otherwise) without the prior written permission of the publisher. Any person who does any unauthorised act in relation to this publication may be liable to criminal prosecution and civil claims for damages.

ISBN 978-93-81836-55-2

Book Editor: Oswald Pereira
Design Editor: Mishta Roy
Layout by Ryan Lynds
Cover Design by Sukh D. H. Khokhar

Typeset in Book Antiqua
Printed at Repro India Ltd, Mumbai

Price — India: Rs 245; Elsewhere: US $10

DEDICATION

Dedicated to my dad, G. S. Deepak, a poet, whose love and light sustains me — and to the Divine in me, awakened by the healing Gurbani, Krishna Consciousness, and Christ in my soul.

THE MYSTERY OF THE ROSE
The Return of the Prince

A mystical adventure of a British family under the spell of India from 1880-1945; their struggle and joy in the rebirth of India.

A magical love story of Pearly Ruby Princessa.

A tale of two nations entering an era of new beginnings, coinciding with the love story of Princessa.

ABOUT THE AUTHOR

Sukh D. H. Khokhar was born, raised and educated in India. She migrated to Canada in 1976, at age twenty-four and became a Canadian citizen in 1982. As Executive Director of the *Thompson Citizenship Council Inc.*, she became a voice of the Canadian vision of multiculturalism, and human rights; her name became synonymous with her organization (from 1985-2008), for undertaking the following initiatives spanning a period of twenty-four years into the millennium:

- A Pioneer of the *Race Relations Movement* in Northern Manitoba and a catalyst in the formation of the *City of Thompson Race Relations Committee, Racial Incidents Policy of the Mystery Lake School Division, Thompson Boys & Girls Club,* and *The Speakers' Bureau*.

- A Race Relations Expert, who worked closely with the most progressive RCMP Commissioner *Norman Inkster and Commissioner Phil Murray* at the national levels, and numerous RCMP officials at the provincial and grassroots levels to advise and assist them in diversifying the national Force and developing more culturally sensitive policing policies, procedures and programs.

- Documented the historical era of policing reforms in her book, *The Changing Face of the RCMP – The Legacy of Norman Inkster,* placed by the *Solicitor-General of Canada, Hon. Herb Grey, in his Departmental Library in Ottawa & RCMP Museum in Saskatchewan, Regina.*

- An educator, who conveyed her vision of *creating an inclusive society* by delivering successful interactive workshops on *Multicultural Communications* across Canada and by compiling, with funding support from the Government of Canada, a series of multicultural education books, namely: *Discovering Faces of Discrimination, Integrating Diversity into the Workforce, Removing Barriers to Equality, A Study of East Indian and Aboriginal Cultures,* and the *Newcomers' Guide to Thompson, Manitoba.*

- A popular community leader, she was profiled in several magazines, and recognized by the local media as the *'Northern Treasure'* and *'A Citizen of the World'* for promoting good citizenship and enhancing the quality of life of hundreds of new Canadians by designing and delivering needs-specific *Citizenship Orientation and English as a Second Language Training Programs* and for raising the platform of *Anti-Racism* to international levels by continuously responding to the challenges of multiculturalism and human rights by writing powerful newspaper articles, hosting Radio Programs and coordinating multicultural concerts and youth empowerment programs.

- Nominated and Awarded *Governor General's Commemorative Medal – Canada 125 Years of Confederation (for making significant contributions to Canada and fellow Canadians)*, and several community development awards at the provincial and local levels including the *City of Thompson Race Relations Award.*

Author Website: www.mysteryoftherose.com.

ACKNOWLEDGEMENTS

Someone once told me that there is a book in all of us; some of us go deeper into our thoughts and bring it out.

Even though I believe this book was conceived in my mind and written from a higher source, it would never have seen the daylight without the intellectual support from a remarkable person named Marcia Carroll, who came into my life like a breath of fresh air, became my mentor, and helped me deliver it.

She owns the "Precambrian Art Centre" in Thompson, Manitoba—a sanctuary and an awesome display gallery for the northern artists from the east and west. She was the first one to see the potential in my paintings and display them at her gallery. She helped me to synthesise my images, concepts, and thoughts, which came to me as multiple pieces of a puzzle; much like the forgotten pieces of memories from another life time.

Marcia, who once worked for the American President Lyndon B. Johnson at the White House, introduced me to a very gifted graphic artist named Ryan Lynds, who works at the local newspaper next door to her. His patience in going through the several drafts is amazing. Ryan photographed many of my illustrations, which you will see in my upcoming illustrated eBook, *Dark Mystery - I'm A Demon. I'm A Ghost*

The encouragement from my cousin bother, J. Deepak, the custodian of our family history and archives, and from my former team-worker at the Manitoba Human Rights Commission, Liz Bennett, was phenomenal. The two special persons in the background have always been my husband and my son.

This book is a tribute to the memory of my mother, a great story-teller, and my father, G. S. Deepak, a gifted singer, song writer, and dancer, who traveled across the world and met with world leaders to promote cross cultural understanding through music and dance. He was the pioneer of the popular Bhangra dance in Punjab and formed the first Folk Dancers of Punjab Cultural Group in 1955.

Accompanied by his movie-star brother, Manohar Deepak who later married the famous Indian screen dancer — Madhumati (my favorite aunt), my father performed on the world stage with his two brothers as the back-up singers, dancers and musicians.

He performed for the Chairman, Mao Zedong (Tse-Tung), Premier Zhou En-Lai in China, Ho Chi-Minn in Vietnam, Emperor Haile Selasse in Ethiopia, Senator Bobby Kennedy in the U.S., Prime Minister Jawahar Lal Nehru, Rashtrapati Rajindra Prasad and the Nawabs and Maharajas of the princely states in India.

Bobby Kennedy, who was campaigning in 1967, was so impressed with my father's ability to hold the audience captive with his voice, energy, and movements that he offered him a job after the performance. My dad accepted the offer, but was killed in a car accident in 1968, before getting back to the U.S. Bobby Kennedy was one of the world leaders who sent a touching letter of condolences at his demise.

Though he died young, his closing words at the concerts still echo in my ears and help me carry on the flame.

"Ladies and gentlemen let us build bridges through music and dance, because the graceful movements of music and dance make the soul graceful."

Sincerely,
Sukh D. H. Khokhar

ABOUT THE MYSTERIES OF MY LIFE...

My life's going to last as long as lasts my book, its pages.
A part of me will die forever; a part of me will live for ages.

Like petals the book unfolds my story, steeped in mysteries. Everything meaningful in my life always began and ended in mystery. Early in my life, I became aware of the sixth sense I had about people, places, and things. An invisible *Third Eye* made me visualise images beyond sight and guided me.

I grew up with a recurring dream, haunting the days and nights of my life. Someone whispered in my dream prophesying that my life's path would be filled with demons, because I was born of a powerful union between a soft-hearted angel and a cold-hearted demon. No wonder I tiptoed through every walk of life followed by a *Demon*—running straight into the arms of an *Angel*, waiting to rescue me at the end of every road.

All my life I was mystified deeply by a strange pattern of curses woven into every blessing of my life. It was hard to differentiate when a blessing revolved into a curse and when a curse evolved into a blessing. I always found myself at the center of a fierce battle between the two powerful forces surrounding me and fighting to take control of me.

Looking back, I realize that no one could have prepared me for the events of my life, which culminated in a saga of a million nightmares. I could not comprehend the strength of the higher source until one day, right before my eyes, the entire physical phenomenon turned metaphysical; the matter turned spirit and my deadly *Demon* turned *Divine*. The very demon that relentlessly had pursued me since my conception had turned divine—melting all my regrets into thin air.

I no longer look at my nightmares as curses, but as magnificent adventures that brought me closer to the higher source. My pursuit to discover the true essence of my life led me to search through the very depths of my soul, until I found myself face to face with my Demon and my Angel Divine, experiencing the depth of the mystical spell that befell me years ago.

This book traces the journey of my life through the enchanted land of India, where I was born and died and was reborn. I was destined to discover and break the power of a spell that liberated my family from a century-old curse and, in the process, liberated my *Demon* — my *Tormentor!*

> *I'm eternally grateful to my angel — my holy man,*
> *who ushered me in this magnificent heaven,*
> *raising me from my ashes again.*

> *Ma 'sodaii hu or mamnoon hu,*
> *us bandaparvar ka, jis mohsan ne,*
> *is muflis ko, Yeh jannat atta kar di.*

My stunning journey of self-discovery made me realize that Shangri-La lies within our reach. We can achieve it by connecting our heart and mind to our soul. May this book help you find your own Shangri-La!

Pearly Ruby Princessa
08/08/1950

CONTENTS

Chapter 1: The Mystery Surrounding Pearly – India, 1887   17
Birth of Pearly – Death of Symoune
Encounter with two Strangers – The Trap
Funeral of Symoune – Meeting with Swami Krishna

Chapter 2: The Aristocrats of the Fort   32
Aristocrats of the Fort – The Birth of Twins
Coronation of King Edward VII – The Preparations
Coronation of King Edward VII – The Historical Look

Chapter 3: The Coronation Week – India, 1902   49
Coronation of King Edward VII – Meeting with Prince
Coronation of King Edward VII – Meeting with Mystery Man
Coronation of King Edward VII – State Durbar

Chapter 4: The Royal Fundraiser   69
Fundraiser 'Fantasy' – Family Secret
Princessa and the Rose – Portrait of Pearly
Fundraiser and the Storm – Mystery of the Birthmark
General Scott Reception – Departure of Prince

Chapter 5: The Ghost of Ashley   98
Reception of the Elite – Ghost of Ashley
Ghost and the Fog – Face of the Hidden One
Door to the Past – Stunning Revelation

Chapter 6: The Haunting   118
Shadow and the Ghost – Haunting of Ashley
Shadow and the Ghost – Haunting of Menaka
Shadow and the Ghost – Haunting of Pearly

Chapter 7: The Search   **141**
The Search – Journey into the Dark
Return of General Scott – The Homecoming
Return of Mystery Woman – The Resolution

Chapter 8: The Return of Priya   **161**
Party at Priya Mansion – Return of Priya
Ghost of Symoune – Birth of Priyanka
Symoune Family Curse – Legacy of Demons

Chapter 9: The End of the Aristocrats   **182**
Mystical Wedding – Curse of the Blackbuck
Fall of Fort Priya – Stunning Proposal
End of the Aristocrats – Marriage of Priya

Chapter 10: The Death and Rebirth of Pearly   **199**
Obsession of Pearly – Mystery of Suzana
Mystery of Priya – Legend of Suttee
Death of Pearly – Rebirth of Pearly

Chapter 11: The Return of the Prince – 1910   **217**
Unfolding of the Divine – The Restoration
Festival of Holi – Return of the Prince
Marriage with Prince – Double Wedding

Chapter 12: The Final Episode – India, 1945   **234**
The Great War, 1914-18 – Promise of Swaraj
Disappearance of Prince, 1935 – The Accident
Return of the Prince, 1945 – Mystery of the Rose

Chapter One
Mystery Surrounding the Birth of Pearly

BIRTH OF PEARLY RUBY BOONE
DEATH OF SYMOUNE RUBY BOONE

In the body I sleep; in the soul I rise.
A part of me renews; a part of me dies.

Since the moment of her conception, a mystery surrounded the life of baby Boone, and all those who encountered her. The family and friends prayed with bated breath around the clock, until the hour she finally arrived.

Symoune had never looked more anxious than she did on the eve of her baby's arrival. There was something mystical about the way she looked that evening with her honey blonde hair framed around her face, her blue melancholy eyes apprehensive and her ivory skin translucent.

She was a stunning sight, lying breathless in anticipation on her mahogany bed, clad in a fresh, long sleeved, white chiffon gown and her favourite string of pearls and rubies shimmering around her neck. The necklace was her husband Daniel's last gift to Symoune, before he died seven months ago, following a hunting accident.

Dr. Ashley's heart went out to Symoune, her beloved sister-in-law, the fragile creature she had grown to care for so deeply during the difficult months of her pregnancy. Symoune's condition had become more complicated after the tragic death of her husband, Daniel Augustus Boone. Her heart was completely shattered.

It took all her strength and will power to hold on to her pregnancy. Each day of her expectancy became eventful as her moods became increasingly unpredictable. Her emotions went from ecstasy to despair in a matter of minutes. Symoune often reminded Ashley of a hunted tigress struggling to hide her fatal wounds, resigned to her fate, yet trying to prolong the inevitable. Symoune took great pains to bond with her unborn child. She talked to her daily. She played the piano for her. She sang songs for her and painted imaginary portraits of her. Sometimes she laughed and sometimes she cried, while thinking of her. She became so immersed in her unborn that they became two entities and one soul.

"Ashley, oh Ashley, hurry—" whispered Symoune weakly, squeezing her hand.

"Just relax, honey. Breathe deeply. Here you go. One, two, and three," said Ashley, steadying her shaking hands.

All through her medical career, Dr. Ashley Rose had never felt her hands shake. However, tonight was not like any other night. So much had happened within the last two years that she had had lost count of the amazing incidents. Ashley had come to India with high hopes. The idea of opening her own clinic and being reunited with her one and only brother, Daniel, and sister-in-law Symoune, were like dreams come true. Little did she know that in less than two years her brother would be gone from their lives forever and her sister-in-law would be struggling with death!

"There, there, Symoune—take heart," whispered Dr. Ashley, disengaging Symoune's fingers from her wrist and reassuring her.

All eyes turned moist as the shrill cries of the baby filled the room with the announcement of her arrival at midnight. Weak and spent, Symoune held out her arms. A gust of wind stole through the window and in one sweeping moment, blew out all the candles. Annie, Dr. Ashley's nurse, rushed to the window to pull aside the curtains. With hungry eyes, Symoune faced the baby—glistening like a diamond in the moonlight.

"My long awaited child, my flesh and blood," murmured Symoune, her voice raw with emotion. "Here we meet for the first and the last time."

She clutched the baby to her breast with one hand, removing her necklace with the other hand. Gathering every ounce of her strength, she slipped the necklace around the baby's neck. She lifted the baby up in the air and whispered:

"I, Symoune Ruby Boone, name you, my child, Pearly Ruby Boone."

Symoune appeared totally ecstatic for a second. Her moments of ecstasy were rare and precious. She savoured every happy moment as if it were an eternity.

"Tonight you deliver me from my *Demons*," Symoune's voice cracked with pain. "You are my deliverer; you are my dawn. How shall I thank you, my little one?"

Her demeanour became prophetic as she alluded, "If only you knew how it grieves me to tell you that tonight is the night when the family curse befalls you. While your arrival sets me free, my *Demon* is waiting in the dark to follow you as he had followed me and all my ancestors."

"Though it is predicted that your life path will be filled with demons," she said, adding, "It's also predicted that you will be protected by your soul. You may be little but your soul is the timeless, ageless, and all-knowing part of you. It'll remind you of my last message at the right time," wailed Symoune.

"Remember me by my legacy of blessings and not by my legacy of demons. I've breathed into your soul a secret gift—the gift of being reborn each time you're destroyed. Turn inwards, when you find yourself at a crossroad. Your soul will awaken the angel in you, who'll help you to be reborn."

"Never give in to despair, my baby, no matter how miserable the family curse makes you feel," she continued, taking a deep breath. "Stay connected with the angel in you because it's he who will help you deliver the ghosts of our past. Your ancestors are depending on you to free them. You're destined to be the dusk of the demon at the turn of the century."

Dr. Ashley stood aghast in disbelief. The touch of finality in Symoune's voice shocked her. With teary eyes, she watched Symoune reach under her pillow and pull out a large golden envelope bearing her name, *Ashley Rose*, scribbled in Symoune's handwriting. It read: *"For Your Eyes Only—My Last Will."*

Ashley hesitated.

"Ashley, hand me that red box on the dresser," she said, breast-feeding her baby for one precious time.

"I must engrave an eternal gift in my baby's flesh. C'mon, my time is running out..."

Ashley smiled faintly. She knew Symoune had loved tattoos

and had planned to put one on Pearly ever since she was conceived.

"What is it gonna be?" Ashley asked, in a dream-like state, handing the box.

"A necklace of pearls and rubies. Please close the door," she replied.

"Do you think you can handle it alone?" Ashley asked, wiping her eyes.

Symoune nodded without taking her eyes off the baby.

Ashley looked up at the sound of footsteps. A sense of relief swept over her as she saw Father Elliot waiting outside the door. She felt she had never needed him more than she needed him at that minute. She walked with him to the porch feeling weak in her knees. They waited outside until Symoune was ready.

"Father Elliot," Symoune held out her trembling arms. She had been watching the door impatiently.

Father Elliot rushed to Symoune's side, placing his rosary and Bible neatly on the table beside her.

"Congratulations, God bless you and the baby, Symoune!" He held out his arms for the baby.

Father Elliot had become a rock of strength for Symoune and Ashley during the period of Danny's injury, which predated a long period of bed rest and later his death. He had visited Symoune every morning. He came in before breakfast every day, with a fresh rose and his Bible clutched under his elbow. Ashley often joined them at the conclusion of the sermon to pray for the mother and the unborn child. Both Symoune and Ashley had become tremendously fond of Father Elliot and leaned on his strength through their tragic circumstances.

Overwhelmed by emotions and fatigue, Ashley sank into the armchair by the bed and closed her eyes. She started to drift over the faint sound of Annie's skirt rustling around the room and Father Elliot's voice baptising the baby and praying by Symoune's bed.

Ashley felt herself slipping slowly from a hazy awareness into a dream state. She dreamed of her dead brother, Daniel. He seemed so real. Ashley had never seen him look happier. Symoune was standing beside him, smiling. She was placing the baby in Daniel's arms. Daniel was caressing the baby and beaming with joy. Symoune was murmuring, "Everything's going to be all right. We are going to be so happy together . . . together . . . together."

Her dream suddenly turned into a nightmare. A ghastly figure broke into the room and snatched the baby from Daniel's arms. Symoune wailed in terror. Daniel frantically followed the figure and Symoune collapsed in horror. Ashley woke up with a start, her heart thumping. The room was in turmoil. It took her a while to take in the scene. Father Elliot was trying to comfort the crying baby. Symoune was lying motionless. Annie was standing by her side, sobbing. A sense of horror swept over Ashley as she started to stand up. She heard Father Elliot's voice, stunningly quiet, as if it came from a far off place.

"Ashley, Symoune is gone," he said. "She died a few minutes ago. We tried to wake you."

Ashley felt as if she had been struck by lightning. She looked around the room in total disbelief, as it spun around her. She fainted.

ENCOUNTER WITH TWO STRANGERS
THE TRAP

*One phase is over; another phase sets in.
And the mysterious tale of woes begins.*

Ashley found herself drifting in and out of sleep all through the evening. Her mind kept going backwards towards Symoune's bedchamber, hoping against hope to find her alive. A gentle tap on her shoulder brought her back to reality. She opened her eyes and saw Annie leaning over her bed with a look of urgency in her voice.

"Dr. Ashley, I hate to disturb you at a time like this, but I need you in the clinic. It's an emergency."

"Annie, I don't think I can see any patients tonight. Could you not handle it, please?"

"No, I can't, Dr. Ashley. There's a young girl waiting for you in the clinic with her mother. The girl is barely an adult. She's in labour. There could be complications. I cannot handle the situation. The girl looks like she's going to die. We cannot possibly move her. Her mother is in shock. They are begging to see you. Please, please!"

"Fine, please tell them I'll be there shortly," said Ashley, getting out of bed swiftly and disappearing into the washroom. As she passed the hallway, she looked back at Symoune's room. Her eyes welled up with tears and she struggled to gain her composure. She entered the clinic, finding herself face to face with an elderly woman, who rose from her seat, looking distraught.

"Hi, I am Dr. Ashley Rose. Please forgive me if I seem disoriented," she said, smoothing a strand of dishevelled hair from her forehead. "We had a death in the family earlier today. What can I possibly do for you?"

The elderly woman straightened her shoulders nervously and moved forward to shake hands. The woman appeared to be in her late fifties. She was dressed in a silver silk outfit and heavy gold jewellery. Dr. Ashley found her deeply engaging eyes disturbing.

"My—my daughter . . ." she muttered, skipping the introductions.

Ashley felt apprehensive as she turned to examine a breathtakingly slender and beautiful woman in labour. A number of questions arose in the doctor's head. For starters, she had never seen these two women in her clinic before. Secondly, they looked as though they belonged to an upper-class society and were loaded with money.

Why had they chosen to sneak into an English clinic to deliver their baby in the middle of the night?

Dr. Ashley's professionalism overtook her frenzy when she started going through the motions of a very difficult and painful delivery. The elderly woman stayed by her daughter's side throughout, occasionally throwing her hands up in the air in what looked like a gesture of crying and praying in the same breath. At 12:00 p.m. Ashley and Annie delivered a tiny, beautiful baby girl. As Ashley turned to say goodbye, leaving her patient and her mother in the good hands of her nurse, Annie, the elderly woman took her by surprise.

"Thank you, Dr. Ashley. Please, I need to discuss something with you in complete confidence."

"Sure, go ahead. Please understand that anything you have to discuss will have to be discussed in front of my nurse. I will not have any secrets from my nurse," replied Ashley.

"In that case, I implore that this conversation remains among the three of us forever. As much as we would like to, we cannot stay here a minute longer. We must leave before daybreak and before anyone sees us. Our coach is waiting outside."

"No, No, No! I cannot allow you to move the baby and her mother," Ashley cut in, interrupting the older woman vehemently. "The lives of your daughter and her newborn could be in complete jeopardy. They are not fit to travel under any circumstances."

"My nurse has been directed to prepare a recovery room," Ashley added, "You're welcome to stay here. Now if you'll forgive me, I really must go—"

"Please, Dr. Ashley," the elderly woman confronted Ashley as she rose to leave. "We aren't going to take the baby with us," she said, pulling out an envelope full of cash from her vest pocket and placing it on the table.

"Why not?" Ashley narrowed her eyes.

"In fact, we can never take the baby with us. Our lives will be in complete jeopardy if our family finds out that my daughter was pregnant and delivered a baby. No one must breathe a word of this to anyone. My daughter and I must entreat you to please find some good adoptive parents for this child. We will pay all the expenses."

"No. I can't do it and I won't do it! I'm going through a personal tragedy of my own. I cannot and will not deal with a messy situation," remarked Dr. Ashley, defending her position.

"Dr. Ashley, you're the kindest and most charitable person in this area. That's the reason we approached you. Please do this kind deed for us. We will forever be indebted to you."

"I can't," replied Dr. Ashley, shaking her head. She was stunned by the request.

"Please, money is not a problem for us. Please find a good noble adoptive parent for this child. We'll pay you more than you can imagine for each day this little baby stays here," she pleaded.

"Please, our lives and family honour are at stake," she said, wiping her tears until her eyes became swollen and red. "My daughter, Saya, has been living with me for a few months due to the difficulties in her marriage. She has made a terrible mistake by trusting someone close to her husband, an English gentleman. Her husband must never find out that she has been unfaithful to him."

The elderly woman started sobbing bitterly. Annie rushed to her side with a handkerchief.

"Saya must return to her husband soon. If her husband finds out that she was an adulteress he will kill her. He'll never accept this child. This child must be put up for adoption. I'm trying to save the child and her mother. I'll pay handsomely to the potential adoptive parents. No one needs to know."

The woman spoke with such humility that Ashley stood aghast.

"May I borrow your pen for a moment, please?" she asked, moving towards the writing desk.

Annie nodded.

"That's my address. I can be reached most discreetly," she said, scribbling a few lines on the blank card and tucking the card neatly on the desk. She took a deep breath and added, "Please let us leave now. I will continue to monitor the situation and keep sending money. Please, do not stop us. I beg you and thank you for your kindness."

Feeling too weak to argue, Ashley left the room quietly, leaving the sleeping baby in the care of Annie. Annie rushed forward to assist the patient with her handbag, long veil, and shawl. Saya took her time, getting up timidly with downcast eyes and trembling hands. She murmured a polite 'thank you' under her breath. The elderly woman thanked Annie before picking up the prescription from the table and wrapping an arm around her daughter's waist to provide support. Annie watched them walk to the carriage.

The coachman jumped to open the door as the women approached the carriage. He stood waiting until they were seated. He then secured the door and moved on, cracking his whip on the horses. Annie stood transfixed by the window with the newborn crying frantically in her arms, until the carriage disappeared into the dark. With her free arm she picked up the note from the table, reading carefully, before dating it Jan. 1, 1887. She catalogued it alphabetically in a box marked 1887-1888.

The card read: Mrs. Chandra Mukhi Thakur - 55 Kalyani Bhawan, Gulam Ali Street, Banaras.

FUNERAL OF SYMOUNE RUBY BOONE
MEETING WITH SWAMI KRISHNA

*I'm as grateful to my demon, as I am to my holy man,
whose relentless pursuit so intrigued my Master,
that I was redeemed by the Master himself.*

Saying farewell to Symoune was one of the most difficult things Ashley ever had to do in her life. A million emotions tore at her heart as she bent over the coffin to take in every detail of the heavenly person, whose presence had dominated two decades of her life. Symoune and Ashley were childhood friends. They were always there for each other all their lives to the extent that they took each other for granted and were proud of it. What was the basis of their friendship? Ashley was not sure.

Symoune and Ashley were poles apart in terms of looks, temperament, and personality. Symoune had often wished she had Ashley's intellect and Ashley had wished she had Symoune's fire and beauty. Perhaps it was the case of two opposites living in complete harmony. Symoune was the unmistakable queen of intrigue, drama, and glamour and Ashley was the epitome of simplicity, predictability, and plainness. Perhaps they were each other's missing links. They were kind and caring friends, who felt like sisters, and, by a stroke of luck, became sisters-in-law.

"Our Lord Jesus Christ and Saviour, we're gathered here to pray for the dearly departed soul of Symoune Ruby Boone — the devoted wife of deceased, Daniel Augustus Boone; sister-in-law of Dr. Ashley Augustus Rose and a friend of all of us in this room and beyond."

Father Elliot took a long pause before continuing, "Shortly after midnight last night, Symoune's soul crossed the threshold of life and moved into the realm of eternal peace by the divine grace," he said, eulogising Symoune.

"*What an eloquent eulogy,*" *whispered Ashley, beneath her breath.*

Despite the depth of her grief, Ashley couldn't help notice the look of peace over Symoune's face, as she lay in the coffin. She looked like an angel asleep. Perhaps Symoune was to find in death the peace which had eluded her all her life. The thought momentarily warmed Ashley's heart.

"Dr. Ashley, please accept our heartfelt condolences at the death of your precious Symoune. We hope that you take comfort in the thought that Symoune has left you with a beautiful baby girl," said Menaka Partap Singh, the next door neighbour, a patient, and a friend.

Menaka and Major Partap Singh were known as the *Aristocrats of the Fort*. Major Partap Singh was a legendary figure and had recently joined the rank of A.D.C. of *'His Highness, the Maharaja of Jodhpur'* of the state of Rajisthan. Their residence in Simla was seasonal. They came to live in Simla every four months in the summer with the Maharaja. Dr. Ashley was the Maharaja's family physician in Simla. The two families socialised regularly over dinners and parties. Menaka was also expecting a baby that was due any time. This was her fourth try. She had three miscarriages, one after the other. She was so afraid to lose this baby that she took every possible preventive step to minimise the chance of another miscarriage. The continuity of her marriage depended on this child, as there were rumours that the Major was under great pressure from his family to remarry, should his wife be unable to produce an offspring from the second marriage. After each miscarriage, Menaka went into long periods of depression. This was a very critical time for the entire Partap Singh family. They needed Dr. Ashley to be in sound emotional and physical health for the sake of Menaka and took great pains in helping her with the funeral arrangements for Symoune.

A gentle tap on Ashley's shoulder made her swing around. It was Major Partap Singh. He gently pulled Ashley towards the chairs. Taking her one hand in his and Menaka's in the other, he sat down facing them.

"Menaka's right, Dr. Ashley," he said, looking directly

into her eyes. "God never takes away anything without giving something in return. It appears that Symoune wanted to go home as much as the God wanted her to come home. She has left you with a beautiful life-long gift in Pearly. View this gift as a new beginning, rather than an ending," he paused, then continued:

"My wife and Symoune became best friends because of their pregnancies. Your Pearly and our unborn baby will bring our families closer."

"It's amazing how my life has changed dramatically after Menaka's pregnancy," he said. "There's nothing in the world more precious to both of us than this baby. Perhaps you don't know how empty and meaningless our lives had become before Menaka became pregnant."

He paused.

"The death of my former wife, Karuna, my deep disappointment with my son, Pooran, the process of re-adjusting to the new marriage, three miscarriages in a row and the thought of having no one to carry on my legacy had totally shattered my heart. But now, we have hope. This child will give us a new hope as Pearly will bring to you."

Ashley nodded in agreement.

"Your Pearly and our baby will bring us closer. You must take heart and focus on this precious gift. We're always here for you, day and night. In fact, I will make sure that I look in on you on daily for all the days we are in Simla," promised the Major.

Ashley felt her bitterness start to melt. Hope has magical qualities.

"*You change the mind and you change the man. It's wonderful to have such healing people around,*" thought Ashley, counting her blessings: "*Annie, Father Elliot, Major Partap Singh and Menaka, whose turbulent life was a true reflection of Symoune's life.*"

"Thank you for your kind words," said Ashley, hugging them and waving a warm goodbye.

The crowd slowly started to disperse. Ashley walked to the window for some fresh air. Her eyes fell over a striking gentleman, walking gracefully towards the main door. He was tall and slender with flowing hair. He seemed to be floating in air, dressed in peach loosely fitting silk attire, with a black and white garland of roses wrapped around one wrist. Their eyes locked for a split second. Ashley stood motionless.

"Symoune was right. There's something stunning about his looks," she thought, *wistfully.*

He blinked and smiled, approaching the church door.

Ashley smiled back, turning quickly to welcome him.

"You're Swami Gopi Krishna from the Krishna Ashram," Ashley spoke in Hindi. It was surprising how quickly Ashley had learned to speak in Hindi. Her ability to speak fluently in the native Hindi language had become an asset with her patients. They felt instantly at ease with her.

"Yes, Dr. Ashley — Ashley Rose? I'm not sure how to address you." He hesitated.

"Dr. Ashley is fine. No one calls me Dr. Rose in India." Ashley smiled back shyly.

"I regret meeting you in such a tragic circumstance!" Swami Krishna spoke in English.

"Symoune was a dear friend. We had many good times together. She spoke very highly of you," he said with a touch of a smile on an otherwise sombre face.

Ashley nodded engagingly.

"I've come to pay my respects to Symoune and am here for you and the baby if you need me," said Swami Krishna, stopping for a moment before walking towards the coffin.

Ashley stood in disbelief. Everyone knew that Swami Krishna never called on anyone. Not much was known about this man except that he was a wealthy, reclusive man who was revered by the people for his great knowledge of the scriptures, Ayurvedic medicines, and his charitable activities.

He was in his early thirties. He lived in a cottage at the foothills of Simla with his mother and father. They were devoted to the running of Krishna Ashram founded by their forefathers many years ago. The Ashram included Krishna Temple, Krishna Ayurvedic Oshdhaliya (Medical Centre), Krishna School for the Blind, Krishna Handicrafts, and Krishna Shelter (for the Orphans).

Symoune had met Swami Krishna quite accidentally at one time. She had sneaked into his garden during one of her long evening walks down the hill. She had felt compelled to pluck

one beautiful flower from his amazing nursery of black and white roses, the likes of which she had never seen before. As Symoune crawled in through the broken fence, she stumbled on Swami Krishna sitting in a meditative yoga posture, chanting:
OMMMMMMMMMMMMMMMM
Ommmm Nama Vasudeva. Ommmmm
"I wonder what Om Nama Vasudeva means?" she murmured, beneath her breath.
"It means, I surrender to the divine in me," he replied, opening his eyes.
That was the beginning of their brief spiritual journey together. Symoune had started gathering new insights into the life of Lord Krishna, becoming gradually a Krishna devotee. During the times when Daniel was away on his travels around India, Symoune would sneak into the Krishna Temple to visit Swami and his parents and would come home with a bunch of beautiful black and white roses, which Ashley now saw around Swami's wrist. The black roses are so rare that Symoune used to take extra care to make them survive longer in the vase.
"Ashley, look how beautiful the black roses seem with the white. Swami has a garden full of them. He grows them himself and calls them, the meeting of the darkness with light, night with the day, just like the darkness and light within our souls," Ashley recalled Symoune words.
"I pray to you, Lord Krishna, for the soul of Symoune Ruby Boone, who's making her way towards her sanctuary, her final resting place after a difficult, lonely and thorn-filled journey," said Swami in his magical voice.
Tears rolled down Ashley's eyes.
"O! Krishna, help Symoune find peace by freeing her from the cycle of life and death. I promise to stand by the family in times of their needs," murmured Swami, placing the garland of black and white roses neatly across Symoune's chest.   He swiftly walked out of the door, raising his right hand high in the air, murmuring, "I will always be there for you, Dr. Ashley, if you need me. May Lord Krishna bless you and little Pearly."
Ashley stood rooted to the ground, staring blankly at the swinging door and the extraordinary man who slipped past it.

Chapter Two
The Aristocrats of the Fort

ARISTOCRATS OF THE FORT
BIRTH OF TWINS

Two strangers in disguise strolled in.
Two-fold treasures appeared in twins.

When Father Elliot escorted Ashley home, her only thought was to run upstairs to the nursery and gather little Pearly in her arms and cuddle with her all night.

"It's been an amazing day," thought Ashley. "It has ended far differently than I had anticipated. I had felt completely crushed at the beginning of the day. Surprisingly, all the dark clouds have melted away. I'm beginning to feel calm again."

"Ashley, there's something much bigger going on here than you know," Father Elliot's words echoed in her ears.

"What do you mean?"

"Symoune has always been your main concern. Maybe she's come back to re-live another life with you in the form of little Pearly. You must start bonding with the baby before she starts to wonder why her mother has suddenly stopped communicating with her."

"Father Elliot's right. Pearly has to be my main concern. The baby needs to feel safe and loved," echoed Ashley, remembering the loving bond Symoune had developed with her baby over her difficult nine months of pregnancy.

"Rest in peace, sweet Symoune," Ashley murmured, tearfully. "I promise to raise Pearly as though you were with her every step of the way." The thought warmed her heart. Ashley rushed upstairs. She was only halfway up when the sound of the telephone made her jump.

"Dr. Ashley, I'm glad you're home. I was worried that you

would be held up at the church." Ashley was struck by the urgency in Major Partap Singh's voice.

"What's wrong, Major?" asked Ashley, feeling apprehensive.

"Menaka's in labour. We're heading to your clinic." He rang off, with a touch of nervousness.

A look of surprise crossed Ashley's face. Annie rushed to the clinic to prepare a room for Menaka. Ashley ran upstairs for a quick wash. She stole a glance at the two babies sleeping snug with each other before heading to the clinic.

Annie had laid out the appliances neatly on the table by the bed. Menaka's mother, Menakshi was nervously massaging her daughter's back between the cycles of pains; this made Menaka scream desperately. Though her feet and arms were tied to the post, she had still managed to slide a corner of the bed-sheet between her teeth to control her screams.

"There's something wrong. I can't feel my baby . . . move," Menaka screamed.

Big beads of sweat broke out on Ashley's forehead and her hands started to shake uncontrollably, when the newborn failed to cry in response to the gentle tapping. Ashley realized with a sense of shock that it was a case of a stillborn baby. Her first instinct was to protect her patient who was lying unconscious in the pool of blood. She felt helpless observing the lifeless baby in her arms.

"The baby looks every bit perfect," she noticed remorsefully. *"She has perfect eyes, perfect ears, perfect nose, beautiful hands, and lovely toes; except for the fact that the infant is lifeless."*

"Oh, God, the cruel hand of the fate has snatched the fourth baby from Menaka," burst out Menakshi, crying bitterly. "Major Singh would be devastated. My daughter's life has been ruined."

"Where's my baby? I want to see . . . my baby," wailed Menaka.

"Your baby is fine. She's being examined," replied Annie, her voice quiet and reassuring.

With tears streaming down her cheeks, Ashley stepped behind the curtains in the back of the room to examine the baby more closely. From across the room, she watched Annie whisper in Menakshi's ear. Menakshi stopped crying and became alert.

Annie approached Ashley.

"Dr. Ashley . . ." she said, after an awkward pause.

"Yes?" replied Ashley, with an uncertain look.

"I may have found a solution to this tragic situation—" she stopped to clear her throat.

"Go on."

"Menaka may not survive this blow," Annie stammered.

"I agree!"

"This tragedy would tear the family apart," whispered Annie. She added. "The rumors of the third marriage of Major Partap Singh might become a reality."

"I'm listening."

"I sort of . . . mentioned to Menakshi that we happen to have a beautiful healthy baby girl in our house waiting to be adopted. She jumped at the idea—" Annie stopped abruptly.

Ashley's eyebrows shot up in surprise. She glanced in Menakshi's direction.

"Dr. Ashley, Menaka's condition is worsening," she said. "Her fate's in your hands now. You can change this tragedy into a blessing for this family. Time is running out . . ."

Ashley did not reply. She needed to weigh the matter rationally before jumping to a hasty decision.

"Dr. Ashley, think about the consequences of this tragedy on Menaka. Please let Menaka have the abandoned baby. You can turn this sad situation into a happy one."

"I cannot rush into any hasty decision," she replied impatiently.

"Please, Dr. Ashley—" Annie pressed on.

"Stop, Annie," Dr. Ashley was adamant. "This might have serious implications. Go to Menaka and tell her that I am still examining the baby."

Annie's jaw dropped. Menakshi rose from her seat with a determined look.

"Please listen to Annie," she said, approaching Ashley. "It's a miracle that God has sent a beautiful baby. We will adopt her," Menakshi murmured emphatically.

Ashley's eyes grew large with surprise.

"Dr. Ashley, please do not hesitate. We'll take the baby at once and will raise her as our own. We will keep it private. I promise never to breathe a word about this to anyone," she declared. "What are we going to do with the dead baby?" demanded Ashley.

"Well, we will make up a story. Something . . ."

Menakshi started to whisper in Annie's ear. Annie nodded. Menakshi cleared her throat.

"Dr. Ashley, please let me tell my family that Menaka has given birth to twins. One baby has died and the other is alive and healthy by the grace of God," pleaded Menakshi.

Ashley turned silent. She left the room to think quietly while the tension mounted.

"It seems like a sensible thing to do. It would be a win-win situation," she thought.

Ashley needed to decide quickly because many lives depended on it, yet she kept dragging her feet until a loud bang on the door interrupted her thoughts.

Annie opened the door. There stood at the door, Major Partap Singh with a train of friends and servants carrying colorful balloons and boxes of sweets and gifts. He leaped towards the bed like a lion. Annie froze with horror. A hush fell over the room.

Ashley had to act quickly. She jumped to Menaka's side and started wiping the tiny beads of sweat on her forehead. She heard herself saying, "Menaka, I bring you good tidings. You, my friend, have just given birth to a beautiful, healthy, bouncing baby girl."

"Hooray!"

Congratulations poured in.

"Thank you, Dr. Ashley, and thank you, Annie. You've given me the greatest news of my life. I can't wait to see my baby," he said, caressing his wife's cheeks, flushed with nerves.

"Annie, would you kindly fetch the baby?" said Ashley, in a trembling voice.

Annie shot out of the room like a rocket. The crowd cheered in jubilation. The atmosphere turned festive.

Menaka and Menakshi clung to each other in a tight embrace. Major Partap Singh took over the center stage.

"My beautiful Menaka," he said. "I will never underestimate you again. Kindly forgive my past mistakes. From now onwards, you will be the queen of my heart. How did you ever know that I had wanted a baby girl?" he demanded, stroking her cheek tenderly.

Menaka let out a visible sigh of relief. She smiled nervously with downcast eyes and became totally calm. Ashley had never seen her look prouder and prettier than she did at the moment. Everyone leaped with joy when the smiling Annie returned with the baby wrapped in a blanket.

"Here's the moment we've been waiting for," remarked Major Partap Singh, raising the baby high in his arms like a trophy. "Gather around folks and meet my beautiful daughter — Priya Partap Singh!"

"Hey!" Everyone cheered.

"You're all invited to the biggest party of the year at my house tonight to celebrate the birth of my daughter, PRIYA," he said, proudly. "Another announcement, folks. Today, I rename my ancestral mansion as the '*Fort Priya*' in honour of my daughter, Priya Partap Singh."

The stunning announcement sent shivers down the people's spines. It was common knowledge that the *Rajputs* favoured boys and frowned upon girls because they viewed girls as liabilities. The *Rajput* community was notorious in India for honour-killings of girls at birth. After a moment of awkward silence the room shook with cheers, whistles, and claps. Pooran Partap Singh left the room in fury. He was crushed by the announcement. He had always hoped that being the only son and heir of Major Partap Singh, he would one day inherit the envious *Fort Partap Singh*. He had hated his stepmother with a passion and had felt relieved each time she had failed to produce an offspring. Now he had to compete against his stepsister. He was furious.

By the strange turn of events, in a matter of minutes, the unwanted, abandoned baby girl became an heiress, the owner of unlimited wealth and grandeur.

The sweets started passing in the room, from hand to hand and rose petals started flying in the air. The cameramen stepped forward to take pictures of the proud parents being showered with rose petals, holding the newborn.

A pundit in a white *Dhoti* and *Kurta* stepped forward chanting some *Mantras*. He bent forward to anoint the baby and her parents with the holy *Tilaka* and blessed the child. Menakshi picked up a *ladoo* (ceremonial sweet) from a plate and put it in Menaka and the Major's mouths.

All faces lit up. Every one clapped.

"One last announcement," roared Major Partap. "I'm organizing the biggest *Food Centre* in front of my house. Free food and blankets will be distributed to the poor and homeless for the next thirty days and nights!"

Loud cheers followed the announcement. Ashley watched the scene in amazement from across the room. It was the sight that was to remain with her forever. She felt like a *Goddess*; overwhelmed by her power to change destiny.

Everyone in the room seemed to be floating in the air. The last thing on Ashley's mind before she collapsed in her bed with complete exhaustion was the sense of ecstasy and power. She kept seeing the overwhelmingly secretive look exchanged by Menakshi and Annie as the two waved their *'lips being sealed'* sign to each other in the air.

All through the night, Ashley's mind kept flooding with the pictures of the lit-up faces, scented candles, stunning procession of men and women, amazing costumes, glittering jewellery, fragrant rose petals, the chanting of Mantras and the proud faces of the parents.

KING EDWARD VII CORONATION WEEK
PREPARATIONS IN INDIA

Gold and glitter, splendour and renown,
I'm an elusive gem in the British Crown.

"Aunt Ashley, can I go to Priya's house?" asked Pearly, brushing her shining white, blonde hair. "The tailor's coming over this evening to try the fittings. I'm invited to dine with the family."

"Hmmm," Ashley nodded.

"Oh! Yes, I need some money for the costume jewellery. We plan to shop before supper. I need some white and red pieces of jewellery to go with all my dresses; the black, the pink and the red one," said Pearly, twisting her hair over the top of her head in a bun and putting golden clips around it.

"You're a sight for sore eyes, Pearly," said Ashley, smiling. She had never seen Pearly look lovelier than she did this evening with glistening curls dangling by the sides of her flushed cheeks and sparkling eyes.

Ashley and Pearly were invited to the biggest gala event being organized in the country by the Viceroy, Lord Curzon to mark the accession to the throne by the new King Edward VII. "I'm so looking forward to my first major public appearance with you, auntie," Pearly exclaimed.

"So am I," declared Ashley, with a touch of nervousness.

As personal physician of the Maharaja of Jodhpur, Ashley was invited to the weeklong festivities. Ashley had felt privileged to be his most trusted physician in Simla. The Maharaja never traveled anywhere without his personal physician(s). She thought back to the day when her brother, Daniel, had recommended Ashley to the Maharaja fifteen years ago.

Daniel was the Maharaja's favourite artist. He used to accompany the Maharaja on his hunting trips to capture his special moments in oil paintings. As ill luck would have it, the Maharaja's last hunting trip turned deadly for her brother, who was trying to capture the scene in oil. Quite unexpectedly, the Maharaja's new elephant turned wild, knocking down Daniel, and nearly crushing him to death. Daniel never recovered from the accident. After being confined to bed and a wheelchair for over a year, he finally succumbed to his wounds. Even though the family was extremely grateful to the Maharaja for his compassionate handling of the unfortunate accident, yet they could never bear to look at the unfinished painting, which remained stored in the *Annexe* as the last testament to the tragic event.

"This is not the time to dwell on the past," Ashley reminded herself, shrugging her shoulders and turning her attention to the excitement on hand.

"What're we going to wear?" was the daily topic of discussion around the dinner table.

"I'm quite nervous at the thought of dressing in some long, fancy gowns," Ashley admitted.

"I feel comfortable in my usual physician uniform, white long coat, plain shirt, jeans, laced boots and no make-up."

"Why don't you look for some conservative yet elegant outfits to match the festive occasion," Annie suggested. "You've several jet-black tuxedos, long frock coats, and snow white frilled shirts with pearl buttons and black ties which would work well with the occasion."

"Yeah. I should try to look as glamorous as the Major does in his traditional uniforms."

Major Partap Singh had to be posted firmly by the Maharaja's side in his glittering A.D.C. (aide-de-camp) uniform, with several medals of bravery pinned to his chest. The family had proudly displayed a large picture of the Major (taken at the royal palace) on the main wall under the magnificent chandelier in their spectacular drawing room filled with expensive ornaments and brocade curtains.

"Why don't you go to the *Kohinoors, over* at the hill near Davico? I saw some great new arrivals. If you like, you could wear some of your mom's dresses," suggested Ashley.

"I don't think I'm quite ready for that. By the way, how are your outfits coming along? I bet you'll look great in whatever you wear. You are a natural beauty!" said Pearly.

"And your mom called me, the *Plain Look,*" replied Ashley.

"Maybe because my mom was so downright gorgeous, judging from her portraits. No wonder, my dad was never tired of painting her. I've never seen anyone prettier than my mom, except Priya."

"Yes, she has an amazing resemblance to Symoune," Ashley agreed.

"Priya looks totally English with her white skin and blue eyes, except for her hairstyle and dress-up which are flat out Indian."

A cloud came over Ashley's face. Her eyes became pensive.

"Auntie, is it true that the reason Priya turned out looking more like my mom than hers is because her mom used to look at my mom's picture daily when she was pregnant?"

"It could be," Ashley shrugged her shoulders feeling uncomfortable with the conversation.

"No wonder, people think we're twins! We both have the same blue eyes, same colour of the skin except the hair. Priya has these gorgeous honey blonde hair, which I envy so much. Don't they look far shinier than my white blond hair?"

Ashley's mind went back to that fateful night, some fifteen years ago, when an unknown beautiful Indian girl gave birth to Priya in her clinic and abandoned her to hide her adulterous affair with an Englishman.

"*I feel sorry for Priya's real parents. They'll never know what they've lost.*" Ashley thought.

"*Priya is an adorable and gifted girl who has great looks and a great soul. She sings like an angel; paints like a professional and is wise beyond years. No wonder there's nothing her adoptive parents wouldn't do for her. The sun rises with her and sets with her.*"

"I feel so drawn to Priya. I wonder if it's a past life connection," Pearly said, powdering her nose. "I'm going now, auntie. Please promise not to worry if I'm late. I don't want you sending a search party each time I am a bit late."

"In that case, you had better take your medication with you, Pearly."

Ashley was prone to worrying about Pearly's health. Pearly was real cool about her heart condition. She hated her aunt fussing over trivial health matters.

Ashley was always concerned if the weather was too cold or too hot for Pearly; and worried whether she had taken her medicine on time, and if her diet contained proper nutrients. Every weekend, she personally cooked Pearly's meals and tried as often as she could to eat with her. Pearly always managed to bring out the mother in Ashley which she had never thought existed. Ashley loved Pearly's innocent ways, her trusting nature, and her very calm and honourable disposition.

"Dr. Ashley, you have no appointments this afternoon. Why don't you go shopping with Pearly and Priya? You might find some latest designs," said Annie, walking in with a pencil tucked behind her ears and carrying a long list of *things to do* before their trip to Delhi the next week.

"No, I'm waiting for Ram Lal, the tailor. He should be here shortly. Annie, why don't you come with me to Symoune's room and help me choose a couple of gowns from her wardrobe? They are so beautiful that it's shame they are not being used. I'm lucky to be the same size as Symoune," replied Ashley, feeling excited.

Ashley and Annie felt a strange sensation inspecting Symoune's huge walk-in closet. Symoune had dresses for every occasion with matching shoes, jewellery and hats. Everything had looked heavenly on her. She loved jewel colours — purple, royal blue, deep red and emerald green. She had worn them well. Ashley's favourites were her collection of ivory white chiffon dresses, embroidered with different colours and beads. Her unique styles and detailed work made her look like an angel in the flesh.

"How about this white silk dress with gold embroidery on it? It will go so well with your blonde hair," Annie suggested, fingering the dress carefully.

"No, I like those two ivory chiffon dresses at the back, which Symoune never got to wear. They are brand new. The ivory frilled outfit with glasswork and the black georgette one with multi beads look conservative and sophisticated at the same time."

"How about this ruby red gown with pearls and rubies embroidered on the neck and sleeves?" asked Annie. "Isn't this the dress in the portrait over the wall?"

"Yes, the very last portrait of Symoune done by my brother in that spectacular gown?" She paused. "I remember clearly the day she had modelled in that outfit with the matching set of pearls and rubies shimmering around her neck," Ashley sighed.

"I've got an idea! Why don't we get the tailor to alter this gown for Pearly? She could get her portrait done in this dress in Delhi," suggested Annie.

"It's a great idea!" Ashley agreed.

"The BAU (British Artists Union) is putting on a fundraiser for the Krishna Orphanage in Simla," she said. "They need some models. I've donated five hundred rupees for one ticket for an oil portrait and signed up Pearly. This would be an excellent opportunity for Pearly to have her portrait done in her mothers' outfit and jewellery," replied Ashley, feeling thrilled.

A loud doorbell interrupted their conversation. Annie ran to answer the bell.

"I bet that's Ram Lal," Annie said.

He walked in timidly wearing his traditional white *Dhoti-Kurta*, a *Sandal Tilaka* and ponytail.

He was a Hindu *Brahman* guy. The '*Brahmans*' were considered to be the upper class caste. They were extremely religious people. They worshipped the cow as the *Mother* symbol of India. One thing strongly common in the British and Indian cultures was that they were built on a similar idea of hierarchy; the British had their classes and the Hindus had their castes.

"Ah! That's a lovely gown, Dr. Ashley," he said, placing his multi-coloured satchel on the table and taking out his measuring tape, getting ready for action. "I remember sewing it for your sister-in-law, Miss Symoune. What are we going to do with this today?" he added, with a wistful look.

"Could you resize this dress for Pearly?" asked Ashley, opening the drawer of Symoune's dressing table and pulling out Pearly's dimensions from the golden box.

"Certainly! When do you need it?" inquired Ram Lal.

"We're leaving for Delhi on Friday. I also need these two

gowns taken in about two inches at the bodice," Ashley said, folding the three gowns neatly and handing them to him.

"You are so lucky to be invited to the coronation event," he remarked, examining the dresses.

"Yes, thank you. I look forward to getting the dresses back on Thursday. Okay?"

"Yes. I read about your accompanying the Maharaja with Major Singh in the 'Distinguished Guest List' column in the newspaper, *Kesri-Hind*. Is Annie going as well?"

"Yes, I'm going as Pearly's chaperone. I might find someone special," Annie giggled.

"Yeah and I will get rid of her," teased Ashley.

"Well, good luck with the trip. I will see myself to the door."

"Annie, I can't seem to find Symoune's pearl and ruby necklace," said Ashley, going through the pieces of jewellery arranged neatly in rows in Symoune's Jewelry box.

"You might have placed it in your safety deposit box," replied Annie.

"No, I did not! It should be here, somewhere . . . but I can't find it. I need to find it because it matches perfectly with that dress being resized for Pearly," said Ashley, going through the contents of the box several times.

"Here, I've found a plain strand of pearls instead. I think it will go well with the earrings. I will settle on this for now and will look for the original necklace when we come back from the trip."

Ashley was glad to have settled the issue of the necklace, because she had a million other important details to take care of before the big trip.

CORONATION OF KING EDWARD VII
HISTORICAL LOOK

*Two powerful cultures matching their might;
one locked in the cage; one roaring outside.*

"Pardon me, did I surprise you with my Hindi?" giggled Annie, opening her appointment book and grabbing a pen from the drawer.

"The clinic is closed for three weeks," she said, observing the appointment book. "Why don't you call us back in mid-January? Fine, Merry Christmas, and a Happy New Year to you," she said, replacing the receiver and picking up the coffeepot.

"Isn't this the greatest Christmas tree or what?" remarked Ashley, putting the finishing touches on the Christmas tree. "This Christmas, Pearly steps into her fifteenth year. The coronation of the new monarch is in the New Year. Two great celebrations!"

"Yes. Can you move the angel up one row?" asked Annie. "The house looks so festive with the decorations. It looks like *Diwali*. Christmas is as important to us as *Diwali* is to the Hindus. It's a shame that we're the only ones celebrating Christmas on this street," said Annie, settling down on the sofa with a cup of coffee.

"We're the only white people on this street, Annie," Ashley replied with a grin.

"We participate in *Diwali* and other Indian festivals. Why don't Indians celebrate Christmas?"

"Christmas is a religious event. The Hindus, Sikhs, and Muslims have their own religious prophets. Why should the English impose their religious beliefs on Indian people when they don't impose their religion on us?" replied Ashley, grabbing a cup of coffee.

"I suppose the British have done one thing right. They've shown tremendous respect for religious freedom in India," observed Annie.

"Because the British understand that India is as diverse religiously as it is linguistically. Indians are generally speaking peaceful people."

"Then why does the British government keep pounding on Indians?"

"They're not pounding on the people. They're pounding on the leaders; nationalists and extremists."

"Why do they do that?"

"They're afraid of the growing Indian nationalist sentiment and nationalist movements. Even though the British have destroyed many such movements, the Indian nationalist sentiment is growing. I bet many movements have just gone underground and are expanding. They are like ticking time bombs ready to explode," said Ashley.

"Why is that so?"

"Because of the love and hate relationship of the Indian masses with the British Empire. What's new in the newspaper, Annie?" asked Ashley, sipping coffee from the Christmas mug.

"The *Splendid Durbar* being organized by the Viceroy is becoming the talk of the town. Entire India, not just the princely states, are getting into frenzy over the *Durbar*. Look at these pictures," remarked Annie, handing over the newspaper to Ashley.

"Interesting!" noted Ashley, turning the pages. "The Coronation Week is certainly being used to create the biggest public relations event in India. Or to proclaim the supremacy of the British Empire over its native Indian rulers and subjects."

"You sound sarcastic, Dr. Ashley!" Annie remarked.

"Despite my loyalty to the crown, I'm a bit skeptical about Lord Curzon's agenda."

"Why?"

"It looks as though he has manipulated the crown to elevate the title of the governor-general into the monarch's viceroy to add more prestige to his position. The viceroy appears to be much more powerful than the monarch he represents," commented Ashley.

"No wonder. He's promising a much more spectacular

Durbar than the one organized in 1877, when Queen Victoria was proclaimed the Empress of India. He could be trying to increase the popularity of the British Raj as well as his own popularity in India," said Annie excitedly.

"Either that or he's trying to minimise the chances of another 1857 Revolution," said Ashley.

"What happened in the 1857 Revolution, Dr. Ashley?" asked Annie, biting her lower lip.

"The Mutiny of 1857, known as the *1857 Ka Gadar* by the Indian people, was a deadly revolution against the British. Though the British were triumphant, they did realize the strength of the masses and the need to improve their image of goodwill towards the Indian masses."

"No wonder there are announcements to improve the British image in the media every day."

"I read in the paper yesterday that they're recruiting more and more Indians into the British Army to combat the growing nationalist sentiment. The proportion of European troops to Indian soldiers or *Sipahis* used to be one to nine. Now there are 75,000 British soldiers and 150,000 Indians wearing the Queen's colours."

"It's a great achievement for the Indian people. Isn't it?"

"Yes. As more and more people are getting educated and moving up in the Indian Administrative Services (IAS), Indian nationalism is growing. The Maharaja rightly pointed out the other day that there's a definite need to build bridges with the masses," remarked Ashley.

"How many princely states are there in India, Dr. Ashley?"

"I believe there are 562 *princely states* in India, occupying one third of the land mass of the sub-continent, which never came under the direct British rule."

"What do the British get in exchange for that?"

"In exchange for such concessions, the princes pay a certain amount of annual fees to the British government and are allowed to raise their own state military forces."

"When did Simla become the British Headquarters?"

"I think it was Captain Kennedy who discovered Simla in 1822 and made Simla his headquarters. Lord Amherst was the first ruler to visit Simla and a few years later, it was Lord William Bentinck who chose Simla as the site for the government."

"The guest list at the coronation looks awesome! Take a look."

"Yes, the list includes world ambassadors, Sheikhs from Arabian countries, Maharajas, Nawabs and lesser chieftains, soldiers, senior men and ladies of the Indian government. The Viceroy is also organizing a very elite reception for the Maharajas of Indian princely states— the entry is by invitation only," said Ashley.

"What's the Maharaja of Jodhpur contributing to this event?"

"Same as the other rulers from the princely states are contributing: elephants, palkies, horses, bands, dancers, and banners. The Major is organizing, on behalf of the Maharaja, a special parade of the Jodhpur contingent of 7,000 soldiers— English and Indian, decorated in colorful, shining uniforms. There will be a 31-gun salute to the royalty and the Viceroy,"

"What else is the Maharaja contributing?" asked Annie.

"He's contributing the decorated elephant on which the Viceroy will make his stunning entrance into the stadium. The Indian people will remember that moment for centuries."

Chapter Three
The Coronation Week - India, 1902

KING EDWARD VII CORONATION WEEK
MEETING WITH PRINCE

He had depth in his voice and magic in his face;
in his body and soul, there was rhythm and grace.

"Annie, I know that Pearly is longing secretly to meet someone special at the Coronation event," whispered Ashley, in her ear.
"I heard that. How can you tell?" Pearly yelled.
"Because the list of the boys you would like to date is growing bigger every day!"
"You've been snooping around. How awful?"
"No, I stumbled on your list—quite accidentally," Ashley laughed.
"Priya, on the other hand, is fully content with the idea of an arranged marriage. She feels that it's the prerogative of her parents to find a suitable match for her," Annie jumped in.
"Because I might not be allowed to see the man I would marry before the big day," Priya replied.
"And you're fine with that, Priya?" Pearly asked.
"I've no choice. I don't want any complications," she smiled.

The two families flew to *Delhi* in a private jet belonging to the *Maharaja of Jodhpur*. Pearly and Priya were excited beyond imagination. They stayed in the *Hotel British Crown*—a magnificent ten-storey building occupying an area of three miles overlooking the famous *Tal Katora Gardens*. Originally, the building was one of the palaces belonging to the Mughal Emperor, *Shah Alam*. The palace fell into the hands of the British rulers after his death in 1805, and was converted into *Hotel British Crown*. The British rulers were known for their keen interest in conserving the historical sites and ancient monuments. No one had worked harder in this endeavour than the reigning *Viceroy, Lord Curzon.* He took tremendous delight in restoring historical sites such as the *Taj Mahal* (the world famous testament of the Mogul Emperor, *Shah Jahan's* love for his queen *Noor Jahan*), the *Temple of Fatehpur Sikri*, the *Temple of Khujuraho*, the *Pearl Mosque of Lahore*, to their original glory.

The Maharaja of Jodhpur and his Maharani occupied the entire west wing on the seventh floor. Next to the Maharaja was his *A.D.C.* Major Partap Singh's suite. Dr. Ashley's suite was adjacent to Major Partap Singh's suite in the corner, near the staircase. In the east wing were staying the Nawab of Malerkotla and the Nizam of Hyrdabad. The *Darbaans* (ushers) in glittering uniforms were posted in front of every suite. A high level of British Indian Security Force was seen posted on all entrances and exits. There was a huge amount of hustle and bustle in the hotel lobby and the corridors.

Ashley's suite faced directly the main hotel entrance; so they could clearly see the guests arriving with great pomp and show. Pearly and Priya had stood for hours with their noses pressed to windows, watching the steady stream of distinguished guests arriving in open carriages, decked in glittering clothes, gold and diamonds — royal costumes and uniforms. The guests included Maharajas, Nawabs from the princely states, Ambassadors, and Sheikhs from the Arabian countries, Chieftains, British, and Indians soldiers accompanying their bosses, aristocrats and senior men and ladies of the Indian government.

"Why don't we slip downstairs to watch the procession of the dignitaries from across the lobby?"

"I'm not sure, Priya!"

"C'mon, Pearly! We can go to the private area beside the entrance of the lobby and pretend to be waiting for our escorts. What do you say? Shall we sneak out while Annie is away on an errand?"

"But Annie told us not to do anything crazy — "

"It's her duty to say so. I'm sure she'll cover for us in case we get caught."

"Let me scribble a note to Annie — something as we're going downstairs to fetch the program schedules," replied Pearly, picking up the note pad from the dresser. "You go and check if the hallway's clear."

"Pearly, the corridor's clear. What the hell are you doing in the closet?" she yelled.

"I'm looking for something."

"What could you be looking for, Pearly?"

"I'm looking for my overcoat. We must be disguised. Wait, I've found something—one for you and one for me," replied Pearly, sneaking out of the closet.

"Here, put this on," she yelled, tossing a black chiffon overcoat to Priya and fumbling with a snow-white brocade overcoat with a hood attached to it.

"I don't want to wear this one."

"C'mon Priya, what's wrong with it?"

"Nothing, except it has your name '*Pearly*' on it."

"No big deal. If anyone asks your name, just pretend that you're Pearly. Now let us move on," Pearly said, slipping a tiny camera into the large pocket.

Pearly and Priya sneaked out of their suite, tiptoeing in the hallway for fear of being stopped by anyone. They were trying to enjoy their new-found freedom. Their suite was stuck in the corner of the hallway and the *Darbaan* posted in front of the *Maharaja's Suite* could not notice them.

"I've an idea, Priya. I'll take the elevator and you take the staircase because, if either of us gets caught, we both won't get grounded at the same time."

"Besides, I need to stop on the sixth floor to take a few, quick pictures of my dad's paintings hanging in the hallway," she said, adding quickly, "I found out last night that this hotel has the unique privilege of displaying my dad's artwork on the sixth floor. I'm dying to see it."

"Pearly, stop! No one is allowed to take pictures of the hotel's artwork. You'll get caught sneaking around and we'll both get into a hell of a lot of trouble for wandering around unchaperoned."

"C'mon, Priya, how can anyone get into trouble with an innocent face like mine?" replied Pearly, disappearing into the elevator with her hair shimmering behind her like a cloud.

Priya took the staircase, whistling a tune and sliding down

the banister, with one hand on the railing. She kept sliding down, floor after floor, until suddenly the door on the second floor swung open, and Priya crashed into a young man, knocking him down and landing on top of him. The big vase of roses he was carrying smashed on the ground as he fell backwards, hitting his head on the cement floor and landing in the middle of the scattered roses and shattered glass.

"I'm so sorry! Please forgive me," Priya muttered, shocked. "Please don't worry," replied the stranger, wiping the blood trickling down his neckline and sitting up.

"My apologies for meeting you in this condition, my lady!" he burst into laughter.

"Please, I'm so embarrassed . . ." replied Priya, kneeling beside the stranger.

"I'm fine . . ." he smiled, reassuring her.

"Do you mind, if I take a look at your head?" she asked, reaching out impulsively and cupping his head with both hands to assess the depth of the cut. She jerked the handkerchief, neatly tucked in his vest pocket and began pressing the spot to stop the bleeding. The stranger raised his elbow to finger the back of his head, which was oozing with blood. His hand accidentally landed over Priya's hand.

Priya turned crimson.

"I'm sorry!" he giggled.

"No, no! Please stay right there until the bleeding stops. You could have a concussion, Mr. —"

"Ryan Hugh Prince, at your service, Ma'am," the stranger replied, with a twinkle in his eyes.

Priya burst into laughter. Ryan picked up a rose from the floor. He extended the rose to Priya.

"May this rose be a reminder of our accidental meeting, Lady Pearly," he said, reading her name tag on her coat.

"So you've read my name tag," Priya giggled. "I blame the person who invented name tags. It takes the mystery out of introductions. Won't you agree?"

"Normally, I hate surprises but this one has been an exception."

"Thanks for the rose! Imagine getting a beautiful reward for knocking you down. I should do that more often. Ouch!" she yelled, pulling a thorn from the finger.

"Looks like the prospect of friendship between us is headed for more disasters," Ryan whispered.

"A friendship? Oh, no, I assure you that I'll never see you again. We could be poles apart."

"How can that be? We're both British and free. What's stopping us from being simple friends?"

"Simple—I may be too young to have a boyfriend!"

"We've become acquainted whether you agree or not. It was destiny!"

"No, it was a coincidence."

"Wouldn't you like to find out if the injured party survived the accident?" He smiled mischievously. "What if my condition becomes critical . . .?"

"Please get a doctor to take a look at the cut. Thanks for the rose. Goodbye Ryan," said Priya, dashing downstairs with the beautiful rose in her hand.

"We'll meet again, Lady Pearly. I assure you. We will," he said, in a deep and crisp voice.

"No, we won't!" she replied, slipping downstairs as fast as her feet could carry her. Her mind kept going back to the embarrassing episode.

"We'll meet again . . . again. We'll meet again . . . again!"

"Do you need any help, Ma'am?" Priya heard the *Bellman* bend over to ask politely with a look of concern. He had seen Priya get off the elevator with a troubled look and he had been watching her sitting in the lobby, looking utterly lost.

"Where's Pearly? Why is she not in the lobby?" Priya woke up from her reverie with a start.

"I beg your pardon. I didn't follow you, Ma'am?"

"How long have I been sitting here?"

"You came here an hour ago, alone. Are you waiting for someone? Can I ring for your relatives?"

"Would you let my friend Pearly know when she arrives here that I've gone back to my suite. I'm not feeling well." Priya rose from her seat, biting her upper lip.

"If you give me a minute, I would be happy to escort you back to your suite, Ma'am."

"Yes, thank you. I'll wait. Would you kindly fetch me the program schedule?"

"Be happy to, Ma'am."

Pulling her hood over her head, Priya followed the Bellman into the elevator. Little did she know that Pearly had gotten into a trouble of her own as soon as she landed on the sixth floor.

KING EDWARD VII CORONATION WEEK
MEETING WITH THE MYSTERY MAN

*This is the story of a woman he ever loved deep;
she was the only one woman, he dreamt in sleep.*

Pulling the hood tightly over her head and keeping a low profile, Pearly jumped off the elevator. The sixth floor looked exquisite in light blue and emerald walls with gold rimmed glass doors and multi-coloured murals on the walls and the ceilings.

Tiptoeing around the empty corridors, Pearly started to examine the nameplates beneath the paintings. She kept moving swiftly until she stopped before one large painting, which took her breath away. It was a very masculine and regal hunting scene, deep into the heart of a jungle. Underneath the painting, she read, *Daniel Augustus Boone - June 1877.*

Tears welled up in her eyes. She looked around for a moment before pulling out her camera. With trembling hands, she took a quick shot of the painting and slid the camera carefully in her pocket. She started gliding in front of the different suites reading the nameplates: Maharaja of Faridkot Suite, His Highness King Bhupindra of Patiala Suite.

Pearly stopped in front of the two large waterfall paintings hung side by side in the balcony and a stunning painting entitled *"Fantasy"* in the middle. She looked closely at the initials on the bottom of the paintings - D. A. Boone, May 1880. A sense of pride filled her heart. With one quick movement, she took several shots of the paintings. She had barely slipped the camera into the long overcoat pocket when a very stern looking *Darbaan* caught her by surprise.

"Excuse me, my lady, May I inspect, what you just slipped

into your pocket?"

"Why? Are you ordering a *search*?" Pearly stood up to the Darbaan.

"This is a private floor and there is fine for RS 1,000 for trespassing."

"I'm not trespassing, I'm visiting," said Pearly flatly.

"Oh yeah, where is your chaperone?"

"She is sick in bed."

"What did you slip into your pocket, a moment ago? Out with it!" he ordered.

"No. I won't! I have the right to my privacy," argued Pearly.

"Well, in that case I'll have to take you into custody until your guardian arrives."

"No, you can't! You'll have to answer to the Maharaja of Patiala. I'm his guest."

Pearly stood her ground firmly, giving no visible sign of being scared. She was thinking quickly to come up with an idea to get her out of the trouble. She knew that if she were caught, she would be grounded and may have to pay the fine out of her pocket money.

"*Please, God, help me,*" *she whispered beneath her breath.*

To her surprise, the elevator door swung open and she saw coming towards her direction a very tall and distinguished British gentleman in army uniform with several medals pinned to his chest. He was followed by two footmen and a dining cart. Pearly jumped to the chance.

"Look!" she pointed to the British gentleman, "That's my uncle."

"What's going on here, Lal Singh?" roared the British gentleman, in a high-pitched voice.

"General Matthew Scott, Sir!" the Darbaan turned sharply, kicking his heels together in a salute and adding, "I must apologise. I didn't realize that My Lady, your niece, was visiting you, Sir."

"Indeed, you didn't. I'll take it from here," said General Scott smiling and extending his arm to Pearly politely.

Pearly jumped to his side.

"Uncle, thank God you came! This man was going to take me into custody," she said, resting her hand on the General's arm and following him until they stopped before an elegant suite. One of the footmen behind the dining cart rushed forward to ring the doorbell. Pearly stood waiting on the arm of General Scott until a very young looking British army officer opened the door. He quickly kicked his heels in a salute to the General.

"Meet my right hand man, Captain George Jones. May I have the pleasure of presenting my niece . . . ?"

"Pearly Ruby Boone, Sir," replied Pearly, quickly covering up, and thinking about her next step—how to get out of the situation with General Scott.

"The pleasure is all mine. I didn't know you had a niece here, General Scott?" Captain Jones said, raising his eyebrows.

"Indeed, you didn't. Can I offer you lunch, Captain Jones?"

"No, Sir. I wouldn't want to intrude on your private lunch with your niece. Ring me, when you're finished, Sir," said the officer, kicking his heels together in a salute, and disappearing from the room.

General Scott remained standing with his back towards Pearly until he heard the sound of the door click shut. Then he swung around to face Pearly. He spoke with a touch of amusement in his voice, seating himself at the dining table, looking handsome with graying hair above his temples and deep set, melancholy blue eyes.

"Now that we're alone, my dear niece, what was the name . . . Oh, yes, Miss Pearly Ruby Boone. Would you do me the honour of serving the lunch?"

"I owe you an explanation, Sir."

"That should be interesting. Why don't we hear it over the lunch? After all it's not every day that my niece drops by for a visit," said General Scott, pulling her leg.

"I can explain it, Sir. You see, it's all very innocent," said Pearly, blushing heavily.

"Uncle!" he corrected her. "Isn't that, what you had said outside that I was . . . your uncle?"

"I'm so sorry for putting you on the spot. I had no way out," said Pearly, preparing to serve lunch.

"I'm listening. Where is your plate?" he asked.

Pearly hesitated.

"Please don't deny me the pleasure of having lunch with my

beautiful niece. Get a plate and sit down at the table with your dear uncle and provide your explanation. No lies, because I'm trained to detect lies quickly. All right, my sweet niece — ?"

"Yes, Sir," said Pearly, picking up a plate from the cart and serving lunch.

"Yes, uncle," he corrected, again.

"Yes, uncle! I give you my word to tell no more lies."

"Indeed. Go on, I'm a good listener."

"My aunt, *Dr. Ashley Rose*, is accompanying the Maharaja of *Jodhpur* to the Coronation event as his personal physician. My friend Priya's dad, *Major Partap Singh* is the *A.D.C. of His Highness*. We're occupying the suite seven on the seventh floor. My aunt and my chaperone were away this afternoon on an errand. Priya and I were just snooping around . . . for fun."

"Snooping around? Where is your friend, Priya?"

"She took the stairs and I took the elevator because we didn't want to get caught together."

"Ha! Ha! Ha . . ." The general rolled into laughter. "This doesn't explain what you were doing on this floor and what was in your pocket. Please try some Indian curd and salad."

"I don't know if you've heard the name, *Daniel Augustus Boone*, a famous British painter? I'm his daughter. There are several paintings of my dad's displayed on this floor. My friend Priya has a rare gift of painting. She had promised to create replicas of my dad's paintings. I was trying to take pictures of my dad's paintings. Is that a crime, Sir?"

"My goodness, you're the daughter of Daniel Boone," the General exclaimed, extending his hand. "It's an honour to make your acquaintance. I've a great collection of your dad's paintings. In fact I made an offer to the hotel owner to buy *Fantasy* to add to my collection."

"*Thank you, God, I'm out of trouble now,*" Pearly jumped with joy.

"What a wonderful surprise! Though I've never met your dad, I am a great fan. Your action was a lovely tribute to the memory of your dad. Your father would be so proud of you."

"You sound like a great father-figure yourself?"

Pearly was curious.

"I'm not married," he said. "I came close to it three times

but fate eluded me. The first time I was engaged to the woman I loved, I was sent to India. When I went back to England, my bride to be met with a car accident and died on the spot. It took me several years to get over her loss."

"The second time I got engaged, my helicopter crashed and I was proclaimed missing in action. When I returned, my fiancée had moved on with another man. The third time I fell in love, I found out that the love of my life was already married. That's my love story. A tough luck! It was my luck to love in vain. To be in love and to be in pain."

"And you've no one in your life now?" Pearly was intrigued.

"I do! I've known Jenny all my life. I seem to be dragging my feet because a part of me won't let go of the woman I can't have. I must decide soon, because it's not right to keep Jenny hanging."

"Who's the other attraction?"

"My attraction to my East Indian friend is very profound and deep. She loves me to death but she is married. There is a mystical bond between us. Why am I talking about this with you? I must escort you back to your suite," said General Scott getting up and looking at his watch and then at the door.

"Wait, do you have a picture of the woman you love so much? I'm curious..."

With a twinkle in his eyes, he fumbled with the locket around his neck. He clicked it open with one hand and motioned Pearly with the other hand to take a look at the picture mounted inside. Pearly's eyes fell over the two most stunning eyes, a gorgeous head full of wavy hair and full lips.

"Oh, Uncle, she's the most beautiful woman I've ever seen. What's her name?"

"Saya Sunaina Surya-wanchi which means—a shadow with stunning sun-lit eyes." He paused.

"Breathtakingly beautiful woman?"

"And a forbidden love story," he sighed. "Her husband is a friend of mine. She doesn't have the strength to break away. Playing hide and seek with her was such a torment that we quit seeing each other. Now I must escort you back to your suite." He rose to his feet, extending his arm.

Pearly stood up, putting her hand on his arm affectionately.

She was amazed at how comfortable she felt with him. She had only met him an hour ago and she felt she had known him forever. The air of familiarity and kindness around the man made her feel secure with him. She felt she could tell him anything and he would understand. She couldn't wait to introduce him to Priya, whom she knew was eagerly awaiting her arrival in her suite.

Ashley looked a bit puzzled to see Pearly walk in on the arm of an army officer.

"Aunt Ashley, may I present General Matthew Scott?"

"My pleasure, General Scott," said Ashley, smiling dubiously. "Has Pearly gotten herself into some trouble, like loitering around in an area where she shouldn't?"

"Something like that. No harm done. I came on the scene in time to rescue her. She told the *Darbaan* that I was her uncle. Isn't it right, Pearly?"

Ashley's cheeks turned crimson. The General followed Ashley into the suite with a big smile.

"Please, have a seat. Can I offer you some tea or coffee? By the way this is Annie Black, my nurse."

"And this must be Priya," he said, seating himself. "Nice meeting you. Please, coffee's fine."

"Thanks for helping Pearly. She's little headstrong but her heart is in the right place."

"Indeed! I'm honoured. I'm a great fan of your brother, Danny Boone. May I invite you all to the *General Scott Reception?*" he asked, handing a small red card to Ashley.

"Thank you. I accept the invitation on behalf of all of us." Ashley smiled.

"The reception's on the New Year's eve on Wednesday, January 1st, 1903," he added. "I'm going to be honoured as *Sir Matthew Scott* by the *Viceroy, Lord Curzon,* earlier in the morning at the Arena."

"What an honour? We would love to join the celebration party." Ashley beamed with excitement.

As he rose to take his leave, Pearly jumped to his side. She walked him to the elevator, placing a hand on his arm. A little sigh escaped from her lips when General Scott bent over to plant a kiss on the back of her hand. Out of nowhere a feeling of sadness engulfed her.

"Take care! You're a fascinating young girl. Call me any time you need me," he winked.

"I feel the same. Please don't ever be a stranger. I was so lucky to meet you . . . uncle."

She noticed a peculiar look in the General's eyes which she could not fathom. She felt an undeniable invisible bond with the mystery man and sighed.

CORONATION OF KING EDWARD VII
STATE DURBAR IN DELHI

Indian gems, Indian soil, British glory;
who's the teller? And who is the story?

New Delhi, the capital of India, was being decorated like a newly-wed bride. A series of events were being planned by the British-Raj in cooperation with the princely-states from December 29, 1902, right through the New Year to celebrate the Coronation of King Edward V11, in India. The actual Coronation event already had taken place in England some six months earlier. This was the second time that the Indian people were going to be treated in large numbers to stunning displays of splendour and glory by the British Monarchy.

"My goodness, auntie, the highly publicised long procession of the native princes and dignitaries from around the world and the *'State Durbar'* are promising to be the two most spectacular events ever seen by anyone in the world," said Pearly, reading the headlines in the newspaper.

"The cooperation which the British have been able to build with the native princes, world leaders and the general public is overwhelming," remarked Ashley, slipping into her night gown.

"According to the newspaper, the area chosen for the *State Durbar is* so large that it could accommodate an audience estimated at 175,000 visitors," replied Pearly, bubbling with excitement.

"I can't wait to visit the variety of pavilions, displaying Indian art and craftsmanship like carpets, pottery, silks, and priceless ornaments," said Annie, joining the conversation.

"Yeah. There's also going to be a big enclosed camp for

the animals and their attendants taking part in the various ceremonies and parades. I'd love to visit some of those camps," said Pearly.

"Enough about the *Parade* and the *Durbar*. Goodnight, ladies," said Ashley, turning out the light.

The precedent of organizing a lavish State Durbar initiated by Queen Victoria was carried on with great pomp and show by the reigning Viceroy, Lord Curzon in 1902. Following the State Durbar Ceremony the Queen had become so popular in India that her gestures of goodwill towards the Indian people continued till the end of her reign. Her popularity soared after the great Mutiny of 1857, when she ended the unpopular rule of the East India Company and established the rule of monarchy in India. The stories of the Queen's deep interest in the day-to-day events of the British-Indian Empire were highly publicised in the media. It was reported that she publicly chided British bureaucrats for their discriminatory attitude towards the Indian people. Her fondness of Indian culture, Indian people, Indian architecture, and food; her campaign to reduce the death rate among Indian women during childbirth and her announcement of special (Kaiser-I-Hind) medals to Indian women doctors in 1900 made her the Queen of the masses. Her openness was demonstrated by her great affection for Abdul Karim, her Indian Muslim servant, whom she referred to as her Munshi. Abdul Karim was mentioned in the Queen's personal diary as her Hindustani Tutor, Hindustani Chef, and Indian Secretary.

The first five days in Delhi slipped away like a dream. The two families would leave right after breakfast and come home exhausted. Pearly, Priya, and Annie kept visiting different pavilions and functions of their choice. The program schedules were readily available at the hotel lobby. There was everything for everyone in the program guide. For men, there were sport events like football, hockey, cricket matches, tent pegging competitions, and wrestling. Interesting events were planned for the general public like dance shows, recitals, firework displays, musical rides, and magic shows. There was to be a *'State Ball'* and a special *'Viceroy Reception'* at which Britons and Indians were going to be decorated for their loyalty to the British Raj. Major Partap Singh accompanied the Maharaja and his train to different sport events while Menaka and Ashley tagged along with the Maharani and went to the musical events, dance shows, lunch buffets, and suppers. The two families would be together every evening to plan next day's schedule before retiring.

Major Partap Singh and Ashley worked round the clock attending to every detail from the decoration of the carriages and horses to the Maharaja's change of uniforms and Maharani's costumes for the *'gala parade'* event.

"Ashley, we must retire early tonight," said the Major, "We've a long day tomorrow!"

"Yes, I'll meet you at the arena at 4:30 tomorrow. Annie will make sure that the Maharani and the girls are fully ready and waiting in the hotel lobby at 7:00 sharp. The carriage will be waiting for them at the foot of the hotel main door."

"Fine, Goodnight," he said, heading to the door, grabbing Menaka's hand.

"Pearly, can you review the program schedule with Priya and Annie and let me know the events you are interested in participating tomorrow?" asked Ashley, laying out her tuxedo suit carefully on the back of the chair and inspecting the contents of the box, to look for a matching tie and breeches.

"It's hard to choose. There's so much happening. I guess we'll attend the *Parade* and the *State Durbar* together tomorrow."

"What about the fundraiser on Wednesday morning?"

"I'm attending that one," said Pearly. "Since the BAU is arranging for the escorts for the models, Priya and Annie would be free to plan whatever they like in the morning. Priya and I are too young to attend the *State Ball* but we would like to attend together the *'Vice regal Reception'* for the native princes and General Scott's Reception on Wednesday night."

"And we're planning to see a few more pavilions after the Parade tomorrow?" Priya said. "I'm sure that's fine as long as Annie keeps an eye on you. Now off to bed."

A soft knock on the door startled Priya out of sleep.

She switched on the bed light.

"Who could be knocking at 5:00 in the morning?" Priya thought, opening the door.

She was astonished to find a single red rose left on the doorstep with a note:

January 1, 1903
Lady Pearly:
I look forward to seeing you at the Parade.
RHP

"Oh, no, Ryan thinks that I'm Pearly. I didn't have a chance to tell Pearly last night because she fell asleep so quickly. She would kill me," she thought.

Priya kept tossing and turning in bed and fingering the rose with uncertain emotions.

"Priya, where on earth did you get that rose?" asked Pearly.

"What rose?"

"Get moving, girls! The parade will start at exactly 8:00. Hurry up!" yelled Annie, pacing impatiently.

Pearly, Priya, and Annie sat proudly in their carriage in elegant gowns. The eye-catching carriage ahead of them carried the Maharaja and Maharani of Jodhpur, adorned with jewels and sparkles. Seated proudly opposite them were Major Singh with a laced turban and sparkling medals and Ashley looking elegant in her black and silver long dress with embroidered collar and sleeves.

The people flooded the streets in large numbers, cheering in utter amazement the long procession of the dignitaries in the open carriages drawn by shining horses and decorated elephants marching through the streets of Delhi.

"Oh, look at the spectacular carriages! I'm so excited," Priya whispered, hiding the rose.

"I've never seen more diamonds in my life," Annie whispered.

"India is a land of gold. I'm dazzled! I'm breathless," remarked Pearly.

The procession moved on, carrying dignitaries: ambassadors and Arabian sheikhs from all over the world in embroidered robes; the maharajas and princesses in shining outfits; chieftains, foot soldiers and other important people in shining uniforms and designer outfits.

"Where did you get that *Rose*, Priya? It looks stunning with your dress. I'm so jealous!"

"I found it on the table last night."

"Why do you keep looking out as if you're waiting for someone to show up?" asked Pearly.

"I'm looking for the *viceroy*," whispered Priya. "There he is — entering the arena, surrounded by shining horsemen on the back of the decorated elephant in the glittering uniform."

The people rose from their seats and cheered until he positioned himself at the most spectacular spot on the stage; representing the king, who was conspicuous by his absence from the *Durbar*. He took salute from various squadrons, British and Indian soldiers, and Indian retainers from the princely states who had generously contributed elephants, horses, camels, palki-bearers, banner bearers, dancers, and bandsmen for the event.

"Pearly, where's the Emperor King?" Priya asked.

"He sent his brother, Duke of Cannaught, and his sister-in-law to represent him," replied Annie.

Her voice drowned as the loud sound of trumpets echoed from four directions. *The Viceroy, Lord Curzon* rose from his seat to address the audience. He took the 101-gun salute, before taking his place on the throne with the Emperor's brother and sister-in-law. Pandemonium fell over people when he started to speak. People tuned in to his message spell-bound. He concluded the proclamation from the throne by thanking the organizers and adding, *"The future of British India can only be realized under the supreme command of the British Crown. Long live the king!"*

"What a pompous guy! He just wants to glorify his own title, Pearly?"

"Yeah, he's trying to look spectacular in gems given to him by Indian princes."

"Girls, I won't have you criticising anyone in the public. Let's get going," Annie frowned.

A gentle tap on the shoulder and a soft whisper had an electrifying effect on Priya. She spun around, catching a glimpse of Ryan disappearing into the crowd; his words ringing in her ear. "Happy New Year, my lady. See you at the Bhopal Pavilion in half an hour."

"Oh, it's Ryan again. He must've seen me holding the rose." She felt breathless.

"Priya, where are you lost? Let's visit the pavilions, we missed yesterday," said Pearly.

"No, I want to visit the Bhopal Pavilion one more time," replied Priya.

"The Bhopal Pavilion? Priya, we've already been there three times."

"Why don't I meet you two in half an hour? I need to pick up a piece for my mom."

"Oh Priya, must you go alone," asked Annie, with a look of displeasure.

"Don't worry, Annie. I read in the paper that a *Special Police Act* is in force. If anyone is found hassling a lady, he will get caught and fined fifty rupees or eight days in jail."

Priya slipped through the crowd before Annie or Pearly could stop her.

"Can I help you with something, my lady?" asked the sales clerk.

"I love that band — the one with a cluster of rubies in it. How much is it?" asked Priya, looking over her shoulder.

"Five hundred rupees. It looks like it's made for you."

"It's over my budget. I need a trinket for my mom. I must get back to my friends, thank you."

Priya stopped at the corner of an antique pottery pavilion and momentarily looked behind, colliding with Ryan who was standing close behind her, smiling. He reached for Priya's hand and held it for a moment before releasing it in slow motion.

"Just a keepsake, a friendship ring, nothing more or . . . less," he whispered softly.

"*Oh, it's the same ruby band, I had been admiring a moment ago at the Bhopal Pavilion,*" thought Priya bending her head to admire the ring.

She lifted her head quickly with a questioning look. There was no sign of Ryan. Instead, she saw Pearly and Annie approaching her with concerned looks.

"There you are, Priya!" Annie remarked. "We've been looking all over for you. Let's get back. Pearly is coming down with flu —"

Chapter Four
The Royal Fundraiser

FUNDRAISER - THE FANTASY FAMILY SECRET

*From a distant world, and a distant land,
I have come to take you to the magic land.*

"It's morning, Pearly. Wake up!" said Priya, shaking her shoulder lightly. "You're supposed to get ready for the royal fundraiser."

"I don't feel like getting up, Priya."

"C'mon Pearly, don't be lazy," Priya insisted. "You've been so looking forward to going to this fundraiser for weeks now. Aunt Ashley has gone into a lot of trouble to get you the ticket. Don't waste it."

Pearly didn't answer.

"Pearly, look at this beautiful gown and jewellery laid out for you." Priya coaxed her, picking up the lovely gown from the chair and placing it in front of her. Pearly looked into the mirror and sighed.

"I feel tired and want to sleep. Please don't bug me, Priya."

"You're in a strange mood this morning," remarked Priya, turning sharply — almost dropping the gown on the floor. "I would give anything to go to the fundraiser."

"Why don't you go instead of me?"

"Do you mean it, Pearly?" asked Priya, jumping at the sound of the telephone.

"Hello, this is Malcolm Smith calling from the BAU. I'm calling about the fundraiser. May I speak with Miss Boone, please?"

"Yeah, this is Pearly Ruby Boone speaking," Priya hesitated before adding, "Is the fundraiser cancelled or something?"

"No, I'm calling to say that your escort will arrive at 11:00 sharp? This gives you exactly two hours to get ready."

"Yeah, 11:00 is fine, thank you," said Priya, hanging up the phone and clapping her hands gleefully. The phone call made her anxious.

"What would it be like to walk into a big hall on the arm of an escort and get my portrait done in the gorgeous ruby red gown?" she wondered.

"Who was on the phone, Priya?" Annie walked in, locking the door.

"I took the call for Pearly. Her escort will pick her up at 11:00 sharp. Annie, can you wake her up? I am going to shower."

Annie looked at her watch and frowned. Pearly was an early riser. It was unlike her to sleep past nine, especially when she was planning to go to a special event. It had been raining steadily all day yesterday and Pearly had started to sneeze and shiver.

Dr. Ashley had examined her thoroughly before going to bed and found no serious cause for concern, except a very mild touch of cold. She had given Pearly a couple of tablets thinking that she would return to her normal self in the morning. Dr. Ashley and Menaka had left early. Priya and Annie were planning to stay indoors the entire afternoon while Pearly went to the fundraiser.

"Pearly, are you okay, dear? Would you rather I called room service and ordered breakfast for the three of us here, than going downstairs," asked Annie, touching Pearly's forehead and checking her pulse. She felt relieved that Pearly had a normal temperature. She added, "You really should be getting up and getting ready, you know."

Priya walked into the room removing the towel around her head. She sat in front of the mirror and started combing her hair.

"Pearly, get up. Don't be lazy. See what a beautiful day it is," she shouted. "My goodness, you've an escort arriving shortly. Don't you want to go? I would be excited, if I were you."

"I told you that I'm not going. Priya; why don't you go in my place?"

"Are you serious?" Priya stood up sharply. "I can't go to a

British function to which I'm not invited. My parents would kill me," replied Priya, toying with the idea.

"Why not? You look very English and you speak English fluently. Just pretend you are Pearly. We have switched identities a million times before and fooled people. It would be fun and the ticket will not go to waste. Your parents will never find out," suggested Pearly, opening her eyes.

"Yes, they will when Priya walks in with her portrait instead of yours," interrupted Annie. "They've left me in charge of you two girls, and I say, no."

"But—"

"No buts. I will get into huge trouble for letting Priya go with an English escort."

"Annie, where is your sense of adventure? Priya is my best friend. We will hide her portrait until I get my portrait done in the near future. Come on; what do you say?" Pearly coaxed Annie.

"No." Annie was adamant. "The idea of letting Priya go to an English event with an English gentleman is asking for trouble. It's against Indian norms. No, I won't do it."

"Please, Annie. Let me go. I want to go and have fun. Here, you could have my favourite broach in exchange?" Priya pleaded. Annie reached back and pushed Priya's hand away.

"On one condition—you must promise to hide your portrait in Pearly's suitcase as soon as you come back and never breathe a word of this to anyone. Do you guys promise?"

"Yes." Pearly and Priya spoke together.

There was a soft knock on the door and a waiter wheeled in the breakfast cart. By the time, Annie poured the tea; Pearly had already wandered into dreamland.

"All right Priya, get into the gown and wait for me in front of the mirror. I will do your hair in English style," said Annie, handing her Pearly's gown, while sipping tea.

Priya ran dancing into the bathroom. She jumped into the gown in no time and came out giggling at the excellent fit. She shivered in excitement over the idea of transforming into Pearly.

"My goodness, you do look like Pearly. I hope that I don't repent doing this."

Priya giggled like a child, catching her beautiful reflection in the mirror. Annie fetched Pearly's jewellery box from the cupboard and started drawing beaded hairpins and placing them neatly on the dresser. She brushed Priya's hair several times before parting it into multiple layers and securing the layers with pins. She stopped suddenly in the middle of securing a curl.

"There's something unusual behind your left ear, Priya?"

"Oh, that's a *Birthmark*."

"I've never seen a birthmark look like this before."

"It's a birthmark, Annie, whether you've ever seen it or not. Go on—"

"It doesn't look like a birthmark," said Annie, examining the spot intently.

"C'mon—"

Annie began braiding the layers with beads before piling them up high over her head, highlighting Priya's long neck and square shoulders.

"My goodness, I do look like Pearly. Don't I, Annie?" Priya said with excitement.

"Wait till I put some lipstick and mascara on you. Now sit very still and close your eyes."

Priya closed her eyes tightly, feeling Annie's cold fingers slipping the pearl and ruby earrings in her ears, the necklace around her neck and fastening the silver sandal clips around her tiny ankles.

Priya rose from the chair glittering like a princess—tall and slender, porcelain face, flushed cheeks, dark blue eyes, and glittering curls. Annie was struck by her beauty.

"Annie, I have a necklace which matches exactly with these earrings. I will go and fetch it."

"Wait—"

Priya glided back into the room with a shimmering necklace in the palm of her hand.

"Look, Annie, the necklace—an exact match with the earrings," Priya exclaimed.

Annie's eyes became two pieces of ice.

"What's the matter, Annie? It's only a necklace, not a ghost!" Priya said, putting the necklace on.

"Where the hell did you get that necklace, Priya?" demanded Annie, fingering the necklace.

"Why? What's wrong? Why are you acting crazy? I hate it when you act like this."

"I'm sorry. You should have asked your mom before taking anything out of her jewellery box."

"Oh, don't worry. It's not my mom's. I found this in my grandma's jewellery box. I was looking for some jewellery to match my red outfit and found this piece. I'm going to replace it when I get back. It's a great coincidence that it matches perfectly with the earrings—as if it were a set."

A knock on the door provided an excellent opportunity to Annie to smooth over the situation. Priya jumped to her feet, reaching for her shawl and purse. She took one quick look at her reflection in the mirror before heading to the door.

"Oh, here is my escort, Annie. God, I'm so nervous. Do I look like Pearly?"

"Yes. Don't act nervous or you'll spoil everything. Wait here. I'll speak with the escort for a moment before you go," said Annie opening the door.

There stood at the door a handsome, six-foot tall youth with curly golden brown hair brushed away from the forehead, deep blue eyes, a full mouth, long neck, and broad shoulders. He was dressed in a black frock coat edged with white trimmings, snow white laced sleeves, and shining shoes.

A look of surprise settled in Annie's eyes.

"Hi, I am Ryan Hugh Prince, the escort for Miss Boone," he said sweeping a curtsy, placing one hand across his chest and bending forward elegantly.

Words stuck in Annie's mouth.

"My pleasure, Mr. Prince..." Annie stammered. "I'm Annie, the nurse at the clinic owned by Miss Boone's Aunt, Dr. Ashley Rose. Please, can I see some identification on you?"

"Certainly! Here's my escort ID from the BAU," he replied, handing the card to Annie. "I'll bring Miss Boone back at exactly 4:00. The portrait sessions will be over at three. There'll be a small get together, following which all the models will be escorted back no later than 4:00."

Annie nodded, looking at the ID briefly, and signalling to

Priya. The sound of his voice brought an alarming reaction in Priya. She started trembling.

"Oh, no. It's Ryan. He thinks I'm Pearly. What have I done?"

"May I present Miss Pearly Ruby Boone, Sir?"

The youth bent forward and curtsied in a most bewitching manner, then looked up, straightening his head. Their eyes met and locked for a split second. The colour drained from Priya's face.

"At your service, Ma'am," he whispered politely, with an elegant bow and sweep of hand across his chest. He then swiftly jumped to Priya's side, extending his right arm.

"Thank you," murmured Priya, her cheeks on fire.

She winked at Annie, before leaning on her escort's arm lightly. At the end of the corridor, Priya stopped abruptly and glanced back. Annie lifted her hand and waved. Priya waved back.

She sensed a strong vibration and magic around those two.

"What have I done? What if, those two fall head over heels in love? That would be the most tragic love story ever written. I pray they don't fall in love. What have I done?" she thought.

"How did Symoune's necklace end up in Priya's grandmother's jewellery box? What could be the connection between the necklace and Priya's grandmother and Symoune?" Annie became troubled.

Annie kept pacing back and forth for a long time. Finally, distraught and tired, with a long face, she sank down into an armchair. The telephone ring made Annie jump.

"Hi, Annie, I'm calling to let you know that I'm on my way back to the hotel. I'm worried about Pearly. She must not exert herself too much or we'll have a very sick lady on our hands."

"Hello . . . hello . . . hello?"

Annie began to shiver.

"Annie, are you there? Annie—?"

"Yes, I'm here. It's a bad connection, Dr. Ashley. You don't have to cut short your day. Everything is fine. Besides, Pearly has gone to the fundraiser."

"She had looked awful when I looked in on her this morning."

"She's fine now. Everything is under control."

"Can you put Priya on the phone? She must be bored out her mind without Pearly."

"Well, she's not here at the moment—"

"Where is she, Annie?"

"She's in the bathroom . . . washing her hair. She will be there for a while."

"Okay. Are you sure you don't want me to come back?"

"I'm positive, Dr. Ashley. Enjoy yourself." Annie slammed the phone down with shaking hands.

What a narrow escape. Please God; bring Priya back before Dr. Ashley gets back."

"Has anyone ever told you, Annie, that you worry too much," remarked Pearly, smiling at Annie's perturbed face. "You're making a big deal out of nothing. Can you bring me some water, please?"

Annie smiled, pouring water from the jug and handing it to Pearly.

"Annie, let's play cards," suggested Pearly, sitting up. "Priya will be back before we can finish one game." She continued, "I will tell auntie that my portrait needed a touch-up and it will arrive next week. I have more than five hundred rupees saved up for the rainy days. I will get my portrait done next week at the BAU. No one will find out. Okay? Now quit worrying and give me a smile."

"Sounds like a plan—" agreed Annie, pulling a deck of cards and a small booklet from her purse.

"C'mon, let's have some fun. I'll read your fortune, Pearly?"

"Okay! I need to find out when will I meet my prince charming?"

"Girl, you just missed your prince charming. He's with Priya. I've never seen anyone more handsome than him," smiled Annie, sitting at the edge of the bed.

A surprised look crossed Pearly's eyes.

"C'mon! It's not as if he's going to propose marriage to Priya in one meeting."

They laughed. The dark cloud of tension slipped away.

"Are you ready to draw your card? I'm finished shuffling."

"Shuffle, one more time. I need accurate information on my Prince Charming," she giggled.

"In that case, concentrate on your question. Pull the card in one quick motion and put it face down."

"It is a black card," Pearly yelled, opening her eyes. "It portends disaster. Shuffle again."

Annie smiled and reshuffled the deck. Pearly closed her eyes again and drew the card.

"It's the 'black jack' again. What does it mean? Is my prince charming going to be an Indian?"

Annie burst into laughter—a hearty laughter. She turned over the pages of the book and read:

"*If you draw this card; it means — the people that are close to you in your life will experience many tragic incidents. A lot of unhappiness will come your way. You will survive if you stay strong.*"

"Annie, shuffle again." Pearly's eyes became pensive.

"No. It's not good to repeat." Annie shook her head.

"Why not? Three strikes are perfectly fair. C'mon, I dare you!"

Annie reshuffled the cards. Pearly drew a 'black ace' and placed it in the middle of the bed.

Annie became alarmed. She read:

"*If you draw this card, you will face many undesirable situations. You will have to draw on your inner strength to face the adversity that awaits you.*"

Pearly's face darkened.

"Now, it's my turn," said Annie, trying to change the atmosphere of gloom in the room. Pearly started to shuffle the cards. Annie drew a 'six of clubs.'

Annie and Pearly bent over the book and read:

"*If you draw this card; a dark and sinister force will surround your life path. A series of disasters will come your way. You will have to be strong to overcome the evil forces.*"

A shiver ran down Pearly's spine. Annie too was scared.

PRINCESSA AND THE ROSE
PORTRAIT OF PEARLY - FACE OF PRIYA

He had named her rose; she was rose like sweet;
So was each meeting, they had planned to meet.

"You're awfully quiet, my lady," said Ryan, breaking the icy silence between the two. "I know that my surprise has come as a shock to you." Ryan shrugged. "Please forgive me."

"Only if you promise to forgive me after you meet with my surprise." Priya sounded preoccupied.

"Planning a surprise for me, how nice?" Ryan laughed, slowing down at the elevator.

"Not all surprises are pleasant," suggested Priya, continuing to walk towards the staircase.

"Allow me to be the judge," said Ryan. "We just passed the elevator," he asked, stopping momentarily and looking sideways. "Do you want us to take the stairs?"

"I'll take the elevator. You'll take the stairs."

"I don't understand —" Ryan blinked in surprise.

"That's my surprise and on my . . . terms."

"In that case, state your terms, Lady Pearly."

"I challenge you to race me to the main floor. If you reach before I get off the elevator, we should start over with proper introductions and you can escort me to the fundraiser. If not, you will never follow me again — no questions asked. Agreed?"

"Aha! Trying to get rid of me? I intend to reach the appointed spot long before you do."

"In that case," smiled Priya. "May I inform you that there are 300 stairs between the seventh floor and the first floor? I know it, because I counted them. It takes less than two minutes to reach the main floor by the elevator. I hope you're planning to do 150 stairs per minute. Any questions?"

"Just one. Why are you ruining the most beautiful moment of our lives?"

"I'm trying to provide us an opportunity to walk away while we can."

"I promise to walk away, if I lose," said Ryan, studying Priya's face closely. "You must promise to do something, if I win."

"Promise you what?" asked Priya, with knit eyebrows.

"To live in the present moment and give me a chance to prove that I'm a perfect gentleman."

"I agree," replied Priya. She added, "Shall I give you a countdown from five? I'm not sure if I should say good luck or goodbye?" Priya teased Ryan.

"Good luck would be fine," winked Ryan, getting ready to move.

"Five. Four. Three. Two. One. Go—"

Ryan dashed out of the door.

Priya ran towards the elevator. She stopped seeing the "occupied" sign.

"It'll be over soon. There's no way Ryan can climb three hundred stairs in a few minutes." *She felt relieved.*

"What if he does?" *A frown crossed her forehead. She started pacing the floor.*

"Even if he's able to, it will still be over after I tell him that I'm not Pearly. He'll be furious. I'm doing the right thing," *she reassured herself.*

The elevator door swung open. Priya hesitated before squeezing her way to the back row to avoid the piercing eyes. The elevator halted on the third floor and two British Security Officers appeared on the scene. One of them quickly stepped forward to push the *stay* button and the second person began to address the crowd in the elevator.

"Ladies and gentleman," he said. "We're conducting a random security check. I must ask everyone to dismount for a few minutes to allow us to check your security passes. Please line up in the hall. We apologise for the inconvenience. We must take every possible step for your safety."

Priya followed the crowd into a medium size hall. She looked abstractedly at the line-up, taking her place in the middle of the hall. A British officer was checking the personal ID's against the list of names on the register.

"May I see your ID, Ma'am?" the officer asked, looking over her shoulder for her escort.

"I don't have it... on me," replied Priya, nervously. "I forgot to bring it. Is that a problem, Sir?"

"What's your name, Ma'am?"

"Pearly Ruby Boone, Sir."

"I'm afraid, I've to ask you to step aside, Ma'am."

"How long will that be? I have an escort waiting for me in the lobby."

"What's the name of your escort, Ma'am?"

"Ryan Hugh Prince."

"Where are you headed, Ma'am?"

"To the *Royal Fundraiser, Fantasy,* in the *Crystal Auditorium.*"

"If you'll step aside for a few minutes, Ma'am, I'll personally escort you to the lobby. It's my duty to ensure the safety of our guests especially someone as young as you are."

Priya was about to step aside when she remembered something. She quickly dived into her purse, and pulled out a ticket. She handed it to the officer, saying, "Excuse me, officer; here is my ticket for the Royal Fundraiser, with my name P. R. Boone on it."

"Ummm..." murmured the officer, studying the ticket and verifying the name and suite number with the register. "It will do, this time. Be sure to carry your ID at all times. Run along." A shadow crossed Priya's face when she got off the elevator.

"Ryan is not here. It's over. I'll have to go back to my suite now, alone. I did the right thing."

As she turned to leave, she caught the reflection of Ryan in the mirror on the wall.

"And you thought I lost —" They burst into laughter.

"It's time to start with a new slate. May I have the permission to introduce myself, my lady?" said Ryan, straightening his shoulders.

Priya nodded.

"I'm Ryan Hugh Prince, your escort to the Royal Fundraiser, my lady," said Ryan, sweeping an elegant curtsy. "Now it's your turn to introduce yourself."

"I — I — I am..." The words stuck in her throat.

"May I have the honour of presenting Miss Pearly Ruby Boone, Sir?" A voice from behind startled them. Priya felt relieved.

"Thank you, Officer Mark, meet Ryan Hugh Prince," she said, taking over the introductions.

"Thank you," replied the officer, shaking Ryan's hand. "You dropped your fundraiser entry ticket on the floor. I found it. This could cause you trouble at the door because of the restricted entry."

"Thank you, Sir, for rescuing me!" Priya let out a deep sigh of relief.

"A word of caution," said the officer, addressing Ryan, "Kindly escort the lady right to her suite, for the sake of security, Sir? Have a nice day!"

Ryan nodded, surveying Priya from head to toe, before extending his arm to her.

"Is something wrong with the dress?" Priya felt apprehensive.

"Something missing would be more like it. Would you mind, if we take a short detour to fix it?"

"Where are you taking me?"

"*Just close your eyes, honey, hold my hand. And step with me into the magic land.*"

"I didn't know we were going to the magic land and that you were a poet?"

"It's a surprise. Close your eyes. Let me guide you. Keep walking."

"I feel like a blind person. Can I open my eyes now?"

"Sure. We've arrived at the *Fantasy Rose Garden Exhibition* put up by the BAU in conjunction with the fundraiser. Step into the paradise, my lady—" Ryan said with sweep of the hand.

"Beautiful," Priya giggled, stepping into a big hall turned into a magical rose garden. Hundreds of roses in all colours, flashed before her eyes against the background of heavenly music and giant murals of green, blue sea with rising and falling waves. The fragrance of the roses, the sound of the water splashing against the rocks, the magnificent murals and bewitching costumes—English and Indian—created a breathtaking atmosphere in the room.

"A single red rose for the lady," ordered Ryan, choosing a flawless, red rose from a bunch.

"Good choice! It comes without thorns and matches with the ruby red dress, Sir," remarked the shopkeeper, placing the single red rose in the middle of a silver tray and extending it to Ryan.

"The rose is ready for presentation to the lady, Sir," said the shopkeeper, placing money in the box.

Picking up the rose from the silver tray, Ryan said, "A symbol of my devotion, to a perfect friend I met by accident. The Princess and the Rose are now ready for the painting session."

"Since countless ages, I had been dreaming for this hour; though the realization of my dreams never seemed in my power," whispered Priya.

"A poetess! What else do we have in common? I can't wait to find out," Ryan said.

Priya stepped into the dazzling hall, making a fairy tale entrance on the arm of Ryan over the announcement in progress:

"Ladies and gentleman welcome to *Fantasy Fundraiser*," the announcer said, "The escorts are requested to present the models at their designated spots identified on the entry tickets. The portrait painting sessions will be three hours long. There will be a ten-minute break every half-hour. Refreshments will be provided to the models. The models are not to converse with anyone other than their escorts and their artists."

"Ready," asked Ryan, studying Priya.

Priya nodded, blushing.

The announcer continued, "A batch of fifty spectators will be allowed in every half-hour to view, judge and suggest themes and poems matching with the paintings of their choice. The first 100 spectators and the escorts are eligible to enter portrait themes and poems. You can enter only one theme or one poem for one painting session of your choice. The poem has to be original. A panel of judges will select the portraits with the matching themes and poems. The winning entries will be published in *The Fantasy Models of the Royal Fundraiser 1903 Book*."

"Oh, No! I can't let that happen. I'll be impeached for false entry," Priya said to herself and trembled.

The *fantasy portraits* created such a stir in the public that the organizing team had to be doubled up to manage the hundreds of spectators trying to gain entry to the *Crystal Auditorium*. Priya had never imagined anything more exciting than watching her image being transported onto canvas under the watchful eyes of hundreds of silent spectators and unforgettable music. Every now and then the hall echoed with rounds of applause for the artists who curtsied elegantly in response.

"Thank you for being an excellent model, Miss Boone. I would be honoured to have my painting published in the *Fantasy Book*. See you at the unveiling of the exhibit. Bye," said the artist, gathering his stuff.

"I must level with Ryan to stop the publication of my portrait," Priya panicked.

"Ryan, I need to speak with you," said Priya, preparing to level with Ryan.

"Why don't you hold the thought? I can't wait to see *Princessa and the Rose*," said Ryan, gently pulling Priya by the arm and leading her through the exhibit.

They leisurely strolled through the breathtaking display of portraits arranged in three sections:

Section 1: Unique Portraits
Section 2: Compelling Portraits
Section 3: Stunning Portraits

"Please, God, don't let my portrait be published. I promise never to lie again." Priya dragged her feet.

They were halfway through the exhibit when the announcer came on the stage to announce the results of the *People's Choice*.

"Welcome, everyone," he said. "I wish to thank all the artists for the donation of their labour. The proceeds from the sale of the tickets and the book of paintings will be donated to the Simla Orphanage, courtesy of the BAU."

Applause.

"We've prominently displayed in *Section (1)* of the exhibit, twenty-five portraits, selected in the category of *Unique Portraits*. Every one of the portraits is one-of-a-kind, real treasure. Please, give a big hand to the *Unique Artists* whose names are listed in *Section (1)* of the exhibit. *The Fantasy Book One* will become a publication of twenty-five *Unique Portraits*."

Applause.

"The Fantasy Book Two will include twenty-three Compelling Portraits and two Stunning Portraits, entitled, The Summer Breeze by Andrew McKenna with Model, Laura King & Mystery by Albert Nigel with Model, Nancy Smith. These portraits were unveiled earlier this afternoon. Please give another big hand of applause to the artists in the categories of *Unique, Compelling,* and *Stunning Portraits.*"

The People clapped as the artists rose from their seats to acknowledge the applause.

"The name of the Award Winning Fantasy Portrait of 1903 is The Princessa and the Rose by Cole Diamond; the fantasy model of this year is Pearly Ruby Boone! The name of the Fantasy Poem of this year is English Rose by Ryan Hugh Prince!"

The room shook with loud applause again.

"May I invite to the stage the artist, Cole Diamond, the model, Pearly Ruby Boone, and the poet, Ryan Hugh Prince for the unveiling of the Fantasy Portrait of the Year, *Princessa and the Rose?*"

Ryan and Cole Diamond jumped to their feet.

Priya rose from her seat looking stunned.

She felt like she had died and gone to heaven. Her mind went blank with two opposing sensations, pulling her in two different directions—a sense of shock at her deception and a sense of elation at her stunning achievement. She couldn't remember how she got on the stage and what she said. The only image that kept flashing in her mind was the Princessa and the Rose and Ryan's voice reciting the English Rose:

You look from a distance or up close,
She looks like a perfect English Rose.

STORM AND THE FUNDRAISER
MYSTERY OF THE BIRTHMARK

The sunny days weren't destined to last.
Their stormy past simply blew them apart.

"Dr. Ashley, What's wrong? You seem a bit anxious," asked Major Singh, observing her standing alone by the large window with a frown on her forehead.

"I was just wondering—"

"Yes?"

"What would be the possibility of the Maharaja missing me if I disappeared for a short while?"

"Why?"

"I would like to surprise Pearly at the fundraiser."

"Wait, I'll check with the Maharaja."

He walked over to the Maharaja who was entertaining a group of friends to a game of Bridge. The Maharaja enjoyed playing cards as much as his friends loved his lavish style and generous stakes. The Major bent over and whispered in his ear. The Maharaja looked up with questioning eyes. He glanced in Ashley's direction and smiled.

"You may go, my dear, and join Pearly at the fundraiser."

"Thanks a million." Ashley rushed to the door, feeling excited. The Major stood by the window watching her until her carriage looked off.

"Can you stop for a minute at that flower stall, Lakshman?"

"Yes, Ma'am. What would you like?"

"A bunch of lilies," said Ashley, pulling two rupees from her purse. The coachman returned in a flash with a bunch of lilies wrapped in a tissue.

"Thank you. My niece likes to wear lilies in her hair on special occasions."

"Unlike the Indian women who wear flowers all the time," the coachman laughed.

Ashley laughed with him. She had never felt more relaxed.

"Who taught you to speak in English, Lakshman?"

"English ladies like you, Ma'am. Are you planning a surprise for your niece?"

"Yes, she is attending a fundraiser at the hotel. Do you know what it means?"

"We call it a *Mela* in India," he said, stopping the coach and waiting for Ashley to dismount.

Ashley rushed up the steps, feeling excited. She couldn't wait to see Pearly in her mother's gown.

"Dr. Ashley, It's wonderful to see you at the wind-up reception. Here follow me," remarked Malcolm, an old friend, shaking her hand and escorting her into the auditorium. They walked together feeling excitement in the air.

"Dr. Ashley, we had no idea that your niece, Pearly, was such an accomplished pianist. Our regular pianist couldn't make it. Something came up. We asked around for a volunteer performer. Guess what? Pearly graciously filled in. The audience is going crazy over her performance. She's playing her third and final piece now. What an exposure!"

"Pearly . . . an accomplished Pianist?" *A puzzled look crossed Ashley's forehead.*

"There she is! Isn't she the most beautiful sight in this room? Why don't you follow me to the vacant seat, right by the stage? You'll have a perfect view of your niece." Malcolm said.

"Thank you," said Ashley, taking a quick peek at the striking back pose before taking the seat.

The stage began to revolve slowly, creating a three-dimensional appearance. Ashley sat mesmerised, taking in every detail — the dazzling gown, the shining hair, and the ivory neck, until her eyes stopped at the strange spot, glistening along the side of her long, slender neck.

Her puzzled look turned into sheer horror as the stage spun, bringing her face to face with Priya.

"*What the hell is Priya doing, impersonating Pearly on the stage?*

Where's Pearly? What's that strange familiar mark on her neck?" Ashley's heart stopped for a second.

Her restless eyes kept wandering until she noticed Symoune's necklace, shimmering around Priya's neck, matching perfectly with the ruby, pearl earrings.

"How did this necklace turn up on Priya? I had come to the fundraiser with intent to surprise my niece but clearly the surprise is on me."

She stood up in confusion, dropping the beautiful lilies on the floor.

"Dr. Ashley, leaving so soon? Please stay for the reception," said Malcolm, approaching her.

"There's something I must take care of. Have a good evening and thank you," muttered Ashley.

She walked straight to her carriage. She asked the coach to drive on.

"Where to, Madam?" he asked, surprised by the speedy return.

"Anywhere! Just drive around. Keep going, until I ask you to turn back to the hotel."

"Yes, Madam," he said, eyeing the dark clouds and feeling the strong wind whipping through him.

Ashley sat still. The tattoo and the necklace kept flashing in her mind's eye.

"Why does that tattoo disturb me so much? It's only a tattoo. What could be the reason?"

"Did you say something, Madam?" asked the coachman. He received no response.

Ashley kept thinking with her chin in her hands. She kept asking the same questions.

"Where did Priya find the necklace? Why do I feel like something awful has happened? Why am I so scared?" Ashley kept trying to connect the dots.

"Why have you stopped?"

"It looks like a storm's on the horizon, Ma'am. If you permit, we should head back."

"Oh, the storm!" exclaimed Ashley, becoming aware of being soaked to the skin.

The only storm she had noticed was the one raging inside her chest.

"You're drenched to the skin, Lakshman."

"So are you, Ma'am. You look troubled. Is something the matter?"

"A bit confused may be. Thank you for your concern. How long have we been driving?"

"A couple of hours, Ma'am! I wish you were feeling better."

"I'm all right. Please, turn back. Thank you again."

The coachman lifted his arms up to take his shirt off; twisting it several times to wring the water out, before putting it back on. They drove back through the pouring rain, getting soaked.

Ashley handed a generous tip and mumbled *many thanks* for the ride, before dismounting.

"You're a very nice lady. May Lord Krishna help you solve your problem. *Jai Shri Krishna!*"

"*Jai Shri Krishna.* I'll see you tomorrow," Ashley replied, moving on with heavy steps towards the hotel without a backward glance, dreading the idea of facing Priya, Pearly, and Annie.

Annie was standing by the window. Her heart skipped a beat at seeing Ashley come up the steps. She rushed to the bathroom and banged on the door.

"Priya, get out of the dress and jewellery... fast. Dr. Ashley's on her way up," she screamed.

A commotion fell over the suite. Pearly's eyes grew large with fear.

"Annie, catch the dress and jewellery. Put it back. Quick—" Priya shouted.

Annie quickly gathered the items and shoved them into the suitcase, oblivious of the sound of the necklace landing on the floor.

"Pearly, help me, with the buttons on my back. Come on quick," Priya screamed.

"Thank God, you got back on time," murmured Pearly, fumbling with the buttons.

Dr. Ashley stepped into the suite looking dishevelled and wet. The telephone rang.

"Hello," said Pearly. "Captain Jones is arriving at 7:00 to escort us to the reception; to meet him at the hotel lobby," she echoed. "Fine, thank you," she quickly replaced the receiver.

Ashley stood at the door dripping.

"There you are, auntie," she shouted, making an eye contact. "You're soaking wet!"

"Why are you shouting?" The icy tone in Ashley's voice made everyone jump.

"Sorry," said Pearly. "I'll fetch your gown in a jiffy."

"Is there some tea in that pot?" Ashley inquired, eyeing Priya sitting in front of the mirror with a guilty look and Annie pretending to fix her curls.

"Plenty. Here, slip into this gown," said Pearly, pushing Ashley gently towards the bathroom.

The three exchanged conspiring looks after Ashley proceeded to the bathroom. Pearly rushed to pour tea as soon as Ashley came out of the bathroom, wearing a big towel around her head.

The three exchanged conspiring looks again. Ashley sank into the armchair and started sipping tea. She began watching Priya intently. Annie took note of the strange look from Ashley and pretended to put finishing touches to Priya's hair.

"Auntie, may we go now to Priya's suite? Our hair's done," Pearly asked.

Ashley kept studying Priya's face, making everyone nervous.

"Auntie, we're wearing white *Saris* and white jewellery and of course, the same hairstyles. I'm going to help Pearly with wrapping the *Sari*. We'll meet you in the hotel lobby at 7:00 sharp. Let's go, Pearly," said Priya, moving quickly to the door.

Pearly followed Priya, looking anxious.

"Wait, how was the fundraiser?" Ashley's eyes searched through Pearly.

"It was awesome. It was the most memorable day of my life, auntie?"

"Where is the portrait?"

"Oh, it will be sent to us later. It needed a little touch up," cut in Annie.

"How do you know that, Annie? I was asking Pearly?" Ashley's tone was hard as nails.

"Pearly told me so, Dr. Ashley," replied Annie, blushing profusely. "I asked her the same thing immediately. I was dying to see the portrait."

"Do you like my hair? Annie put it up for the reception tonight," Priya cut in.

"Very nice, except you need to fix those curls in the back. Can I help?"

"Sure, that would be very nice. Do you want me to come over to you, auntie?"

"No; stay right there. I'll come over," said Ashley in a voice cold as ice. Priya trembled.

At the pretext of rearranging the curl, Ashley peeked at the mark on her bare neck. She froze.

She remembered handing Symoune the tattoo box on the eve of her death. "A gift in the flesh? What is it going to be, Symoune?" Ashley flashed back. "A necklace of rubies and pearls," Symoune had replied.

She remembered that Symoune was a skilled tattoo master and had the similar tattoo engraved behind her neck. She had intended to put that tattoo on Pearly ever since she was conceived.

Ashley stepped back in horror, feeling something under her foot. She bent down, opening her hand. It was Symoune's necklace. Ashley gazed at the necklace in her palm in utter disbelief.

Annie and the girls shuddered. "What is Symoune's necklace doing on the floor? How did it get there?" asked Ashley.

A complete hush fell over the room.

Ashley stood in the middle of the room looking formidable.

"I asked a question. Can someone tell me, who found this necklace and where?" Ashley demanded.

"I found this," said Priya, stepping forward.

Ashley lifted her eyes in surprise. Annie and Pearly looked on blankly.

"Why is everyone freaking out at seeing a simple necklace," shouted Priya, rebelliously.

"A simple necklace?" roared Ashley, like a lion.

"Yes, a simple necklace—I found it in my grandma's jewellery box before coming on this trip. I was looking for a piece of jewellery to match my red and white dress and found this. What's the big deal about it?" asked Priya, throwing her arms up in the air in a frustrated gesture.

"You found it in your grandma's jewellery box?" Ashley's tone was ruthless and her eyes bloodshot.

"Yes, I did," Priya, shouted back at Ashley like a rebel, fighting the tears and biting her upper lip. "Why don't you question my grandma when we get back? Maybe she and Aunt Symoune bought the same pieces together or something. I don't know and I don't care! Pearly, let's go to my suite."

Priya stormed out of the suite, slamming the door.

Pearly remembered the gypsy warning.

Annie looked troubled.

"May I go now, Aunt Ashley?" Pearly asked hesitantly.

"Yes," Annie interjected, making light of the situation. "Go now or you two will be late for the reception. Don't worry; we'll sort out this mix-up. It's just something sentimental for Dr. Ashley."

Pearly stopped at the door, looking back apologetically before walking out of the door. She had never heard Ashley raise her voice, let alone lose control. She was perplexed. Annie rushed to close the door behind Pearly. With an agonizing look, she faced Ashley standing still under the glittering chandelier.

In a gesture of extreme rage, Ashley picked up the cup from the table and smashed it on the floor. The room shook with the sound of shattered china. Annie shivered in fear as she kneeled down to pick up the pieces. Ashley sank down on the floor and started crying incoherently ...

"I remember everything. What have we done? Priya is Symoune's baby." Ashley was inconsolable.

Annie blinked her eyes, trying to make out the conversation.

"What are you trying to say, Dr. Ashley? Are you saying what I think you're saying?" she said, wrapping an arm around Ashley's shoulders.

"Annie, try to guess why we couldn't find Symoune's necklace?" Ashley murmured in anguish.

"Because when I gave away the baby, she was wearing it." Annie replied, with a sense of deep shock.

Ashley nodded. She hesitated before continuing, "Menakshi had seen that necklace on Symoune a hundred times when she was pregnant. It is a one-of-a-kind necklace. Why did she hide the fact from the very people who helped her? I wonder if Menaka knows the secret as well—"

"We never knew that the secret we were carrying all these years held another devastating secret underneath, and that it would come back to haunt us forever," said Ashley clinging to Annie on the floor and crying bitterly.

RECEPTION OF THE ELITE
DEPARTURE OF PRINCE

Why can't I forget you; I am deeply amazed.
Why your memory haunts me nights and days.

"May I have the pleasure of presenting Miss Pearly Ruby Boone and her friend, Miss Priya Partap Singh, Sir General Scott?" announced Captain Jones, bending forward gracefully.

The girls stepped forward shyly.

They lit up the room with their sparkling looks.

General Scott leaped to his feet, holding a cigar and flashing his diamond-studded rings.

"Indeed, I'm honoured!" he replied, sweeping the girls in a warm embrace.

A complete hush fell across the room. The guests looked on mesmerised.

"And now, may I present Miss Annie Beth Black, the chaperone, Sir?"

"Welcome to my reception, Miss Black," replied General Scott, graciously shaking Annie's hand and looking over her shoulder.

"Where is Dr. Ashley?"

"She's running a bit late, Sir," Annie stammered, with downcast eyes and a shy look.

"Indeed," nodded General Scott, eyeing the girls.

"May I have your attention, please?" he said, positioning himself in the middle of the two girls and grabbing their hands.

"Tonight, I've the unique honour of presenting my lovely niece, Miss Pearly Ruby Boone," he said, straightening his shoulders. "And her best friend—Miss Priya Partap Singh."

Everyone clapped. Pearly and Priya curtsied shyly. Women started whispering . . .

"General Scott has a niece? What a beautiful niece? Who is the other one?"

"Ladies and gentlemen," said General Scott, raising a glass of champagne to the audience. "Please, join me in proposing a toast to our two most beautiful Goddesses—Pearly and Priya."

The room shook with cheers and whistles.

"Now, ladies and gentlemen, look for your dance partners quickly, because in exactly one minute, the drums are going to roll and I'll open the floor for the dance. So, have a great evening!"

The guests rose from their seats, looking for their dance partners.

"May I have this dance, Miss Pearly?" asked Captain Jones, flashing a smile.

"My pleasure," Pearly replied graciously, placing her hand on his arm.

Annie's eyes settled on a middle-aged officer standing close to her. He leaped towards Annie.

Priya felt a breeze sweep across her neck, followed by a whisper in her ear. She jumped out of her skin, swirling around. Her eyes dived into two most unforgettable eyes.

"It's Ryan Hugh Prince at your service, Lady Pearly?" he said, emerging out of the shadows.

Priya was on fire. She looked away in confusion and then looked back at him.

"May I have the honour of this dance, my lady?"

Priya felt being swung on the dance floor. She gazed at the shimmering blonde hair neatly brushed back from the forehead and tied in a ponytail with a tiny ribbon. Her eyes studied every detail—the expensive texture of the black velvet coat trimmed with white lace, the snow-white breeches, and the perfectly polished high-heeled shoes. Ryan gazed back, amused.

Time stood still.

Not one word passed between the two.

How long they danced. They had no idea. Suddenly the music stopped. Priya came out of her trance at being swung out of the dance floor into a quiet garden as smoothly as she was swung in. Ryan extended his arm to steady her as she slipped out of the encircling arms.

They sat down on the steps. Ryan cleared his throat to say something.

Priya became apprehensive.

"I'm sorry, Lady Pearly, I've to take your leave now. My uncle's waiting for me as we speak. Tomorrow, I head back to England. I won't be back for another eight years."

"Eight Years? Who's your uncle?" Priya heard her voice, weak and frail.

"Brigadier Edward Hugh Prince. He is the Commanding Officer of the Second British Indian Battalion at Calcutta Headquarters. After my father's death last year, my uncle brought me with him to India for one year. I'll be back in eight years to serve as a trained army officer in India. When I come back, I'll find you."

Priya felt like someone threw a glass of icy water on her face and she turned into ice. Ryan pulled out a perfect rose from inside his vest and smiled.

"May this Rose remind you of the moment we met and built a bond of friendship. I'll come back in eight years to seek your hand in marriage," he whispered, stepping back into the shadows, leaving her standing alone with his scent in the air and the image of the two deep set blue eyes.

Priya was stunned.

"I didn't even tell him my real name. He thinks I'm Pearly. Oh, God, what would Pearly say?"

She lay down on the steps, looking deep into the sky, studded with stars.

"Oh, God, I would give anything to trade places with Pearly; to have the freedom to choose my own life partner. My parents will never let me accept a proposal from Ryan," Priya moaned to herself.

The images floated across her eyes . . .

Ryan handing the rose . . . Ryan escorting her to the fundraiser . . . Ryan gazing at her at the fundraiser . . . Ryan escorting her back to the suite . . . Ryan meeting her at the Bhopal Pavilion . . . Ryan dancing with her . . . the moist eyes . . . the abrupt goodbye . . .

"There you are, Priya. We've been looking all over for you. What the hell are you doing lying on the steps like a *tragic Greek Goddess?*" Pearly shouted.

"I came out for some air."

"What are you writing in the dark?"

"I'm writing a lyric."

"Oh, really? Let's go inside. Annie and Aunt Ashley are getting concerned—"

"It's too stuffy inside."

"Are you nuts, Priya? Get up and let's go."

Pearly kept eyeing the rose and writing.

"Where did you get that rose? Who's giving you roses daily?"

"I found it." Priya lied.

"The hell you did. Priya, level with me—who's giving you the roses?" Pearly was furious.

"An Englishman! I met him at the fundraiser—"

"And you're writing a lyric for him. How old is he?" remarked Pearly.

"He's eighteen. We're just friends."

'Do you know the consequences if you pursue this madness?"

"My parents would kill me. The *Rajputs* are known to kill for honour." Priya said in anguish. "I'm scared, Pearly. Promise me that you will save me. You always do."

"I promise to die for you, if it makes you feel better," Pearly replied, snatching the paper from Priya's hands. "Excellent lyric, Priya! I hope he loves you as much as you love him."

"That's the problem. He loves Pearly."

"What the hell, I've never met him—"

"He thinks I'm Pearly. The day I crashed into him on the stairs, I was wearing the jacket with your name-tag, Pearly, on it. The day he escorted me to the fundraiser, I was impersonating you."

"And you never corrected your name when you met him today. My God, Priya?"

"There was no time. I was too overwhelmed. He left suddenly."

"And you let him go away thinking of you as Pearly. I've never seen this side of you before."

"That's why I've been sitting here, wishing that I was Pearly."

"Gosh, Priya! What have you done? I advise you to get him out of your head at once."

"No. He'll be back in eight years to seek my hand in marriage." Priya was adamant.

"Priya, we must never switch identities again. Never! Are you listening?"

"The damage is done. My family will kill me for wanting to marry out of caste."

"Don't worry, Priya, you'll forget him in eight years. We must leave."

Pearly grabbed Priya's arm and shook it hard.

"Ouch . . ." Priya screamed.

"Please, let's go Priya. I need to find my own mystery man somewhere in this party after losing my Englishman to you. You cheater . . ." Pearly lashed out at Priya.

Priya didn't move. Pearly took a swing at Priya, kicking her in the stomach.

'Ouchhhh, that hurt—"

"Seriously, Priya, I'll reveal your secret if you don't get up at once. Consider this an order!"

Priya stood up, holding onto her rose.

Pearly grabbed her hand and pulled Priya along with an angry face. The strange turn of events had made her jealous and angry at the same time. She snatched the paper from Priya's hands and started reading it:

So softly he whispered, so gently he touched,
   so warmly he kissed and held my hand.
      I felt like a most beautiful woman,
         he felt like an angel from the magic land.

He touched me — just like in the dreams,
   I forgot everything and I forgot everyone.
      Just the kind of love that held me spellbound,
         And made me towards him wildly run.

I believe my love was a gift from God,
   a gift for being so good through the years.
      A kind of love one reads in the books.
      A kind of story one likes to hear.

Chapter Five
The Ghost of Ashley

RECEPTION OF THE ELITE
GHOST OF ASHLEY

She opened her arms in a loving embrace.
There stood her ghost, staring in the face.

Pearly and Priya walked in hand in hand, through the long corridor illuminated by multicolored chandeliers. Halfway through the corridor, they caught a glimpse of Ashley pacing back and forth in an agitated manner.

"Priya, you had better hide the rose," whispered Pearly, letting go of Priya's hand.

The door at the end of the hallway opened unexpectedly. Ashley stopped abruptly, colliding with a slender woman emerging out of the door. Her purse fell to the floor with a thud and the contents scattered on the floor.

"I'm so sorry," she muttered, kneeling on the floor.

As Annie rushed to help the stranger recover the contents from the floor, their eyes met.

"My goodness, it's you—Miss S?" Annie shrieked.

"Oh, I'm surprised . . . to see you here, Miss . . . Annie?"

Ashley rose from the floor facing the stranger with a handful of items.

"It's my fault. I'm so sorry!"

Her eyes stayed on her face, staring, until Pearly intervened.

"Auntie, aren't you going to introduce me to your friend?"

The stranger turned her head, moving her eyes from Pearly to Priya and from Priya to Pearly.

"Is she . . . mmmmm . . . ?" She murmured, without taking her eyes off Pearly.

"I'm . . . sorry, this is my niece, Pearly," Ashley spoke without moving her lips. "And that one is — Priya Partap Singh, a friend of the family."

"And you are Saya Surya-Wanshi," Pearly smiled, extending her hand to the stranger.

With a startled look, the stranger held her hand and kept it. Their eyes locked for a spilt second and kept appraising each other from head to toe.

"How do you know my name?" the stranger spoke in perfect English, appearing visibly shaken.

"I can't believe that you've appeared in the flesh. You're much more beautiful in person."

A cloud passed over the stranger's beautiful face.

"I know everything about you. I was longing to see you," burst out Pearly.

The stranger's eyes grew large in her face with surprise.

"I would like to speak with you in private . . . if I may?" Pearly sounded excited.

The stranger hesitated, attempting to smile politely.

"Please, may I see you, in private? I need to ask you something personal, if you don't mind?"

The stranger looked alarmed. She stepped back turning her eyes squarely on Ashley and then on Annie giving them an accusatory look.

Ashley blinked her eyes in total surprise.

The stranger cupped her face in her hands, momentarily.

Pearly touched her shoulder.

She lifted her head and fled out of the corridor without a backward glance.

"Wait a minute. Wait, we are not finished yet — " screamed Pearly, following her.

Annie grabbed Pearly's arm to stop her from following her. Pearly pulled her arm free and ran behind the stranger. Annie and Priya followed Pearly. Pearly kept following the stranger until she disappeared through the doors. Ashley froze.

"There you are, Dr. Ashley. I've been looking all over for you and the girls. What are you doing here standing alone?" asked General Scott.

Ashley neither moved nor answered.

"My dear, you look like you've seen a ghost," he said, grabbing Ashley by the shoulder.

"I have! I have seen a . . . ghost." Ashley spoke under her breath.

"Where?"

"There! She was there a moment ago. She walked out that corridor."

"There's no one there," he replied, eying the corridor. "Are you under some kind of a strain?"

"No, I'm not imagining. The ghost from my past was definitely there," she said, sobbing.

General Scott bent his head to pull a silky-soft, clean handkerchief from his pocket.

"Dr. Ashley, I've big shoulders," he said, handing the handkerchief to Ashley. "Would you like to borrow them for a minute to lean on until you are not afraid of the ghost anymore?"

"Thanks," replied Ashley, resting her head on his shoulder and sobbing into his handkerchief.

"There, there, Ashley! You're not alone any more. There is no such thing as a ghost."

"I was going to escort the ladies to the Hall—" cut in Captain Jones curtly, walking in on the scene. "Is something wrong, Sir?"

"Yes, Captain," replied General Scott. "I'm relieved to see Pearly, Priya, and Annie safely by your side. Dr. Ashley has been taken ill. I'll personally escort her to the hotel suite. Could you follow me with the ladies?" he asked, wrapping one arm firmly around Ashley's waist and heading towards the exit door.

"Yes, Sir."

"Captain Jones, could you stop by the hall for a minute to inform my guests that I had to leave to deal with an emergency. Kindly ask Captain Mark to fully entertain the guests for as long as they wish to stay. I'll wait for you at the foot of the hotel steps to assist me in escorting the ladies to their suite. Is that clear?"

"Crystal clear, Sir."

General Scott remained silent until Ashley was comfortably settled in the carriage beside him. "Dr. Ashley, may I ask a personal question?"

"Please call me Ashley," she interrupted, touching his hand

politely.

"Well, Ashley," he smiled. "I'm a good listener and a great problem solver. I might be able to help you explore your options in dealing with whatever's bothering you."

Ashley sighed.

"It's not good to keep things bottled up inside. Your secret will remain safe with me."

"Thank you, General. I'm sorry. I can't."

"Please think of me as your extended family in India. Don't be afraid to open up to me. Even though we have met recently, I've become very fond of you and Pearly. She's blithe spirit. This issue might have serious repercussions on Pearly," urged General Scott.

Ashley considered his sentiments for a few minutes. Then taking a long, deep breath, she replied, "Well, I was drawn into a secret, quite inadvertently, some fifteen years ago, in the dead of the night," she paused.

"A secret—?"

"Yes. A ruthless stranger forced me to witness a young girl discard her most valuable possession—for the fear of dishonour, right at my doorstep. I was forced to find someone who would accept the discarded possession as their own. I'll say no more because I may have already said too much."

"And, you saw the ruthless ghost tonight—" said General Scott finishing the sentence.

Ashley nodded.

"And what are you going to do about that ghost?"

"I've no idea."

"I believe that it would be most therapeutic for you to take a few deep breaths and let out the name of the so-called ghost."

Ashley hesitated.

"Yes, Ashley, you must deal with your fear by bringing it out into the open. Close your eyes and tell your fears that you're going to face your ghost without flinching. Take a few deep breaths and let out the name of the so called ghost. You'll come out of this exercise feeling stronger. Ready?"

"I'm not sure—"

"Hold on to my hand to draw on my strength. I'll withdraw my hand when you no longer need it. Keep your eyes closed until you are ready."

"Yes, I must destroy my ghost before my ghost destroys me," affirmed Ashley, closing her eyes and leaning her head on the cushion.

"Ashley, open your eyes slowly and let out the name of your ghost."

Ashley opened her eyes, reaching for the General's hand before opening her mouth and whispering . . .

"Why have you come back to haunt me? I wish had never met you and your daughter, CHANDRA MUKHI."

She whispered the name under her breath before burying her head in his shoulder; unaware of the bombshell she had dropped on the unsuspecting General. The explosion hit the General like a ton of bricks. He sat completely still. His hand slipped out of Ashley's fingers and his head slid backwards with a stunned look.

The General remained silent until the carriage came to halt at the hotel. He swiftly managed to compose his face before waking Ashley, lying peacefully, resting her head on his shoulder.

"Here we are," said Captain Jones opening the door to help Ashley dismount from the coach. The General smiled politely, extending his arm.

"Are you all right, auntie?" asked Pearly, leaping forward, absent-mindedly.

Captain Jones and General Scott walked the ladies to their suite in silence.

"Thank you, General Scott. Thank you, Captain Jones. Good night and Good Bye," said Ashley, extending her hand first to General Scott and then to Captain Jones.

"Goodbye, ladies. Please call me, day or night, if there's anything I can do. I'm only a phone call away," said General Scott, with a preoccupied look.

He then walked straight through the corridor towards the staircase and said, "Good night, Captain Jones. I'm going out for some fresh air—"

"Sir," Captain Jones blinked, "It's raining outside. You mustn't venture alone."

The General had disappeared into the staircase, leaving Captain Jones alone with a baffled look. He stepped out into the pouring rain and walked for hours, getting drenched to the skin. Captain Jones kept looking for him until he found him at midnight, sitting on a bench, soaking wet. He managed to drag the disoriented General to his suite and helped him to bed. He sat by his side all night, monitoring his high temperature and watching him murmur incoherently in a delirious state.

"Chandra Mukhi . . . Chandra Mukhi . . . Chandra Mukhi, what have you done?"

The General kept having nightmare after nightmare about Chandra Mukhi and Saya Surya-Wanshi all night. His state of mind remained tangled and precarious as if he was trying to piece together a puzzle.

Ashley's words kept pounding on him in the sleep . . .

"Some fifteen years ago, I was drawn into a secret by a ruthless stranger, in the dead of the night. I was made to witness a very young girl discard her most valuable possession, right at my doorstep, for the fear of dishonour. The same stranger forced me to find someone who would fully accept this possession as their own—"

"What did the cruel Chandra-Mukhi do to my beloved, this time? What did she force her to give up at the dead of the night? What could that be?"

The mystery kept eating at the General's s heart. The more he tried to resolve the mystery the more it deepened, taking him deeper with it.

GHOST AND THE FOG
FACE OF THE HIDDEN ONE

*Come out of the shadows; I want to see,
the face of the one, who's haunting me.*

Pearly had been sitting cross-legged, with a frown between her eyebrows all morning, reading her book. She had been very quiet in the jet, all the way back from Delhi to Simla. She went straight to her room as soon as she arrived home and to bed without saying 'Goodnight' to Ashley. Her breakfast was found untouched on the tray next morning. She appeared determined to avoid her aunt ever since she had returned from the school with a pale face and a pre-occupied look.

"Pearly, you owe me an explanation," demanded Ashley, looking concerned.

"No, I don't!"

"Where is this attitude coming from?" Ashley felt uncomfortable with the sharp tone.

"I'm entitled to my privacy. Do you mind, auntie?" Pearly replied sharply.

Ashley's jaw dropped.

Pearly had been keeping her anger buried deep inside for days. Somehow her anger burst out at her aunt's prying comments. She knew that her aunt was hiding something formidable. She was trying to connect the dots and was furious with Annie for being evasive.

"Pearly, I need to know how you know Saya Surya-Wanshi." Ashley insisted, pacing the floor nervously and eyeing the door as if she was expecting someone important.

"Why this sudden interest in someone you barely knew?" Pearly's obstinate streak was showing.

"I asked the question first. I'll ask again. How do you know Saya Surya-Wanshi?"

"I just do—" Pearly replied flatly, without lifting her head from the book.

"Who told you about her?" Ashley kept pressing to get information from her mouth.

"Let me see. It wasn't you, and it definitely was not Annie, because she's sworn to secrecy," replied Pearly, raising her head from the book. "Oh, I remember who told me. It was that little birdie outside that window who told me," said Pearly, pointing to the window, in a sarcastic tone.

Ashley fell silent. She knew that if she pushed too hard, the situation would get messy. She felt troubled at the thought of being put on the spot by Pearly.

"The less I discuss the topic of Saya with Pearly, the better it would be for me," she thought.

Pearly was feeling terribly frustrated by the conspiracy of silence between Annie and Ashley. She had noticed Ashley gazing at Priya in the 'jet' with a questioning look. She had also observed a sudden change in Ashley's demeanour since the day of the fundraiser. Ashley had become overly interested in Priya and terribly stand-offish with Pearly.

"What's the mystery?" Pearly thought with a growing suspicion.

Ashley was too absorbed in her own thoughts to notice that Pearly was monitoring her every move. Pearly had noticed that her aunt was eagerly eyeing the door from time to time as if she was expecting someone to walk in any minute.

"Pearly, don't you think that you'll be more comfortable reading your book upstairs? The lighting is much better in your room," said Ashley.

Pearly's suspicions deepened at Ashley's abrupt remark. Pearly kept reading the book.

Annie walked into the room to look for Ashley. She paused at the door, and then whispered in her ear. Ashley looked shifty-eyed to check if Pearly was listening. Pearly pretended to look absorbed in the book. Her suspicions deepened when Ashley left the room quickly after Annie.

Pearly recalled the dreaded warning signalled by the cards: *"The people that are close to you in your life will experience tragic* incidents. A lot of unhappiness will come your way."

Pearly started to feel sick. She tried to feel her pulse, but her bangles got in the way. One by one, she slipped her bangles into her lap. Her pulse was racing as fast as her heartbeat. She folded the book over her chest and closed her eyes.

She kept tossing and turning until she drifted into sleep. The book and the bangles slipped from her lap over the jug of water making a tingling sound, shaking Pearly out of sleep. Pearly picked up her book and started to walk towards her bedroom. She had barely climbed the first step when something unusual made her turn back.

She had caught a glimpse of her aunt whispering in someone's ear with an envelope tucked in her hand. Pearly tiptoed back and crawled behind the curtains to overhear the conversation.

Ashley looked up to ensure that no one was close by.

"Make sure, that you hand the note to Miss Menakshi and no one else, Okay?" whispered Ashley in her quietest tone. "And come back straight to me through the back door."

"Yes, Ma'am!"

Pearly was deeply shaken by what she had heard and seen. Her aunt was obviously trying to hide some deep secret from Pearly. Her spirits sank down to a zero degree. With a sinking heart and weak knees, she tiptoed upstairs to her room. Pearly's curiosity peaked. She fell on the bed thinking about the mystery. Pearly drifted in and out of sleep with a high temperature and shivering spells—faintly conscious of her aunt and Annie's deeply alarmed faces. She felt their nervous hands on her forehead several times, changing the cold compresses to bring down her temperature. She kept complying with their instructions until her eyelids grew heavier and heavier with sleep.

The last thing she remembered before sinking into a deep sleep was—being picked waist up on the bed to prop her pillows and to open her mouth slightly to push some bitter tasting pills.

Suddenly, her body began to shiver and her mind started to slip into a series of nightmares. In her sleep, she was playing cards.

"It's a black jack," she screamed, drawing a black card.

Then a horrid creature leaned over her shoulder and

whispered in a ghastly voice . . .

"If you draw this card; a dark and sinister force will surround your life path. The people that are close to you in your life will experience tragic incidents. A series of disasters will come your way . . . come your way . . . come your way."

The words echoed in her head. She reshuffled the deck of cards and drew another *black card*. She kept tossing the number upside down to determine if that card was a *Six of Spades* or a *Nine of Spades*, until she observed an ancient looking dark door opening with a squeaking sound.

Placing one hand below her forehead, she focused on the approaching figure in the dim light.

A very tall and beautiful woman emerged out of the shadows into the room with an overpowering smile and cloud like tresses shimmering around her tiny waist. She moved with a feline like grace, in slow movements.

She stopped in front of Pearly and jerked the card out of her fingers in a quick motion, flashing her striking signet ring. Pearly read the initials 'MS' on the finger.

The beautiful woman stood still for several seconds studying the card. She slowly lifted a pair of breathtaking hazel eyes and gazed at Pearly. She looked deep into Pearly's eyes as if she was trying to choose the right words to express her thoughts.

"Ohhhhhhh," she sighed, pressing the card to her heart and started crying.

Pearly stood looking at the steady stream of crystals trickling down her magical eyes. She reached out and slipped an arm around her shoulder. The woman kept crying incoherently. Pearly watched in deep amazement, the crystals flowing from the woman's eyes. A few crystals fell inside Pearly's palm and rolled into one big grape-sized crystal.

"Oh, the amazing crystal . . ." yelled Pearly.

"Keep the crystal in your pocket for good luck," the beautiful woman whispered. "It will give you the wisdom and strength to right all wrongs and face the adversity which awaits you and me."

"You and me?"

The beautiful woman nodded.

Pearly kept staring at her unearthly beauty and grace—her

arresting eyes, deep red mouth, long wavy hair, flowing gown, and her black shimmering veil.

"I know who you are!" Pearly shrieked, recognizing her.

The beautiful woman lifted her perfectly arched, long, and beautiful eyebrows in surprise.

"We met before. You are, Saya Surya-Wanshi."

A gorgeous smile illuminated the beautiful woman's face. The crystals started to roll down her eyes again. Pearly lurched forward to gather the crystals in her palms, until her hands started to overflow with the glistening crystals. The beautiful woman bent her head and blew the crystals into the air. They glistened like diamonds before they disappeared. Pearly watched spellbound.

"Why are you crying?" she asked, feeling comfortable in her presence.

"I'm afraid that the number six card is the sign of the devil," she said, taking Pearly's hands.

Pearly shivered.

"My sweet girl, you'll have to be brave, strong, and fearless. The more strongly you face adversity, the less there will be danger that faces you. I've come to warn you!"

With teary eyes, Pearly watched the beautiful woman let go of her hands and proceed toward the dark door through which she had emerged. She watched her walk out of the door, into the dark jungle, covered with thick white fog. Pearly watched the beautiful woman move farther and farther away.

"Stop, my beautiful woman. Don't leave me again. I need you." Pearly screamed.

The beautiful woman kept moving away with her hair flying in the air and her veil trailing behind her like a cloud with a million stars.

"Stop. You cannot leave me hanging like this. I need you," Pearly kept screaming.

Suddenly, the woman stopped and warned, "My child, don't follow me," she sighed. "I want to spare you the pain of seeing the dark, hidden sight of me."

"Please, stop—" Pearly implored, catching her veil.

"No. I'm nothing more than a lonely, shattered ghost," she replied, freeing her veil from Pearly's hands. "My prolonged suffering and tortured soul have turned me into a ghost, who haunts me, day and night; in this never ending thick . . . thick . . . fog."

"Thick, thick fog . . ." *the chilling words echoed into the air.*

The woman let out an agonising scream at seeing the dispersing clouds and the full moon. She started to struggle harder and harder to free her veil out of Pearly's tight grip. It was too late. The shining rays of the moonlight had started to bathe the beautiful woman from head to toe. She ceased to struggle, looking helpless and shedding a stream of crystals from her eyes.

Pearly froze with fear.

The beautiful woman started to transform into a crystal clear statue, reflecting the surrounding images through her. Slowly she began to rise above the ground and turn into a ghost before melting and disappearing into the white, white fog.

"No!" Pearly let out a heart-wrenching scream.

She woke up screaming at the top of her lungs, shivering, and remembering every tiny detail of her dream. She found the room in darkness. She slipped into her nightgown and looked at the clock glowing in the dark. It was midnight. She called out aloud for her aunt and Annie. She heard no response except the sound of her own voice echoing back through the empty corridors.

"Where's everyone?" *she asked.*

She walked towards Ashley's room. The corridor was drenched in darkness. She tried turning on the lights, one by one. The lights wouldn't come on. "*Perhaps there's a power failure,*" she thought. A loud thunder followed by lightning struck the room. Pearly grabbed the kerosene lamp, matches from the corridor shelf, and lit the lamp, twisting the glass screen with shaking hands around the hinges.

The main window blew open, storming in the howling wind, blowing the curtains out of place with a ghastly sound. Putting the lamp on the floor she began to wrestle with the wind to secure the window. Her eyes fell over the flickering candlelight in the window of the Annexe. The Annexe door was wide open and a couple of figures were moving around.

"Who could be walking around the forbidden ground at midnight?"

She was told that the Annexe held nothing more than a few unfinished, unlucky paintings of her dad and some of Symoune's tragic belongings. The Annexe had long been the keeper of sad memories and was kept under the lock and key. No one was allowed to set foot into the Annexe.

With a sinking heart, she looked at Ashley's empty room and her unslept in bed. She rushed over to Annie's room, and found her bed was not slept in either. Crying and sobbing with fear, she slipped downstairs, hoping to find someone. Everything was drenched in darkness. She opened the main door, letting in a torrent of wind push her backwards. Putting the lamp on the floor, she started to struggle with the wind to secure the door before walking barefoot, towards the flickering candlelight and wondering if she was still in the nightmare.

DOOR INTO THE PAST
STUNNING REVELATION

*The stunning secret sealed in the past;
blew up in her face like a volcano blast.*

Pearly was drawn towards the flickering candlelight through the narrow and twisting slopes of the hill, unstopped by the savage, howling wind. She had never been more determined and frightened in her life. She had no idea whose face she would see or what secrets would be awaiting her inside the door, which had suddenly opened after remaining closed for twelve long years.

"Maybe I should turn back. What if there're some prowlers there? What if Aunt Ashley and Annie are being held hostage by the prowlers?"

Fears started to crop up in Pearly's mind, weakening her resolve. She hesitated for a while. Then her determination overtook her and she decided to confront her demons head on.
"I'll go in and let the chips fall wherever they may," said Pearly, renewing her resolve.

Burning with fever, weak and dishevelled, Pearly arrived at the doorstep of the abandoned *Annexe* to confront her past. She crept behind the shadows, beside the door and peeked inside. She was relieved to see Ashley, Annie, and Menakshi sitting in the large room with their heads together, discussing something in low and quiet tones.
"So, that's where the secret meeting is being held. At least they all seem to be safe."

She peeked into the dimly lit, dusty room, decorated in deep red and chocolate furnishings.

She felt a feeling of warmth surge through her body at seeing a huge picture of her mom and dad framed over the fireplace. They looked immensely happy, standing snug with each other in a loving way. Pearly had never seen that picture before.

She wondered why such a precious keepsake was so carelessly left in the abandoned place, gathering dust. She had always felt proud of her handsome and exquisitely gifted dad and her outrageously beautiful mother. Ashley had raised Pearly learning every detail about her parents, making them real and alive to her in the spirit.

"No, no, no!" She heard Ashley scream at Menakshi, terrifying Pearly and breaking her chain of loving thoughts about her parents. It was not what she said, rather how she said it that shocked Pearly.

"You stole my Pearly away from me. You're responsible for this tragedy," Ashley yelled again, pointing a finger at Menakshi.

Menakshi's sat motionless with downcast eyes and a guilty look.

"Why didn't you come to me immediately when you had discovered Symoune's necklace on the baby? Surely, you must have realized an abandoned, orphan baby could not have arrived with Symoune's necklace on her. Did you or did you not realize that? Answer me!"

"I didn't realize it right away," replied Menakshi. "I had simply kicked the necklace into my jewellery box without looking at it in a state of rush. I simply forgot about it."

"Then what?"

"When I did realize, which was after several weeks, it was too late to exchange the babies. Menaka had by that time become acquainted with every little detail of the baby. She had been led to believe that she gave birth to a healthy, kicking baby rather than another dead child."

"And you did not notice the peculiar tattoo or just decided to keep it a secret?"

"To snatch the baby away from Menaka or to have told her the truth at that late stage would have been very suicidal to her and Major Partap Singh," explained Menakshi, in a tortured voice.

"So what am I supposed to do now?" Ashley said, pounding on the table in a dreadful rage.

"We can't do anything except accept *Karma*," replied Menakshi, avoiding Ashley's eyes.

"And, leave my real Pearly to be raised by you people, while I live with an abandoned, orphan, pretending that she is Symoune's and Danny's baby. Never! Never! Never! I'll knock the door of the law to get my Pearly back and restore my baby to her original roots, even if this is the last thing I've to do on this earth."

The lamp dropped from Pearly's hand onto the wooden floor. She stormed off into the dark night, not knowing where. The stunning revelation from Ashley pierced through her heart like a dagger. What she had heard was way beyond her wildest fears. She felt her whole world collapse around her in million pieces. The loving picture of her mom and dad standing arm in arm over the fireplace blew up into flames right before her eyes, sending excruciating pain through her body. She kept running and hearing the dreadful words from Ashley over and over and over again:

"*And leave my real Pearly to be raised by you people, while I live with an abandoned, orphan child, pretending her to be Symoune's and Danny's baby. Never! Never! Never! I'll knock the door of the law to get my Pearly back even if this is the last thing I do on this earth.*"

In a traumatized state of mind, she kept repeating in her mind: "I am an orphan – an abandoned child. Priya is the real Pearly."

"How can I live knowing that I robbed Pearly of her rightful place? No wonder, she looks so English; she has English blood in her. I'm an orphan – a nobody. My own mother didn't want me. She kicked me out of her life right after my birth. What kind of a mother would do such a thing to an innocent child?"

She kept running until she reached home. In an unbelievable state of agony, she sank down on her knees, burying her head deep into her lap before she collapsed flat on the floor.

In the meantime, the floor of the Annex started to burn with the flames of fire, reaching over the top of the Annexe like a hungry wolf.

"Fire! Fire! Fire!" Annie shrieked in horror, noticing the flames through the window. Ashley and Annie ran helter and skelter in a state of utter confusion.

Menakshi stood up feeling dizzy. She took to the door, running blindly. She had barely reached half way through the door when a big wave of flames caught onto her dress, setting it ablaze.

She let out an agonizing scream, watching the flames rise towards her to engulf her.

"Please, someone, help me," she shrieked.

She kept screaming at the top of her lungs and pounding on the flames with her feet. The fire wouldn't let her escape. She decided to extinguish the fire by rolling out of the room. A large wood panel broke loose from the ceiling and shot towards Menakshi. The panel fell squarely over her, knocking her unconscious.

Ashley jumped out the door, over the balcony steps, on to the safe ground in one swift movement, with terrified Annie attempting to follow suit. Unfortunately, Annie's foot got caught inside a broken hole on the steps and she fell backwards screaming like a child. Ashley ran backwards at top speed to rescue Annie.

The harder Ashley pulled her foot out of the hole, the more it went deeper and deeper with maddening flames getting closer and closer. Ashley managed to get Annie out of the flames by dragging the entire wooden step. She then picked up a stone, broke open the wooden hole, and freed Annie's foot out of the panel.

"Where is Menakshi?" asked Annie, remembering suddenly.

"Dear God, she might be trapped inside the Annexe. She could be killed."

Ashley jumped into the burning flames like a tiger, to search for Menakshi, over the terrified screams of Annie behind her.

"Help! Help! Help!"

Annie kept on screaming. A bunch of neighbours came running, armed with whatever they could find, to put out the fire. Major Partap Singh, Menaka, and Priya came rushing in a highly agitated state. The Major pulled the water hose and started to fiddle with the sprinkler. Raising his arms high in the air, he started sprinkling the water over the rooftop, subduing the gigantic circle of flames, turning it into a thick, smoky cloud over the building. A thick concentration of smoke blew towards

Priya, hitting her directly in the face, sparking off a non-stop coughing fit. Menaka pushed Priya out of the smoke to a safe distance.

The neighbours surrounded Annie and started bombarding her with all kinds of questions. Some spectators simply stood by and observed the flames. A huge ball of flames exploded out of the rooftop, spreading a million sparks around. The burning rooftop came crushing down, making a high pitched bomb-blast like sound, shaking the ground beneath the feet of the spectators. All eyes turned to the partially burnt door when Ashley leaped out of the flames like a ferocious tiger, carrying someone in her arms.

The people stepped back in horror.

"Oh, God, who is she carrying in her arms?" shouted Major Partap Singh, rushing with a water hose in his hand towards the badly bruised and unrecognisable Ashley covered from head to foot with smoke, kneeling over Menakshi, who lay unconscious on the cold, wet ground, wrapped up to her neck in a huge, big blanket. The water hose slipped from his hands on the floor with a bang and the Major stood stunned.

"What the hell was 'Ma' doing at the Annexe at the middle of the night?" shouted Menaka, joining Ashley on the floor.

The Ambulance and the Fire Brigade rolled in with flashing lights and noisy sirens. The crowd stepped aside to let the firefighters take over the scene. Menakshi and Annie were rushed to the hospital accompanied by Major Partap Singh and Menaka.

Ashley stood transfixed, watching the flames until she was helped into another vehicle by the ambulance staff.

"Where is Pearly?" yelled someone in the crowd.

"Oh, Pearly! Oh, God. Oh, Pearly!" screamed Ashley, jumping out of the moving vehicle.

She began to run blindly towards her house with a frantic Priya and the neighbours following her. She tore inside the house like a maniac. Pearly lay unconscious on the floor.

"Pearlyyyy," Ashley let out a heart-wrenching scream. She dropped down on her knees, gathering Pearly's cold and unconscious body in her arms and sobbing fiercely.

"Someone, call the ambulance," she screamed, breathing heavily.

She kept cradling her body in her arms, murmuring incoherently and watching through the swinging door and the howling wind, the sight of her beautiful Annexe burnt to the ground. Priya slipped into a state of shock at seeing Pearly's lifeless body hanging in Ashley's arms.

Chapter Six
The Haunting

SHADOW AND THE GHOST
HAUNTING OF ASHLEY

The Ghost of Ashley knocks on the door.
The long, dark shadow falls on the floor.

"Please, let me go, Dr. White. My place is with Pearly during this tragic ordeal."

"Ashley, you must stay in bed until you're fit to watch over Pearly."

"No! I won't be chained to a hospital bed when my niece is fighting for her life."

"Ashley, you must get back to bed," he demanded, looking deep into her perturbed eyes.

"May I remind you that I am a doctor and as such, I can look after myself."

"But you're not looking after yourself. You're wandering around, if you'll pardon my expression, like a lunatic, disturbing my entire recovery ward."

"What would you do if you were me, Dr. White? My baby had a major stroke."

"And your baby has survived the stroke," he replied, pulling his chair closer to her.

"I will not be confined to a hospital bed at a time like this." Ashley was adamant.

"You should be relieved that Pearly is in a safe and stable mode," he argued, grabbing Ashley's hand. "What she needs at the moment is an uninterrupted rest. Do you understand?"

"What about Annie?"

"Annie's foot is in a cast and she needs to rest as well."

"Menakshi needs me. I feel responsible for her predicament."

"Because of your brave and timely intervention, Menakshi

has survived the fire with non-life threatening burns on her legs and arms. However, she has been deeply traumatised by the fire and needs to deal with this tragedy on her own terms. The less you visit her at this time, the better it would be for everyone concerned. Is that clear?"

"Please, can I visit Pearly, one more time?"

"You haven't heard anything I've said. You leave me with no choice but to sedate you," reflected Dr. White, glancing at the nurse, who approached the doctor swiftly with the tray.

Ashley's face turned white.

"Please, I would like to see Pearly, one more time. Please, please, please!"

"No, no, no! I won't allow you to risk your own welfare. Ashley, we happen to have an excellent *Burn Specialist* right here within our hospital. I've spoken with him. He will personally oversee Menakshi's skin-grafting process, as soon as possible."

A look of relief crossed Ashley's face.

"We will be transferring Menakshi to *Amritsar Burns Hospital* within two weeks to ensure that she recovers with as little scarring as possible. We're doing everything humanly possible."

"I can't win with you. Can I, Dr. White?" Ashley relaxed her clenched fists, accepting defeat.

"That's my girl! Just close your eyes and rest, Ashley. I must sedate you to keep you from wandering around the ward all night. I'll look in on you tomorrow morning. Ring the bell if you need anything. Okay?"

Ashley nodded her approval.

Deeply exhausted by the thirty-six-hour, non-stop vigil at Pearly's side, Ashley's tired body yielded to sleep quickly. She slept soundly for several hours until the clock struck midnight.

Ashley stirred out of sleep, feeling dry in the mouth.

"Water . . . water . . . water," she murmured, feeling relieved to see someone approaching her bed.

"Thank you," murmured Ashley, raising her head on one elbow and gathering the glass.

"You're welcome."

"*I've heard this quiet voice before.*" Ashley shuddered, lifting her eyes over the glass.

"Who are you? Why are you standing in the dark?" she asked, gulping the water down her throat.

The shadowy figure did not respond.

"Who are you? Please step into light so that I can see your face."

The shadowy figure began to move . . . slowly. A feeling of fear surged through Ashley. She peered into the dark to take a good look at the person. With bated breath, she watched the figure step into light and begin to remove the hood.

"No! The ghost from my past—"

The glass slipped from her fingers and shattered on the floor. The dark figure stood still.

"Why have you chosen to haunt me?" Ashley screamed, shaking her head in frustration.

"I've come to be with my baby. My baby needs me."

"Liar, liar, liar! Move back. Move back! You abandoned your baby in cold blood as soon as she was born. I'm the only mother she knows and needs," yelled Ashley, shivering like a leaf.

The shadowy figure stood still.

"I was the one who nursed the baby during her coughs and colds. I was the one who read stories and lullabies to her at night. I was the one who raised her. I'm her mother. You're nothing but a ghost from the past. You don't exist. You are only a dark shadow."

The shadowy figure started to approach the bed. Ashley was alarmed.

"Don't you dare to come near me? Get out . . . Get out. I'll ring for the nurse."

Ashley started ringing the bell and beating up on the sheets. A bunch of nurses came running into the room. Ashley kept on screaming.

"Calm down, Dr. Ashley. Calm down," said one of the nurses, wrapping an arm around her.

"Get that ghost out of my room," yelled Ashley, burying her head in her elbows.

"Please, open your eyes, Dr. Ashley. You had a bad dream. Look, there's no one here," said the nurse, gently taking Ashley's hands away from her face.

Ashley opened her eyes wide. The shadowy figure was nowhere to be seen. She glanced at the floor. There were no traces of the spilled water or pieces of the shattered glass. She stared blankly at the crowd of nurses surrounding her bed. They kept looking back politely.

"I'm . . . sorry. I must be dreaming. I apologise."

"Yes, Dr. Ashley, it was just a dream, a very bad dream. Just go back to sleep. Don't be afraid. The front door is firmly locked. Rest assured we wouldn't let anyone get past us. Is that okay?" replied her nurse, pulling Ashley's hand out of the tangled sheet.

"Yes, thank you," Ashley stammered, laying her head back on the pillow and closing her eyes.

She slipped back into sleep almost immediately, opening her eyes once or twice hearing the sound of the raging wind. She wrapped the blanket tightly around her body to keep warm. Her eyes flew open at the sound of thunder in the sky. She caught a glimpse of the shadowy figure lurking in the corner of her room.

"It's only my imagination," she thought.

She quickly closed her eyes to block the sight of the figure from her mind. She opened her eyes slowly, peering into the dark and saw the shadowy figure again.

"Get out. Get out. Get Out!" she yelled, pointing a finger at the figure in the darkness.

The figure did not move. A shiver ran through her spine. Ashley started pounding on the sheets with her eyes closed. She opened her eyes momentarily when the thunder and lightning struck. There was no one in the room. She ceased to scream.

"Oh, it was just my imagination! There's no one in the room." Ashley burst into laughter.

She wrapped her body from head to foot in blankets and began to relax, hearing the steady sound of the rain. She found herself slipping into a soothing sleep.

"Aunt Ashley, I need you. I'm scared. Aunt Ashley—"

Ashley jumped out of the bed and turned on the lights. The room was empty. Ashley was stunned.

"I heard Pearly's voice and felt her hand over my shoulder. She was in the room," reflected Ashley.

"Could she have left because I was in a deep sleep? I must go to Pearly at once."

Bare feet and bare shouldered, Ashley began to walk towards Pearly's room. She stopped momentarily, catching a glimpse of the shadowy figure moving in quick, long strides in the dark corridor towards the rear-exit, with something hung over his left shoulder. Taking quick steps, Ashley began to follow the figure but slipped and she fell backwards, hurting her foot.

She got up dragging her feet.

"Please, someone, stop that figure. Stop the dark figure," she screamed, watching in horror the shadowy figure slip through the back door, slamming the door shut. Limping heavily, Ashley managed to reach the door.

"Someone, please help! My baby has been kidnapped," she screamed, pounding on the door.

A security guard came rushing to her side, followed by a bunch of nurses.

"My child has been abducted through this door," she shouted, throwing her arms up in the air.

"I will inspect the door quickly, Ma'am," replied the security guard, rushing to the door.

"Catch him please. Hurry!"

"That's impossible. The lock on the door is fully intact," he exclaimed.

All eyebrows went up. The crowd of nurses started whispering . . .

"*The lock has not been tempered with—*"

"Please break the door open. Go after the intruder, the ghost—"

Ashley sank to the floor, murmuring incoherently. "Why don't you understand that my baby has been kidnapped. I saw it with my own eyes."

"Would you mind describing the intruder, Ma'am?" asked the security guard.

"I couldn't see the face due the power failure and the storm. I only saw a glimpse of the shadowy figure, when the lightning struck."

"But, there was no power failure tonight, Ma'am, nor was there any storm or lightning."

"Yes, Dr. Ashley," said nurse, in a soothing voice, "There's a clear sky tonight. See for yourself."

Ashley was stunned to see the clear sky and stars.

"I don't believe this," she said, with a puzzled expression. "I saw my baby being kidnapped right through that door," she affirmed, pointing to the door.

"But Pearly is sleeping soundly in her bed in her room, Ma'am," a voice from behind confirmed.

"How can it be possible?" murmured Ashley.

"Believe me, I just left Pearly sleeping peacefully in her bed," said the nurse, approaching her.

"Dr. Ashley, you had another nightmare. In fact, you had a series of nightmares tonight."

"What? How did I get to the corridor?" asked Ashley, becoming totally disoriented.

"You sleep-walked to the corridor. Perhaps, it was a reaction to the drug the doctor had prescribed to you tonight. Your mind was already in turmoil. The drug compounded the trauma. It made you hallucinate. Why don't I let you personally inspect Pearly? After that, I will sit by your bed for the rest of the night. Okay?"

Feeling deeply embarrassed, Ashley walked back to her room with a puzzled look.

SHADOW AND THE GHOST
HAUNTING OF MENAKA

Ghost of Menaka lingers on the door;
many more skeletons waiting in store.

"I must thank you, Dr. White, for saving my mother's life," said Menaka.

"No. It was Ashley who risked her own life to save your mother's. She deserves the thanks—"

"Ashley is the one who put my mother's life at risk in the first place," snapped Menaka. "I wish my mother would tell me what she was doing at Ashley's Annexe at midnight."

Menakshi opened her arms to Priya, ignoring the remark. "Priya, my sweetie—"

"Nana, can I go to see Pearly while you visit with Maa?"

"No, no, no!" interrupted Menakshi. "You must stay away till Pearly is better."

"Nana, why won't you let Maa and I visit Pearly?" argued Priya, putting Menakshi on the spot.

"Excuse me," interrupted the nurse, with a soft knock. "Dr. Ashley is here to see you, Mrs. M."

"Please, tell her—tell her that I'm not receiving any visitors ...yet."

"Mother, why are you avoiding Ashley," asked Menaka, with a touch of suspicion.

Menakshi did not respond.

"Mother, you ignored the question I asked earlier. What were you doing out at midnight?"

"Annie asked me to give her a hand with reorganising the Annexe."

"Really? At midnight? Why didn't you tell me before you left?"

"I couldn't find you anywhere."

"Then why are you avoiding Ashley? Why won't you allow us to visit Pearly? What's the mystery?"

"Pearly needs to heal. Is it hard to understand?" Menakshi responded angrily, arousing suspicion.

"All the more reason for Pearly to be surrounded by people who love her. You are hiding something. I'm very concerned about your behaviour," Menaka lashed out.

"My behaviour? Shouldn't you be concerned about your behaviour — the way you are treating me?"

"I want to know the truth. You sneaked out of the house like a thief at midnight. Why? I don't buy your story. It does not ring true," said Menaka, getting into a heated argument.

"I know what nana was doing at aunt Ashley's house at night," Priya jumped in. "Nana and aunt Ashley were fighting over aunt Symoune's pearl necklace."

Menakshi became alarmed. Menaka narrowed her eyes.

"Whhaaat? Why?"

"Because," Priya paused, eying her grandma. "The necklace went missing after aunt Symoune died. I found the necklace in grandma's jewellery box. Aunt Ashley wanted to know how it got there."

Menakshi averted her eyes. Menaka's face became serious.

"Priya, why don't you go ahead and visit with Pearly and I'll join you later? I need to straighten this mystery with your grandma, alone," said Menaka, giving Menakshi a cold look.

Menakshi lost no time in complaining about chest pains and started ringing for the nurse. The nurse responded quickly to the call and ordered Menaka to leave the room.

Menaka returned home, feeling terribly upset.

"*How did the necklace travel from Symoune's neck to my mother's drawer? My mother never wears jewellery. What's the mystery behind the necklace?*" muttered Menaka, studying Symoune's picture on the wall.

"Still upset about the necklace, Maa?"

"Oh, God, Priya, don't sneak up on me like that. I'm pregnant, honey."

"Sorry. Are you still freaked out about the necklace?"

"I'm concerned — "

"Why is everyone freaking out about a simple necklace? Even Annie remarked that my birthmark matched the necklace — a ridiculous coincidence, she admitted later on?"

"What, let me see," said Menaka becoming alarmed. She jumped to Pearly's side to examine the birthmark by sweeping her hair back from her neck. She stepped back in horror and doubled up with pain, wrapping her arms around her belly.

"Maa, are you okay? You look like you're going to faint."

"Priya, call someone. I don't feel well. Run!"

The household turned into turmoil as Menaka fainted, trickling blood all over the floor. She was rushed to the hospital and remained in a critical condition overnight.

"Where is my baby? My baby?" murmured Menaka, opening her eyes the next day.

"Your baby is fine, Mrs. Singh. The bleeding has stopped. You are physically fine."

Menaka felt relieved that the baby was fine. The memory of the necklace came flooding back to her but she waited to confront her mother until she was stronger and safely home.

"Mother," she hesitated, "Now that I'm feeling stronger, can I ask you something?"

"Menaka, I hope it's not about the midnight episode again," replied Menakshi, sipping tea.

"No, it's about the necklace!"

The cup slipped from Menakshi's fingers, spilling tea all over her dress.

"Mother, how did the necklace end up in your jewellery box? And where did Priya get the tattoo matching the necklace?"

"Why are you digging out old skeletons from the closet?"

"So, you do agree that there are old skeletons in the closet?"

"I didn't mean that—"

"What did you mean, mother?"

Menakshi got up and walked to the window for fresh air.

"Mother, I'm beginning to remember things I had blocked out of my head. I remember that my baby was not moving in my womb and it didn't cry after birth."

Menakshi's face darkened.

"My question is — why didn't she cry? I remember the whispers . . ."

"What whispers? You're losing your mind."

"And you are stammering—why?" Menaka paused.

Menakshi blinked, moving her eyeballs several times.

"Mother, either you give me a straight answer or I go to Ashley. What is it gonna be?"

"Back off, Menaka. The truth will destroy you. It will not . . . deliver you," replied Menakshi wiping the beads of sweat from her forehead.

"Mother, I'm damned if I do and damned if I don't. The ghost of Symoune haunts me day and night. I've decided to face my ghost."

"Even if . . . the ghost destroys you, Menaka?"

"I have no choice. I stay awake at nights. I live with fear."

"All right. I'll tell you the truth, even though I'll live to regret this." Menakshi walked to the window and took a long pause.

"The children are gifts from God. They are not possessions," she said, facing the window.

"Yeah—"

"They come through mothers but don't necessarily belong with them," she added slowly.

Menaka clutched at her belly, preparing for the blow.

"Priya was a gift and she belongs with you even though she didn't COME through you. We didn't steal her. We are not guilty. There was an abandoned newborn waiting to be adopted at Ashley's clinic the day you gave birth to another STILL-BORN . . ." Menakshi paused.

Menaka felt as though a bomb exploded in front of her eyes and she was blown away.

"I chose that baby for you. Somehow the babies got switched. I didn't realize until it was too late. I have accepted this as 'karma' and you should do likewise," said Menakshi, turning to face Menaka.

Menaka lay on the floor with her mouth wide open and eyes fixed on the ceiling.

"Menaka," she screamed at the top of her voice, summoning the whole household to the scene.

Menaka's condition remained precarious at the hospital and her state of mind delirious for weeks. She kept drifting in and out of reality. Menakshi worked long hours to convince Menaka that the necklace incident was merely a recurring bad dream. Slowly Menaka became convinced and her condition started to improve. The doctor ordered her discharge.

Ashley rushed to the hospital to visit Menaka.

"Congratulations. Menaka is feeling stronger. The pieces are falling in place," said Ashley.

"She is still weak," Menakshi stopped Ashley at the door. "You can't see Menaka, yet."

"She'll have her own baby soon. I think she's coming to grips with the reality. It is the right time to tell her the truth?"

"No, no, no! The time's not right," Menakshi whispered, escorting Ashley out of the door.

"Why not? Menaka is strong now. The time has come to restore Priya to her proper place. We must make things right for Priya and Symoune. Priya belongs with us."

"She also belongs with Menaka and us. It's not our fault. It was *Karma*."

"I don't believe in your *Karma* superstition. We can't keep this a secret forever. I think I should speak with the Major instead. He will understand my concern. I will talk to him tonight."

"No, I won't let you talk to him. The time is not right. We must wait a little longer."

"I must free myself from this torment. The truth must be told."

"No, I can't let you do that," said Menakshi grabbing Ashley by the arm; shoving her out of the door.

"Priya belongs with me," argued Ashley, freeing her arm. "She is my brother and Symoune's blood — not Menaka's."

A horrid scream from behind turned their heads, ending the heated argument. Menaka stood at the door, wide eyed and dazed with one hand over her mouth.

She began to slip in slow motion, fainting in front of their eyes, into a pool of blood. Her face turned white as a ghost and her eyes sunk. Ashley jumped to catch her. Menakshi screamed, kneeling on the floor beside her.

"Ashley, you've killed Menaka's baby," yelled Menakshi, pointing a finger at Ashley.

"Murderer! Murderer! I told you to wait. I'll never ever forgive you, Ashley."

"Oh, God, I'm so sorry. So sorry . . ." Ashley burst out, crying.

"Nurse, please get her out. Out—" screamed Menakshi, burying her face in Menaka's hair.

Ashley sank down on her knees in horror with Menakshi's words ringing in her ears,

"Murderer! Murderer! I'll never ever forgive you, Ashley."

SHADOW AND THE GHOST
HAUNTING OF PEARLY

In the raging fire, my life was lost.
My own shadow became my ghost.

"Annie, Annie, where are you? Oh, my God, Pearly's missing again," yelled Ashley, dashing downstairs, slipping on the steps several times and bruising her elbow.

"I'm right here," Annie rushed out of the washroom with dripping hands and a baffled look.

"Oh, Annie, Pearly is not in her room. She has disappeared again."

"Calm down. Calm down," replied Annie, dragging Ashley by her arm to the main window overlooking the thick green plantation surrounding the burnt down Annexe.

"Look, Pearly is sitting on her usual spot. Stop worrying."

"Oh, I'm sorry, Annie," said Ashley, putting an arm around her.

Annie reluctantly yielded to the embrace to communicate her non-verbal acceptance of the apology. She was beginning to get deeply concerned about Ashley's increasing panic attacks.

"I wonder what Pearly is thinking about?" wondered Ashley, absent-mindedly.

"She keeps staring blankly into the dark woods as if she's waiting for someone to materialise out of the thick, dark fog," replied Annie, studying the lines of anguish across Ashley's face.

"How completely our lives have changed in the last four years. When we set out for the trip to Delhi, we had no idea that it would be a life altering experience," Ashley reminisced.

"Yes, there is no way to make any amends now," replied Annie, wiping her teary eyes.

"Annie, we had five wonderful days in Delhi as best friends with the Singh family. On the sixth day, we became adversaries. With a wink of an eye, we lost the mysterious link, which bound us together for fourteen years," murmured Ashley, her eyes soaking with grief.

"Symoune was the reason we became friends; Symoune is the reason we became apart. She was the mysterious link then and she is the mysterious link now." Ashley poured out her grief.

"I think I should bring in Pearly. It's getting a bit foggy outside."

Ashley nodded, without taking her eyes off Pearly. She stayed at the window, watching Sita Ram, her gardener, work on a beautiful bouquet. He lifted his head at the sound of the footsteps and rushed to present the bouquet to Pearly.

"Look, Miss Pearly, your favourite lilies. I am making bouquets for your birthday tomorrow."

A faint smile touched Pearly's eyes. She extended her hand to grab the bouquet. Sita Ram smiled. Pearly lifted the bouquet to her chin and walked on, leaving him and Annie chatting behind. She slipped through the open doors like a spirit and walked past Ashley, who stood poised at the foot of the stairs to welcome her with outstretched arms. She moved up the marble staircase, without making a sound. At the top of the stairs, she paused to smell the flowers. Then resuming her quiet pace, she disappeared into her room.

"Why is it, Auntie, that whenever I'm most peaceful I begin to feel restless as if something awful is going to happen. My mind is always on the guard." Pearly's words hit Ashley.

Ashley followed Pearly upstairs with a glass of warm milk. As usual, she found her standing motionless, staring at the *'Priya Mansion'*.

"Pearly, do you miss Priya?" asked Ashley, placing the milk beside her bedside without expecting a reply. Even though she had become accustomed to holding one-sided conversations, she always hoped that one day Pearly would speak up.

"Why is Priya no longer . . . there?" whispered Pearly, without taking her eyes off the mansion.

Ashley could not believe her ears. Her face lit up. The sound of Pearly's voice brought tears to Ashley's eyes.

"Those are Pearly's first few words in the last two years," she thought. *"It's an omen; the cloud's lifting over the fateful night, which had rendered Pearly silent two years ago."*

"Would you like to see Priya, Pearly?" Ashley asked, stealing a quick glance at Annie standing still at the door.

"Yeah, to make things right with her," Pearly whispered again, very softly.

"Yes, honey. The family blames me for the loss of Menaka's baby."

Pearly nodded.

"Pearly, do you know that it is your seventeenth birthday tomorrow."

"It's Priya's seventeenth birthday, too. Why is she not here?"

"She called several times when you were ill, honey," Annie jumped in joyfully.

"Who else do you want to see at your birthday party, honey?" Ashley asked.

"The beautiful woman—"

"Where does the beautiful woman live, dear?" asked Annie, with a look of caution.

"Out there, in the fog." Pearly pointed to the plantation. "She visits me on that rock."

"Honey, you must be imagining . . ."

"No. She's real. Look, she gave me this crystal," she said, fumbling with her hands around her neck.

"Oh, my God," shrieked Pearly crying. "I've lost my crystal."

"Honey, Don't cry. We'll find your crystal. Annie, can you look for the crystal?" asked

Ashley, resting Pearly's head on her shoulder and patting her back like a baby. Annie pretended to look for the crystal under the bed.

"Tell me honey, who else do you want to invite?"

Pearly moved to the edge of the bed with her chin in her hands, as if in deep thought.

"Father Elliot," she murmured, picking up her head. "Swami Krishna, Priya, Sita Ram, and the beautiful woman."

"We'll go and make the phone calls now if you promise to close your eyes. Okay, honey."

Pearly closed her eyes instantly.

"Good night, sweetie. We'll make a new beginning tomorrow. I love you!"

Ashley and Annie winked at each other in delight.

PEARLY'S "POOJA" CEREMONY

Ashley had left no stone unturned in arranging a perfect Hindu style Pooja ceremony to seek the blessings of Lord Krishna on her seventeenth birthday. A rich and colorful mix of dignitaries arrived in a steady stream throughout the morning to participate in Pearly's 'Pooja' ceremony.

Swami Krishna, the guest of honour, was the first one to arrive with a train of disciples and devotees from his Ashram. He was ushered in with a shower of rose petals, holy water, and ceremonial 'Aarti'. Ashley eyes lingered on Swami Krishna — a mesmerising figure with a mystical glow, flowing hair, and a miraculous voice. His presence seemed to fill the room.

"Congratulations, Dr. Ashley," he said, extending a single white rose to Ashley.

"Symoune's favorite rose. Thank you."

"Symoune is in a place filled with roses," he replied, in a voice of an angel.

"Thank you, Swami, for the help of your disciples in arranging this holy veneration. I thank the Lord for restoring Pearly's speech."

"I'm hoping for another miracle after the Pooja. Where is the birthday Goddess?"

"I will fetch her." Annie rushed upstairs to fetch Pearly.

Pundit Vasudeva and his disciples started to set up the place of worship. Pearly came gliding downstairs in a white sari, sandal-tilka, and lilies in her hair. She bent waist down Indian-style to receive the blessing from the Swami. The Swami moved gracefully to recite a holy Mantra by placing his hand over Pearly's head.

"Om Vijaya Bhva. Om Nama Krishna, Om Nama Rama!" he said. "Here's your own copy of the *'Holy Geeta'*, in English — a birthday gift from the higher source!"

"You remembered. Thank you," murmured Pearly softly.

A disciple stepped forward to guide the Swami and Pearly to their seats in front of the holy urn *(Havan-Kunda)*. The Swami assumed the meditation 'Asana' and closed his eyes.

Pundit Vasudeva rose, looking conspicuous in a white *Dhoti-Kurta and sandal-tilka*, to take his place next to Swami, in front of the big Asian urn, set against the gigantic murals of Lord Krishna. He examined the *Samagri* (meditation items) placed meticulously in front of the urn: holy water (from river Ganges), ghee (shortening), rose petals, almonds, fruits, sweets, sandal-tilka, red-moli, and flowers.

Folding his hands across his chest and assuming the lotus position, he began to chant the prologue to the 'Gayatri-Mantra'. The audience tuned into the discourse in pin drop silence.

He opened his eyes briefly to acknowledge all the partakers of the ceremony seated around the holy fire, in a square seating arrangement on the floor and to watch the disciples shower the deities (placed on a raised platform in the middle of the murals) with rose petals. He then picked up a large spoon from the tray and started dropping 'Ghee' into the fire.

"We will commence this holy ceremony in accordance with the ancient Hindu tradition, by reciting in Sanskrit, the Gayatri Mantra," he said. "The *Gayatri Mantra is* the most potent and supreme of all Mantras. It is a prayer for the liberation of the sprit from the materialistic world called, *Maya.*"

"*Om Bhui Om Bhuhu Om Bhuvaha Om Suvaha*
    Om Mahava Om Janaha Om Tapaha Om SatyaM."

He explained in a soft voice, the meaning of the *Gayatri-Mantra* and the seven Lokas:

Gaya means vital energies. T*rayate* means to preserve. *Mantra* means the sacred text.

OM Tat Savitar VareNayaM Bhargo Devasya Dhimhhi
Dhiyo Yo Nah Prachodayat Bhur Bhuvas Suvar OM.

Om: Supreme spirit. *Bhu'hu':* Physical world. *Bhuvaha:* World of becoming *Suvaha:* thinking. *Mahaha:* emotions. *Janaha:* creativity. Tapaha: intuition. Satayam: truth.

"It means, we ask the God to unfold himself unto us. Just as the fire remains hidden until one fire-stick rubs across another. The God also remains hidden until the chanting of the Mantra."

With eyes closed, Pundit Vasudeva began to clap and chant,

encouraging everyone to join in:
Hare Rama, Hare Krishna Hare Krishna, Hare Hare.
Hare Krishna, Hare Rama, Hare Rama, Hare Hare.

The audience joined him in singing several versions of the Mantra. The ceremony ended with an offering of *Parsada* and a vegetarian lunch, served on the banana leaves. At the end of the ceremony, Pundit Vasudeva walked over to Pearly to impart his blessing.

"May you be successful in your search," he said, placing his hand over Pearly's head. "The God will undoubtedly help you find what you want, if so is your wish," he added.

Pearly's eyes grew large with amazement.

She averted her eyes and proceeded to the rock with her sketchbook and box of crayons, unaware of the footsteps following her.

MYSTERY OF THE CRYSTAL

"Swami, may I join you, and Pearly?" whispered Father Elliot, approaching Swami Krishna, who stood watching Pearly's sketch in progress.

"If Pearly doesn't mind us watching her sketch."

"Not if you promise not to discuss my sketches with anyone," said Pearly, lifting her head.

Father Elliot and Swami Krishna exchanged quick glances.

"We promise. Don't we, Father Elliot?"

"Yeah," said Father Elliot, slipping beside Pearly on the rock.

"I can't determine, what is more striking—the wording of the riddles or the images in the sketches," remarked Swami.

"Both are striking," exclaimed Father Elliot. "Pearly, may I read out the riddle?"

Pearly nodded.

Father Elliot read out loud with a rhythmic beat.

Riddle One: Who am I?
Traveling back in time, to recover and retrace,
the footprints, which sands and winds have erased;
like the pencil marks, like the tiny snowflakes.
I'm riddled with mystery, asleep or awake.

"A mystery riddle and a mystery sketch. Can you unravel the two mysteries, Swami?"

"Let us first examine the sketch and then we'll focus on the riddle—one piece at a time."

Two women are pulling away from the baby. The older woman has a moon over her face and is naked in the back. The young woman depicted as a shadow is watching the baby with gorgeous sunlit eyes. The baby has a grown up face and is gazing through a giant crystal held by a crystal figure. The sunlight through the crystal is illuminating the dark scene.

"I got the answer."

"I can't wait."

"The giant crystal is the mystical medium through which the grown up is revisiting a disturbing childhood episode. A mother is being forced to abandon her baby by an older woman. The partial dress-up suggests a cover-up. Sunlight represents revelation; the moon and the shadow symbols could be clues to the identities/names of the two women."

"Excellent!"

"Now we need to find the answer to the heading of the riddle, Who Am I?"

"The baby is focal point in the entire episode," affirmed Swami.

"Whom does the image of the baby represent? Any clues?"

"The answer lies in the next riddle," whispered Pearly, turning over a page.

Riddle Two: Am I the One?
The picture of the child is the picture of me,
  I'm the one, who is depicting me.
    Top of the mountain to the bottom of the sea,
    I'm the one, who is searching for me.

"Let us first examine the sketch and then review the riddle," advised Swami.

"Fine."

"It's a sketch of the same baby looking at a woman trapped inside a giant crystal. It appears to be the story of the painter who painted the scene."

"That would be Pearly. She painted the scene," replied Father Elliot.

"But Pearly's mom did not abandon her; she died. What

connection could Pearly have with two mystery women, the baby, and a cover-up? It makes no sense."

"My mom did not die. The answer lies in the next sketch," said Pearly, turning over the page.

"Another riddle and a sketch. I'll read the riddle; you unlock the sketch," suggested Father Elliot.

Riddle Three: Nothing to Say?
On the steps of heaven, the skeletons lay.
  My mighty God had feet of clay.
    My demons drove me to my doomsday,
      I was rendered speechless; had nothing to say.

"It's your turn to unlock the riddle now, Swami?"
"I accept the challenge, Father?"
"Go ahead."
"The steps mean the metamorphoses; the heaven/mighty God mean the place of security; the skeletons mean secrets; feet of clay means broken faith; the demons means dreadful encounters; the doomsday means depression; rendered silent means a state of shock."

"I guess, it means that the person who painted the picture became privy to a deadly secret from the past which threw her into a state of deep shock and depression. According to the sketch, a story is unfolding on the steps of a house," observed Swami.

"A girl is fleeing in horror; the dropped lantern is igniting fire; there are figures trapped inside. The words — *Rendered Silent* point to someone we know — "

"Whom?"

"I would say, though most cautiously, that this is the exact scene of the fire at the Annexe."

A complete hush fell over the scene.

Father Elliot's eyes turned into ice.

Pearly turned into stone.

"Honey, I'm afraid, this sketch places you at the scene of the fire," whispered Swami...

Pearly did not move.

"I must ask if you were at the scene of the fire," asked Swami, placing an arm around Pearly.

Pearly did not respond.

"What made you flee the scene, honey?" Father Elliot's voice cracked with pain.

Pearly blinked.

"Did you overhear something disturbing which made you drop the lantern on the floor?"

"Yes," Pearly sobbed, rubbing her eyes.

"You must promise . . . not to reveal this to anyone."

They both nodded.

Father Elliot placed an arm around Pearly's shoulder.

The Swami held her hand.

Pearly hesitated before speaking.

"I overheard a dreadful secret. I heard that there was an abandoned newborn waiting to be adopted at Aunt Ashley's clinic the night Aunt Menaka gave birth to a fourth stillborn."

"And —" Tears welled up in Father Elliot's eyes. He pulled his handkerchief from the pocket.

"The baby was handed to Aunt Menaka. The babies got switched accidentally. I ended up with Aunt Ashley. I'm the abandoned baby." Pearly buried her face in Swami's shoulders and cried. A sense of shock swept their faces. They kept their arms around Pearly until she stopped crying.

"Poor, baby! You've been living with the horror alone since that evening. You're not alone anymore. We'll help you find your mother and will do it most discreetly. Won't we Father."

"Yes, I promise to help you find your mother."

"Yes. We will provide Pearly full support," Swami Krishna affirmed, stroking Pearly's head. "Let us now get back to the house and act normal. Your secret is safe with us, honey."

Pearly felt like a weight was lifted from her soul. She walked back, feeling safe.

A very nervous Ashley greeted them at the door.

"There you are! I was worried about the chill in the air. Here, put this jacket on, honey," she said, handing the jacket to Pearly. As she extended her hand, something shiny slipped from the pocket and landed on the floor with a tinkling sound.

"Ummmm! What's that sound?"

She bent waist-down to retrieve it and stood up with a sparkling crystal on her palm.

All heads turned in amazement.

"I found my crystal!" Pearly jumped in the air. "The 'Beautiful Woman' gave it to me.

Perhaps now you would believe that my Beautiful Woman is real. She does exist!"

With a wink, she had strung the crystal into the chain and snapped it shut around

her neck.

All eyes gazed at Pearly with stunned looks.

Pearly stood tall like a mystical Goddess with the big crystal shimmering around her ivory neck.

Chapter Seven
The Search

THE SEARCH
JOURNEY INTO THE DARK

A part of me doesn't know you at all; a part of me knows you so well.
A part of me wishes to forget you; a part of me searches you like hell.

"Looks like a lead in the old log Swami?" asked Father Elliot, knocking on the door.

"More than one lead, Father," smiled Swami, lifting his head. "Come on in."

"What have we got?" asked Father Elliot, closing the door and removing his hat.

"Our PI confirmed that a woman did contact several high profile ashrams in Delhi, Punjab, and Simla including ours in the year 1887, leading up to December fifteenth."

"Go on—"

"The calls originated from the one place—Banaras," he paused.

"However, the trail gets cold because the people she dealt with are either gone, dead, moved or they were paid heavily to buy their silence."

"You indicated that she contacted your ashram."

"That's right. Our record reveals that a woman did contact our ashram several times in 1877, and met privately with Vishnu Das on three separate occasions in December."

"That's good lead. Isn't it?"

"Yes and no! There's no description of the woman in question except that she stayed at the hotel, Luxury."

"So she belonged to an upper class family. Anything else?"

"We've been able to find one clue," said Swami, tapping his fingers on the desk.

"Go on."

"I decided to review the old photographs in our archives and stumbled on an old picture dated December fourteenth, 1877—the night of the *Jagarta* ceremony we observe annually and take pictures. Take a look," he added, opening the drawer and lifting a picture.

"Ummmm."

"Vishnu Das is seen in a meeting with a lady and a man in the *private office*. It's a casual picture taken through the window and the *private office* sign is visible on the door."

"It's quite blurred," replied Father Elliot, adjusting his glasses and trying to focus. "The lady is caught with the back pose."

"But the face of the man beside her is clear. Why don't we focus on finding the man? He might lead us to our mystery woman. The picture needs to be blown up and cleared."

"Why don't I get it done? I know a great photographer."

"Sure," he nodded. I'll commence the search for the man after I get the picture back."

"By the way, Pearly's doing a great job of teaching English at the Krishna school. Thanks for donating the resources," Swami said, walking Father Elliot to the door.

You're welcome! Pearly and I are working on bringing in Dr. White regularly for medical checks at the orphanage. He's devoted to the Indo-British Charity for Children."

"I'm most grateful to you and Dr. White for all the help. Take care and *Namaste*."

"Annie, what are those bags doing outside?" Ashley asked, walking in through the door.

"Pearly is taking clothes to the Krishna Orphanage," Annie replied, dragging another bag.

"Again? Give me the bag," said Ashley, grabbing the bag and opening it, "These are the new dresses I bought her last week!"

"And the orphans only deserve second hand things. Right, auntie? Give me that bag."

"Really . . . ?" Ashley stepped back, throwing her arms up in frustration.

"I don't expect you to understand how an orphan feels, auntie. I could very well be an orphan. Have you ever thought about that?"

"But you're not."

"And you will tell me if I was. Won't you?"

"Where's that coming from?"

"You have double standards. You love orphans as long as you don't have to live with one," replied Pearly, storming out of the door, adding, "I'm going to the fundraiser at the Krishna Ashram. Father Elliot will bring me back around seven. For your information, I like orphans because I do feel like one . . ."

"That's an unfair statement; Pearly, take that back!" Ashley followed Pearly, watching her drive off with father Elliot without looking back.

"Calm down, Dr. Ashley; ignore that," said Annie, pulling Ashley's arm.

"I can't! There's something going on in her head. She's not herself."

"I agree. I was surprised at her remarks about the orphans—quite unusual."

"Whatever it is, she has confided in Father Elliot and Swami Krishna because I've caught the three with heads together more than once, as if they're plotting something."

"I've observed the hush-hush attitude around me," Annie confirmed Ashley's suspicions.

"We must find out what's going on. Why don't we sneak up on them tonight?"

"And pretend to surprise them if we get caught. Let's do it."

"Aha, there you are Father," greeted Swami, with folded hands. "Pearly, why don't you go to your group and start setting up the booth while father and I talk in private?"

"Can I join you?"

"Honey, you've got to be patient and let us complete our findings." Swami smiled. "Why don't you join us for tea in half an hour in my office?"

"What do you want first—the good news or the bad news?" asked Swami Krishna, leading Father Elliot to his office and closing the door.

"How about the good news?" Father Elliot replied, removing his hat.

"We've been able to trace the man. An old worker led me to the man in question."

"Good news. Did you meet with the man?"

"Yes. He remembers bringing an older lady to meet with Vishnu Das more than once."

"Did he reveal her name?"

"He only remembered two things—the lady came from Banaras and was loaded."

"We already determined that."

"Yes, but he provided a detailed description of the lady or should I say two ladies. He met with two ladies—the older one had a round shaped face and the younger woman was dark and slender with exceptionally large eyes and she was pregnant."

"Large eyes and pregnant?" asked Father, narrowing his eyes. "No names?"

"No, he doesn't remember any names. However, he did say that the name of the older woman was associated with something ... like light."

"Light? That's a good clue, don't you think?"

Swami nodded. Silence fell across the table for a few seconds.

"Something has struck me, Swami. It might be a long shot," Father Elliot broke the silence.

"Do you have the sketch book of Pearly handy?"

"Yeah, why?"

"The description reminds me of the picture Pearly drew—the slender, dark woman with large eyes and the older woman with the moon over her face."

The Swami pulled the sketchbook from the drawer and they began to study the drawing.

"What are words *moon* and *face* called in Hindi?"

"The word *moon* is called *Chandra* in our language," said Swami, "The word face is called *Mukh*. The name of the older woman could be, *Chandra Mukhi*."

"Excellent! What is the *dark shadow* and *sunlight* called?"

"Shadow is called *Saya* and sunlight is called *Surya*. The name of the younger woman could be something like, *Saya Surya*."

"We got it!" They jumped, hearing a knock on the door. The Swami got up to answer the knock. He chatted with someone briefly at the door and said, eyeing Father Elliot, "Excellent timing! Send him in. Please Father, stay. I want you to meet this man."

The Swami waited at the door until an old and skinny *Hindu Brahman* guy walked in timidly, wearing the traditional *dhoti-kurta* and *sandal-tilka*.

"Thank you for coming to see me, Jaya Ram," said Swami. "Please meet my friend, Father Elliot. We're working together on this search project."

Jaya Singh nodded briefly before sitting down awkwardly on the edge of the chair.

"Have you remembered any other detail—like the names of the ladies?"

"No."

"We were reviewing a drawing before you came in, which might trigger your memory? Would you like to take a look, please," asked Swami, pointing to the drawing on the table.

The man took a long pause before lifting his head. "That's an unusual drawing," he said, scratching his beard. "It has made me remember one name—*Chandra Mukhi*. I'm sure of it."

A look of triumph lit up their faces.

"Swami," he hesitated. "I came here to share with you another detail. The two ladies dropped by my house again next morning and my wife took them to see your father."

"My father? Are you sure?" Swami blinked his eyes in surprise.

"Yes, Swami. Your father met with the two ladies the next day for two hours. The pregnant woman fainted in your father's office and he drove them somewhere in the car."

The Swami stared at the man in disbelief.

The Father stared at Swami.

"Thank you for the valuable lead," Swami said, recovering his composure and pulling a bundle of money from his wallet.

"No, no, no," said the man walking to the door "I just wanted to help. *Jai shri Krishna.*"

"Please, accept it," insisted Swami, walking to the door. "I'll talk to Baba tonight. "*Shukria* and *Jai Sri Krishna!*"

The conversation became guarded when Pearly joined them for tea. They kept sipping tea and conversing quietly; oblivious of the piercing eyes of Ashley and Annie spying on them through the key hole.

"Hello, father," said Swami, picking up the receiver. "The story keeps getting deeper."

"I'm afraid to ask—"

"Jaya Ram was correct. Baba confirmed seeing the ladies. He declined to get involved because it's against the ashram policy to make differential arrangements. He dropped the ladies at Dr. White's residence because the younger lady was too close to delivery."

"We need to follow up with Dr. White?"

"I already did. The story gets downright shocking and closer to home."

"What?"

"Dr. White referred the ladies to Dr. Ashley because he was leaving for England next morning and the lady was on the verge of delivering her child."

"My goodness. It all fits! The two women went to Ashley's clinic and the baby was born and left there. That's how the tale of woes began..."

"Now you know where to find the address—in Ashley's archives."

"Yes. Ashley and Annie are going out of town this morning. I'm staying at the residence to look after Pearly. Why don't you meet us there tonight to dig into the archives?"

"I've to stop by at Dr. White's to pick up something. I will join you later."

"Annie, why are you eavesdropping at the door?" murmured Ashley.

"Shush. It was... Father Elliot on the phone."

"What?"

"Shush. I'll tell you in a minute," whispered Annie, tiptoeing away with Ashley.

"You're not going to believe what I've heard."

"It concerns Pearly. Doesn't it?"

A look of panic reflected on Ashley's face.

"Dr. Ashley," she whispered, looking over her shoulder. "Father Elliot was talking to Swami about the two ladies and the baby who was born and left in the clinic. They're planning to dig into our medical records to find their address tonight."

Ashley was aghast.

"Please say something, Dr. Ashley. You keep staring into nothing. You're scaring me."

"My nightmare is back. I'm not going to lose Pearly. We've

to think of something."

"Why don't we cancel the trip and put a lock on the archives storage?"

"No. That'll arouse suspicion." Ashley replied. She started pacing back and forth.

"I got an idea," she said. "Why don't you move the information to another box? We'll cut short our visit and catch them red-handed. What do you think?"

"Consider it done. We'll turn the tables on them tonight."

Father Elliot and Pearly waited to raid the archives until Ashley and Annie drove off. They were utterly surprised to find no record of December 1887 or beyond. They kept going over the records again and again until the door opened and they were caught in action.

"What's going on here, Father?" yelled Ashley. "You should know better than to sneak into my private storage? You owe me an apology."

"Ashley, it's not what you think. I can explain . . ." Father Elliot turned pale.

"Pearly, you go to bed at once," she shouted. "Annie, take those boxes from Father."

"No. I won't! And Father Elliot will not apologise." Pearly stood up tall in defiance.

"What did you say?"

"You are the one who's going to apologise," Pearly screamed, pointing a finger at Ashley.

"Apologise for keeping me in the dark about the identity of my mother. Apologise for destroying her medical record. My mother did give birth to me in this clinic and you destroyed the record to keep me from finding her."

Blood drained from Ashley's face.

"You're accusing me of destroying the record?"

"Yes." Pearly's eyes turned red with fiery sparks. "And for following me to the charity hall and spying on me through the key hole."

Ashley felt the walls crumble around her. Tears flooded her face.

"There's no medical record because no one who gave birth in my. . . my. . ."

"You're lying. I heard every word of your secret meeting on the night of the fire."

Ashley and Annie felt the earth shatter beneath their feet. They clung to each other.

"Ashley, stop," said Father Elliot, shielding Pearly. "Pearly knows everything."

"I'll never find my . . . mother . . . now." Pearly stated to cry vehemently.

"We've found your mother," Swami stepped in with a book clutched under his arm. "No more tears, honey," Swami added, lifting a picture from the book. "Take a look. We found your mother and in the process, we found your dad."

Everyone turned in disbelief.

Pearly grabbed the picture and looked deeply through tears. "It's the beautiful woman—Saya Surya-Wanchi. Is she my mother?" she sobbed. "She has her arms around General Scott—he's my dad. How did you find them?"

Ashley felt the walls crumble around her.

Annie stared in disbelief.

"Your mother forgot her book at Dr. White's residence. Her address is on it," Swami said, slipping an arm around Pearly. "Honey, you must forgive Ashley. Whatever she did; she did out of love for you. She was afraid of losing you. She loves you deeply."

"Ashley," said Swami, turning to her. "It's time to put Pearly's welfare first—time to focus on what we've found rather than what we've lost and to accept this as *Karma*."

Ashley nodded, opening her arms. Pearly rushed to embrace her. Annie hesitated.

"Come here, Annie and Father," Swami said. "Let's rejoice in Pearly's happiness."

Ashley gathered Pearly, Annie, Father Elliot, and Swami in the circle of her arms. They shed tears of joy together.

RETURN OF GENERAL SCOTT
THE HOMECOMING

There's nothing to me dearer; prettier to my eyes.
You're my whole world and you are my paradise.

"Sir Matthew, shall I leave the keys on the table?" asked Dev Das, his cook. "The truck is ready to leave. Are you sure you want us to go on ahead and you'll join us later?"

"Yes. I want the *mansion* to be in top-notch condition before I arrive. Make sure that all my art collections are stored impeccably in the hall upstairs and all the furnishings and paintings in the *Priya Mansion* are fully intact, as per the list provided by the realtor," he said, picking up the lighter.

He bent his head to light a cigarette, walked slowly to the window and stood looking at the heart-shaped pond surrounding the fountain, located in the middle of the garden. The trickling sound of the water, the swaying trees and the setting sun, created an eerie sight. He watched the movers run back and forth; loading the last batch of his priceless art collection into the truck. A feeling of sadness swept over him at the thought of leaving the place he had come to believe as home away from home. *"I can't believe that in few short hours I'll leave this place forever,"* he thought.

Banaras had become a part of his soul. He had loved the streets of *Banaras*. After all this was the place where he had lost his heart forever to a woman he could never attain. He felt like he was leaving a piece of his heart behind and never would be whole again.

"An early retirement from the army and the new career move will be uplifting for me," he reassured himself. *"I can't wait to spearhead the British Indian Museum in Simla."*

"Is there something else that's pulling me in that direction?" he examined his motives. "It is. . . Ashley. She's always on my mind."

He thought back to his last encounter with Ashley. He had often pondered over her secret ghost, *Chandra Mukhi* and tried to figure out the mystery of the discarded possession. Ashley's words had remained engraved in his mind. He recalled: *"I was made to witness a young girl discard her most valuable possession at my doorstep. The stranger forced me to find someone who would accept this possession — "*

The mystery haunted him. He dared not arrive at a wrong conclusion. He had tried so hard to reach Ashley to determine the truth, but there was no answer. He felt sad thinking about that.

"If only I could reach Ashley," he thought.

"Sir Matthew, there's one Miss Ashley on the phone," the servant startled him out of reverie. *"I don't believe it,"* General Scott crushed the cigarette butt with his heel and grabbed the phone.

"Ashley, I was just thinking about you," he said, lifting the receiver. "I tried so hard to get hold of you before I left for England. There was never any answer at your place."

"A lot happened after you departed. There was a fire at the Annexe. The three of us ended up in the hospital for months. A long story! Every thing's fine now."

"Ashley, I've been thinking a great deal about our last conversation," he felt his heart pounding in his chest. "I regret not mentioning before I left that . . . I knew the woman you were concerned about. I should've stayed and helped you bring closure to the issue."

"Actually, I do need your help in bringing closure to the issue that's still haunting me."

"Oh, Ashley, I've been trying to unravel the mystery of the discarded possession. I can't shake the feeling that somehow I'm connected to the mystery?"

A complete hush fell across the line and he became anxious.

"The mystery is connected to you, General." Ashley paused. "The gift the woman left at my door . . . belongs to you."

The blow hit the General hard. He felt his heart stop for a second.

"Can you be more direct, Ashley? The suspense has been killing me!"

"The name of the woman with *Chandra Mukhi* was *Saya Surya-Wanchi* and the gift she left at my door was—your baby. Pearly is your daughter; your flesh and blood, General!"

The words echoed in the General's ears. He heard in disbelief.

"I thought . . . Pearly was your brother's daughter?" he stammered.

"No. Symoune and Saya gave birth to their babies the same day. The babies got switched quite accidentally. My niece got adopted by Major Partap Singh instead of—"

"Oh, my God! What you must be going through, Ashley," he started crying. "My suspicions were correct. It was my baby! Pearly's my baby . . . girl. My baby!"

Ashley broke down and cried on the line.

"Ashley," he said between sobs. "I felt the strange bond each time I met Pearly. I—I can't wait to be with my daughter. Tell her that her dad's on his way. I'm heading for Simla within an hour. This is the best news I've received in ages." He rang off.

Ashley and Pearly clung to each other and cried their hearts out.

Ashley's residence was lit up like *Diwali* for the reception of General Scott. Every corner of the house was filled with flowers. Sita Ram was working on a garland. Annie was busy looking over the dinner preparations. Father Elliot was looking out of the window.

"How do I look," asked Pearly, gliding downstairs in a white long sleeved gown and lilies in her hair. "I wore this dress when I met the General the first time. I mean my uncle, my dad."

"You look like an angel descending from heaven," Ashley smiled, smoothing a wrinkle in her dress. "What do you think about my dress? Does my hair look all right?"

"If I didn't know better, I would say you've a crush on the General."

"Is there anyone who wouldn't? I can hardly compete with your beautiful woman—"

"Come on out, everyone!" alerted Swami Krishna. "There's a car pulling up outside."

General Scott and Pearly flew to each other as soon as the

car stopped. He swirled Pearly in his arms, sobbing and kissing her forehead.

"My baby! My baby! I found my heaven! I found my paradise!"

"Daddy, Daddy, Daddy! I love you, dad! We must find mom! We must!"

"Yes! Yes! Yes! We'll find her together, honey. We'll bring her back."

"Ashley," he finally looked up, extending an arm around her.

"Thank you for uniting me with my daughter. You've ushered me into paradise."

"General, meet Swami Krishna and Father Elliot. They're the ones who've found you."

"No. It was the persistence of Pearly," said Swami Krishna, folding hands, Indian style.

"Yes," nodded Father Elliot, shaking hands. "Pearly never gave up. She's the hero."

"Please all of you, call me Matthew," he smiled, shaking Annie's hand. "I left the army and have taken up a civilian position as head of the *British Indian Museum* in Simla."

His news was greeted with smiles. Sita Ram stepped forward, placing the beautiful garland around his head. "*Jai Shri Krishna, Sir Matthew,*" Sita Ram giggled, folding his hands.

"*Shukria,*" he said, pulling a fifty-rupee bill from his pocket and handing to him.

"I'm eternally grateful to all of you for the miracle reunion," he said, holding Pearly in the circle of his arm. "Pearly is my heart and her mother is my soul and I want to let you know that I'll move heaven and earth to unite Pearly with her mother. I've bought the *Priya Mansion* and will be your neighbor next door." He paused.

"Daddy, we saw a lot of activity at the mansion. We didn't know that you had bought it."

"I will also fight for Ashley's right," he said, slipping an arm around Ashley. "Pearly and I will restore Priya back to Ashley. Together we will right this wrong."

Ashley and Pearly buried their faces in his shoulders and cried.

RETURN OF MYSTERY WOMAN
THE RESOLUTION

The Paradise of the two worlds seems to surround me;
I had drifted into the forgotten land until you found me.

"Krishna Sanctuary is an amazing facility," said Matthew Scott, handing the donation cheque to Swami, "The caring staff and the well-nurtured children are exemplary. A recreation hall would be a great addition to the Krishna Sanctuary. I hope my contribution will help."

"Thank you for the generous donation."

"Thank you Swami for the sensitivity and support you provided to Pearly and Ashley through the delicate circumstances. We seek your direction on the next step."

"I'm waiting for an update from the private investigator. He's in the middle of his findings; working as a servant at the *Surya-Wanchi* mansion."

"Swami, we think that Ashley must accompany us to Banaras?"

"Good idea! But none of you are in a position to march into the *Surya-Wanchi* mansion without consequences. The Indian people react very strongly to the invasion of privacy particularly in their marital affairs. We must wait for the report from the PI and proceed with caution."

"And we will," Matthew said, getting up. "How about a supper with us at the *Priya Mansion* on Sunday? Father Elliot will be joining us."

"Absolutely. Is it still called the *Priya Mansion*?"

"Yes, it is Pearly's wish to keep the name intact and find Priya. She wants to be the one to tell her the truth and find ways to make amends..."

"It's so like Pearly. She could do no wrong. God is leading her towards a resolution.
Namaste!"

Ashley and Annie were playing cards. Pearly was lying on the sofa, resting her head on her dad's lap. He was reading the story, *The Crowning of Glenda* from the book of fairy tales.
Glenda sat down on the throne with a smile. "I chose you to be the princess," whispered Mother Fate in Glenda's ear.
"Look, my magic has turned the real princess into a helpless peasant girl."
Glenda looked at the peasant girl standing alone with tears in her eyes.
The prince got up to place the crown over Glenda's head.
Glenda grabbed the crown from the prince and walked over to the peasant girl.
"The crown belongs with the real princess," she said, placing the crown over her head. "This is the real princess and she belongs with the real prince."
"Glenda, you could've had it all," shouted Mother Fate. "Why didn't you?"
"The essence of living lies in not what you have but who you are," replied Glenda. "I chose to be myself. I couldn't live with myself or the prince if I hurt anyone."
"Daddy, can you read the part again . . . about the essence?"
"Yes, honey," replied Matthew, reading the part again.

"Storytelling is a terrific way of bonding," remarked Swami, entering the cozy family scene.
"I agree." Father Elliot joined in. "Look. What an amazing display on the wall."
They stood looking at the pictures on the main wall—Danny and Symoune in the middle; Swami Krishna and Father Elliot on each side; on the second row, Ashley and two girls in the middle, Matthew and Saya on one side and Partap Singh and Menaka on the other side.
"It is so thoughtful," remarked Swami. "The place feels like Priya will come out any minute."
"Priya is right in front of you. Don't you think I'm Priya?" Pearly said, walking towards him.

"Swami, I figured out why Priya and I constantly switched identities. Priya enjoyed playing Pearly because she was Pearly. I feel comfortable in the Priya mansion because I am Priya. We grew up as sisters; our birthday got intertwined. We look like identical twins with two names. We feel like two bodies and one soul. I can't tell her apart from me because Priya is the reflection of Pearly and Pearly is the extension of Priya. Both of us are Pearly; both of us are Priya."

"Yes, honey. I see Priya in you and Pearly in Priya," said Ashley. Everyone nodded.

"Auntie, I promise to bring Priya back and tell her the truth at any cost."

"We both promise," confirmed Matthew Scott. "Now we must proceed to dinner."

Following the meal, they retired to the drawing room for coffee. Swami Krishna and Father Elliot withdrew into a corner and started whispering. Pearly jumped on the sofa, placing her head on her dad's lap. Ashley snuggled beside Matthew. Annie started pouring coffee.

"Swami, what's the update from the private investigator?" asked Matthew, sipping tea.

"He was able to trace a close confidant of Saya—a distant aunt who has revealed many details."

"Go on . . ."

"Saya was 20, when she married Sagar Surya-Wanchi. Sagar was forced into the second marriage to fulfill a death-bed promise to his first wife, who was dying of a terminal illness. She wanted to see her husband remarried before dying. However, the first wife did not die and the bond between the two remained strong. Saya became more and more isolated each day, leading to her separation from her husband. She was living with her mother and working as an art instructor at the *Bella Institute* where she met *Matthew*."

Matthew nodded, pulling a handkerchief from his pocket.

"Saya was twenty-three when she gave birth to Pearly under the most traumatising circumstances. Her mother forced her to give up the baby and return to her husband. Her husband found out about the affair and threatened to kill the other man if she ever left him again. Saya stayed with him to protect both—her baby and the father. She suffered enormous abuse at his hands but did not reveal the name of Matthew."

A hush fell across the room. Swami took a long pause.

"After she ran into the three of you at the hotel, she became determined to leave her husband and seek out Pearly. Her husband was so preoccupied with the critical condition of his first wife that he didn't realize that Saya had left him. The first wife died and the husband came back to reclaim her. Saya refused to go back. He met with a car accident and died a week later. Saya became a widow."

"Please don't stop . . ." Pearly said.

"Saya began writing letters to Ashley. There was no answer. She urged her mother to visit Ashley to seek her permission to see Pearly. Chandra Mukhi returned from the trip, telling her that Pearly hated her mother for abandoning her and wouldn't see her. Saya's heart broke and she became ill."

"But that incident never happened," Pearly and Ashley reacted sharply.

"You're right," Swami continued. "Saya found out that her mother was lying because she found the hidden letters in a suitcase. She walked out on her mother and no one knows where she went. According to her aunt, Saya was extremely ill that night and needed medical attention."

"Oh, daddy, how are we going to find her?" Pearly sobbed.

"Wait," Swami, said. "The private investigator went to the *Bella Art Institute*. Saya left her job last week. They didn't know her address."

"I think it's time to confront Chandra Mukhi," said Matthew. "The three of us should leave tomorrow. Saya could be ill and in need of immediate medical attention."

Pearly sat quietly in the front seat watching her dad drive through the long and narrow road until the sign *Gulam Ali Street* flashed before her eyes. She turned nervously in her seat. Ashley felt her heart pounding in her breast as Matthew slammed on the brakes in front of 55 *Kalyani Bhawan*. Pearly offered to go on ahead. She walked up to the porch and rang the bell.

A servant answered the door.

"Is Ma'am Chandra Mukhi home?" Pearly asked quietly.

"Yes, please. Come in."

Pearly was shown into a large drawing room. An older lady lay on the sofa with her eyes closed. A cup of tea was sitting in front of her. A large picture of her mother was mounted on the wall.

"Beji, someone is here to see you," the servant said, withdrawing into a corner.

The older lady opened her eyes slowly and looked in her direction with a questioning look.

"Nana," she said, pointing to the picture. "I've come to see my mother, Saya Surya-Wanchi."

Chandra Mukhi's expression turned into surprise. She dismissed the servant with her hand.

"You've come to a wrong house," she said, dryly. "I couldn't possibly be your Nana."

"No. I've come to the right house. That's the picture of my mother, Saya Surya-Wanchi."

"She's not your mother," she said, shaking her head. "My daughter has no children."

'Yes, she does," said Ashley, stepping inside. "Remember me, Chandra Mukhi? I delivered this child in my clinic 17 years ago and here is her father, General Matthew Scott."

Chandra Mukhi stared in utter astonishment, shaking uncontrollably.

"Dr. Ashley, I thought we had an understanding . . ."

"No, you had tricked me. I raised Pearly as my own daughter. She has found her father. She has the right to find her mother. You must tell us where she is before it's too late."

"I don't know where she is," she shouted, pointing at Pearly. "The moment she crossed my threshold, she was dead to me. I did what I had to do to protect you, your mother, and your father from a dangerous situation. I left you in safe hands. You've no right to judge me."

"I don't know how God will judge you," Pearly shouted back. "I judge you very harshly for all the pain you've inflicted on us all. Even if God forgives you; I never will—"

Pearly stormed out of the door, sobbing. The servant followed her. As she looked back, he slipped a paper in Pearly's hand and rushed back in. Matthew and Ashley walked to the car in dead silence.

"Daddy," said Pearly, opening the paper. "Look, the servant slipped in mom's address."

"God is great!" exclaimed Matthew, studying the address and turning the wheels sharply.

They drove in nerve-racking silence until Matthew stopped in front of the *Sunder Mukhi Bhawan*. An elderly lady in her late fifties answered the door.

"We've come to see Saya Surya-Wanchi," said Ashley. "I'm Dr. Ashley Rose and this is Matthew Scott," she said, politely.

"I've seen your picture with Saya. I was waiting for you."

"This is Pearly. She has come to meet with her . . ." Ashley spoke.

"Mother," said Sunder Mukhi, opening her arms to Pearly. "And her mother is pining for her.

I thank God for sending you back. You must have received my letter. We were told that a man was looking for Saya. We hoped that it was Matthew," she paused.

"Yes," said Matthew. "We were looking for Saya."

"I had asked Chandra Mukhi's servant to let me know discreetly, if someone comes by looking for Saya. Your mother's asleep right now. I must warn you before you look in on her, that she's in a volatile state. She has not been herself since she saw Pearly at the hotel." Sunder Mukhi paused.

"She is pining for her daughter day and night. She was drawing a sketch of Pearly before she fell asleep. Her sketchbook is filled with drawings of Pearly. She's very fragile, physically and emotionally."

They tiptoed into the room and stood transfixed, watching the sleeping beauty. Saya looked like a mermaid asleep; her beautiful eyes deeply shut and her long hair spread around her body like a veil. Her sketchbook lay open beside her.

Matthew picked up the book. Pearly and Ashley began to view the unfinished sketch and read the couplet together:

I wait for the day, when he will come for me.
From the bonds and chains he'll set me free.

Matthew turned over the page; revealing another sketch and the couplet underneath:

Lamps shall keep on burning low; my days shall remain lone and grey.
My heart shall keep on burning too, until the end of my days.

Saya stirred in her sleep; wrapping one arm over her eyes and murmuring:

"Pearly, I can't play hide and seek. Pearly . . . come out now. I'm tired," she winced, placing her hand on the chest.

Ashley slipped on the chair to observe her breathing. She opened her eyes.

"Dr. Ashley?" Saya blinked in disbelief

"I received your letter and have brought your baby girl . . ."

Saya moved her eyes, as in a dream.

'It's not a dream," she murmured, raising herself on her elbow. "You've found me."

"Mom . . ." Pearly and Matthew rushed to the bed.

"My baby, my baby. Matthew, Matthew," she embraced them "Thank you Dr. Ashley. Thank you."

"We've come to take you back to Simla with us," said Matthew.

Sunder Mukhi arranged a simple wedding ceremony at her temple the following day with the help of Ashley and Pearly. Matthew and Saya were married in accordance with the Hindu tradition of 'Saat Phere' (seven circles) around the sacred fi re.

"Who gives the bride?" asked the priest.

"I will," said Sunder Mukhi, wiping the tears of joy.

"May the God fill your life with happiness," said Sunder Mukhi, shedding tears of joy, "And give you the strength to forgive my sister, Chandra Mukhi. God bless and goodbye."

Chapter Eight
The Return of Priya

PARTY AT PRIYA MANSION
RETURN OF PRIYA

You've driven my darkness away by lighting a thousand candles of love.
Made me look around shiny eyes by drawing stars from the skies above.

Matthew slipped out of the bed quietly, reaching for his bathrobe. He looked at Saya sound asleep with her arms wrapped around her breasts and her lustrous hair cascading around her body like a cloud. He smiled through his eyes, grabbing the packet of cigarettes and lighter and stepping out on the balcony. He lit the cigarette and started watching, between the puffs, the tall green trees filled with early morning fog, feeling the soothing peace emanating from the trees, sky, and the garden.

"*Everything looks so peaceful,*" he thought.

"*My life has finally come together. I never could've imagined a year ago that the love of my life would be sharing my bed and my beautiful daughter would have me wrapped around her fingers. The pieces of my puzzle have finally come together.*"

"*My heart goes out to Ashley. As always she's on my mind. I can feel her broken heart in her eyes when she looks at Saya, Pearly and me. I wish I could make her whole again.*"

"*All the women in my life are deeply wounded inside and hiding their pain. Saya and I have each other. But what about Ashley and Pearly? They're still searching for their missing piece — Priya.*"

"Swami is right," he murmured, discarding the cigarette butt. "God is leading us towards the missing piece. Something is bound to happen tomorrow, when I visit Major Partap Singh."

Matthew tiptoed out of the bathroom; dressed up and started

packing his suitcase.

Saya stirred in bed.

"Matthew?"

"Darling . . . you look like a mermaid . . . emerging from the sea."

"And the mermaid is surprised to see her prince deserting her," she smiled, sitting up.

"Only for two days. Duty calls."

"Two days without you, my love, would be like two centuries. How will I survive two centuries?"

"Remembering this," he whispered, kissing her forehead. "We've all our lives together."

"That's what I'm afraid of Matthew," she sighed. "I feel like, I'm slipping away . . ."

"Shush, darling," Matthew said. "You're my soul. I can't live without my soul."

"Matthew," she buried her head in his shoulder. "The depth of our love frightens me. It might make my soul shiver at the time of its departure from my body. I'm so afraid of losing my paradise."

"Darling, why don't you focus on the paradise gained rather than the paradise lost?

Why don't you hold that thought until I return? Now go back to sleep," he said, walking out of the door.

Saya nodded, pulling up the quilt.

Matthew had barely reached the door when he saw Saya on the steps.

"Matthew, wait. You forgot your watch?" she stopped suddenly, feeling dizzy.

"Ma'am Sahib," Dev Das and Meera jumped to steady her. Matthew leaped back upstairs like a lion, gathering Saya in his arms. "Dev Das, get . . . Ashley. Quick!" he screamed, taking her into the bedroom. He kept pacing back and forth outside the bedroom until Ashley came out.

"Good news, Matthew," she smiled. "Your loving wife is about to give you another special gift that takes nine months to arrive. You're going to be a daddy again."

"Oh, Ashley, Ashley, Ashley!" Matthew picked her up and swirled her around until she shouted, "Matthew, please put me down or I will smack your head."

"Oh, Matthew," Saya opened her arms. "God has given us another chance to create life. Wait 'til Pearly finds out. Please, hurry back. I promise I'll take care of our baby."

Matthew was in deep thought as his car pulled closer to Ram Garh. He was carefully considering the way to resolve the conflict between Ashley and Menaka without adding more pain than had been caused. He reflected on the feelings of everyone involved: Annie was powerless, Saya was guilty, Matthew was torn, Ashley was angry and Pearly was lost. On the other hand, Menakshi was adamant, Menaka was possessive, Partap Singh was unaware, and Priya was in the dark.

Ashley blamed Menakshi for concealing the truth and stealing her child. Menakshi blamed Ashley for rushing the truth and killing her unborn child. Menakshi believed in *Karma;* Ashley believed in the truth. Life without Priya was hell for Ashley and it was a death knell for Menaka.

He weighed in his mind the arguments for Ashley to bring Priya back against the right of Menaka to hold on to Priya. He knew that the clock was ticking and Ashley could lose Priya forever if the parents married her off without telling the truth.

"*I may be the only person who could reconnect the two families because I'm at the heart of the conflict, being the real father of Pearly; yet I'm afraid of the reaction from the Singh family.*"

"Sir Matthew, we've arrived at *Fort Priya,*" said the driver stopping in front of a magnificent building. Matthew raised his head slowly. Someone was opening the gate. The driver pulled into the driveway. A servant rushed forward to open the car door.

"Would you inform Major Sahib that General Scott has arrived," the driver said.

"Yes, *Namaskar,* General Sahib," replied the servant. "Major Sahib and Priya are held up at the farmhouse due to an accident. Menaka ji is expecting you in the drawing room, Sir."

"Can you bring in the boxes from the car, please?" asked Matthew, walking into the empty drawing room. He stopped in front of a large picture of Partap Singh, Priya, and Menaka.

"General Scott," Menaka walked in with her mother. "Meet my mother, Menakshi Singh."

"*Namaskar*," said Matthew, turning around and sinking into the sofa.

"Thanks for bringing the paintings," Menaka smiled. "I hope you like living in the *Priya Mansion*."

"Thank you. We enjoy living in the mansion very much."

"We?" she laughed. "I thought you were a confirmed bachelor."

"Actually, I'm not a bachelor any more. I got married last year. My wife, Saya, Pearly, and I live in the mansion and there's a baby on the way."

Matthew regretted mentioning Pearly.

"Pearly is living with you and your wife?"

"Well, we are very fond of Pearly. So she —"

"Chose to live with you?" completed Menaka, pouring tea.

"Not exactly," said Matthew, deciding to level with her. "We recently found out that my wife, Saya, was Pearly's biological mother and I was her biological father."

"Oh, your wife was the one who gave birth and left —" Menaka's hand shook uncontrollably, spilling tea over her dress.

Menakshi's eyes grew large with surprise.

"And you . . . didn't just visit to return . . . the paintings," Menaka stammered. "Did you?"

"No — but I didn't want it to come out like this," said Matthew, studying Menaka. "I'm sorry."

"But you did want something to come . . . out?"

"Yes."

"What do you know about my Priya?" Menaka whispered beneath her breath.

"Everything — the baby mix up, the necklace, the fire, and the loss of your child."

"So you are here . . . on behalf of Ashley?" Menaka's eyes froze on his face.

"And on behalf of my daughter and wife. Pearly found out the truth on the night of the fire. She remained in shock for two years. For the sake of Pearly and Ashley, the truth must come out —"

"For the sake of my family it cannot. I beg you not say a

word to my husband and Priya—"

"Priya has the right to know the truth. She mustn't be kept in the dark."

"The so called truth will destroy her like it destroyed my baby," Menaka pleaded. "Priya is our daughter and we've raised her. We've built our lives around her. She is the heartbeat of this family. My husband and I will have no reason to live without her. Priya could end up in a state of shock like Pearly. Do you want to see a happy family ruined?"

"No. Please, calm down."

"Not until you promise to say nothing or I will jump into the well outside and kill myself."

Matthew slid backward onto the sofa.

The tension mounted in the room.

Menakshi started to cry.

"If I promise to remain silent for now," said Matthew quietly. "Would you promise to be the one to tell Priya the truth in the near future?"

"Yes," replied Menaka, getting back to her seat. "I would rather she hears it from me."

"I can arrange for the silence, if you can arrange for Priya to spend the entire next week with Pearly in Simla. Ashley wants to celebrate their eighteenth birthday together at any cost."

"Do you promise on their behalf that they'll wait until I find the right moment to tell her?"

"I will obtain their promise. We'll honour our promise if you will honour yours."

"I will. It's a deal. I'll let Priya go with you and no one will breathe a word to her."

"It's a deal."

The Krishna Sanctuary was bubbling with excitement. Swami Krishna had called a general assembly. The kids rushed to the hall, as soon as the bell rang. The side table was filled with boxes of candies, fabrics, and multi-coloured envelopes. The headmaster signaled the kids to seal their lips as soon as the Swami walked in with his special guests.

"*Namaskar* and *Jai Shri Krishna* everyone," said Swami Krishna.

"*Namaskar, Jai Shri Krishna*, Swami," the kids spoke with one voice.

"I've called this assembly to make a few exciting announcements," he smiled. "First, I want you to extend a warm welcome to our special guests — Dr. Ashley and Father Elliot."

"Welcome, Dr. Ashley. Welcome, Father Elliot."

"How would you like to go to a birthday party at the *Priya Mansion*?"

Everyone clapped.

"Should I take it as yes?"

"Yes, Swami."

"Dr. Ashley and Father Elliot have come to invite each and every one of you to the eighteenth birthday party of Miss Pearly and her friend, Miss Priya at the *Priya Mansion*. Now I would like you to line up in front of the table set up in the corner and introduce yourself individually to them. Each one of you will get your own individual invitation card and a box of candies. You've to stop by the next table to give measurements to the tailor, so that he can get your new outfits ready by the weekend. You may select your own design and the colour of the fabric. Is that clear?"

"Yes, Swami," they said with a loud applause.

The Priya mansion was being lit from wall to wall. The west wing of the building was opened for the guests. A stage was set up for the dance presentations. The kids from the Krishna Sanctuary were busy rehearsing the dance items and making garlands for the family. An enclosed kitchen was set up under a huge tent outside the main house. The cooks were busy preparing a fabulous feast.

Ashley and Annie cleared the dishes from the breakfast table and joined Pearly and Priya in inspecting the piles of gifts on the table. Matthew and Saya walked in carrying more boxes.

"Good morning ladies. Care for more gifts?"

The girls jumped with joy, hugging them. "Can we open the gifts now, auntie?"

"Sure," smiled Ashley. "You may want to wear some of the stuff in the boxes."

Annie gave them a memento of the coronation event. Matthew and Saya gave them beautiful *saris*. Ashley gave them identical charm bracelets, bearing their names.

"Oh, Pearly, I got the wrong bracelet," said Priya. "I got the one with your name, *Pearly* on it."

"Why don't you keep that one? I love to wear the one with *Priya* on it," said Pearly, opening her gift. "That way we won't forget each other."

"Fine. Now I can officially lie that I'm Pearly," laughed Priya. "Pearly, you may want to keep my gift private, because I'm not sure how Aunt Ashley will react. She might get upset."

"I promise that I won't," said Ashley.

"I want to be sure. Remember you got so upset about the necklace—"

"It's all behind us. I promise not to get upset."

Pearly quickly unwrapped the gift; proudly displaying the painting, *Princessa and the Rose with the* inscription underneath— *Pearly Ruby Boone, Fantasy Model 1903.*

A silence fell across the room for a brief second.

"C'mon, it was meant in . . . good humor," said Priya. "Auntie, you promised not to get upset. It was Pearly who sent me to the *Fantasy Fundraiser* . . . because she was sick."

"I was just thinking how beautiful you look in Symoune's gown," Ashley hugged Priya. "What a wonderful surprise. We'll treasure this painting."

"Priya, why don't you go to the party as Pearly and I go as Priya. We'll have fun confusing everyone once again. I want you to wear the same dress you wore at the fundraiser."

"I'll help Priya with her hair and dress," said Annie.

"I'll help Pearly with the *sari* and hair,' exclaimed Saya, winking at Matthew.

A big round of applause greeted Pearly and Priya as they entered the hall with Ashley by their sides. Priya looked stunning in Symounes's dress, rubies, and pearls. Pearly looked like a nymph in her white Sari and lilies in her hair. Matthew and Saya kept their excitement under control and remained in the background to allow Ashley to stay close to the girls. Many times Ashley and Pearly felt an overwhelming urge to spill the truth but they restrained themselves under the watchful eyes of Matthew and Saya.

"Swami, can you tell which one is Pearly and which one is Priya?" asked Father Elliot.

"Amazing resemblance," said Swami, nodding his head.

"Pearly, this dress reminds me of the fantasy fundraiser and Ryan. I can't forget him. I've decided to confide in my mother. I won't marry anyone else."

"What if your parents don't agree?"

"I've to hope they will."

"Priya I need to tell you . . . something," said Pearly, lowering her voice suddenly. "I think you need to know that I'm not really Aunt Symoune's niece. Their real niece . . ."

"Pearly . . ." Matthew interrupted, putting a finger on his lips. "Ashley is looking for you."

"Oh, yes. Priya, don't look so serious. I was just joking," said Pearly, changing the subject.

"Pearly, why do I feel that you were not joking? I've had this feeling all week that Aunt Ashley and you were on the verge of telling me something but pulled back. My mother was so adamant against any contact with you and blamed Aunt Ashley for the death of her unborn, yet she allowed me to come. There could be more to her change of heart than I know. Are you guys hiding something?"

"Priya, I can't answer that question but your mom can. Promise me that you will ask her and call me if they don't approve of Ryan. I'm sure I'll be able to convince them."

"How? I don't understand . . . but I promise."

"Ashley, you're crying . . ." said Matthew, pulling his handkerchief.

"Oh, Matthew, thank you for bringing Priya back? It means so much to me to see her
wearing her mother's gown and celebrating her birthday in her house. Thank you."

"I'll do anything for you, Ashley," said Matthew, wiping a tear from her eyes. "Thanks for bringing Pearly into my life. It means a lot to us to be with our daughter on her birthday."

He stood by Ashley watching the kids finish the dance items by garlanding Pearly and Priya.

"Friends of Pearly and Priya," said Matthew, at the end of the stage show, "In light of the excellent performances by the kids, my wife and I have decided to open the *Priya Mansion* to all our kids at the Krishna Sanctuary once a month. The Ashram will arrange for the volunteer instructors and activities and we will arrange for the monthly lunches and refreshments."

"Hooray," the kids jumped.

"Let's pray that Priya will come back to visit our newborn and us soon. My wife and I have decided to name the baby—Priyanka, if it is a girl."

Applause.

GHOST OF SYMOUNE
BIRTH OF PRIYANKA

The Shangri-La to me is to have your arms around me.
If there is any paradise beyond this, my eyes don't see.

The *Priya Mansion* was in full bloom with children from the Krishna Sanctuary jumping around, enjoying their monthly visit. The forty boys and girls between the ages of five to fifteen came every month to pursue the fun activities. The volunteer instructors were carefully selected by the Ashram to assist the children in mastering the skills of their choice: yoga, classical dancing, musical instruments, art and crafts, singing and gardening. The two gardening groups were busy in their own individual areas; growing flowers and vegetables and competing with each other in the gardening skills. The six Christian children were sitting with Father Elliot listening to the stories from the Bible. Pundit Vasudeva was instructing the yoga group and Ram Maharaj was teaching harmonica and classical dance. Saya was sitting on the verandah, preparing fruit baskets for the children.

"Darling," Matthew whispered, sneaking up behind her. "Why don't I take out the baskets and you put your feet up. I can't have you fainting again . . ."

"Please, Matthew," Saya blushed. "Let me finish the baskets. I love being with children."

"I know, my beauty, but I'm concerned about you and the baby . . ."

"Dad, we need more fruits — Mom, can you free dad from your spell for a second?"

"Exactly," smiled Matthew, carrying the fruit basket.

"Your mom is a real sorcerer, honey — "

"Look who's talking," exclaimed Saya, hearing the breathing sound on her neck again.

"Matthew, please, let me finish . . ."

"Strange," she whispered, placing the basket on the table. "I'm sure I felt a breathing sound on my neck. There was no one behind me."

"Mom, can you play *hide and seek* with us?" yelled Pearly, approaching her.

"Honey, this pregnancy is making me feel so tired. Why don't I watch you play?" replied Saya, sinking into the lounging chair. She looked behind, hearing the breathing sound again.

"Whoever is hiding behind my chair, please come out," Saya smiled, closing her eyes.

"Susana . . . Susana . . . Susana!" the voice echoed in her ears.

Saya jumped out of her skin, opening her eyes.

There was no one to be seen.

"*It's funny. I heard someone . . . twice,*" she frowned.

"Mom, come and play with us," Pearly pleaded, pulling Saya to her feet and blindfolding her.

"Now everyone, go and hide quickly—"

The children disappeared giggling. Their laughter echoed in all directions. Saya stood unsure with outstretched arms for a while. She moved slowly, picking up on the giggling sound. Pearly kept leading Saya farther and farther away until she stopped abruptly.

"There you are," said Saya, removing her blindfold. I've found you—"

There stood in front of her the ghost of Symoune in white flowing gown, holding Pearly's hand.

Saya screamed in horror.

Symoune gazed through her for a while and led Pearly into the woods.

"No, no, no, stop!" Saya screamed again. "Don't take my Pearly away from me."

Symoune stopped momentarily and smiled before disappearing with Pearly.

"No, no, I'll die without Pearly," *Saya screamed at the top of her lungs.*

"Pearly . . . Pearly."

"Mom, what's wrong?" asked Pearly, shaking her out of sleep.

Saya opened her eyes wide.

The children were bending over her.
Saya stared back blankly.
"Mom, are you all right?"
"It was a dream!" exclaimed Saya, embracing Pearly tightly. "Please, don't leave me."

"Please Chandra Mukhi, this is the last spoonful," said Sunder Mukhi, wiping her mouth with the napkin. "Doctor Ahmad is here to check up on you. He's going to make you well."
Chandra Mukhi lay motionless like a corpse.
The doctor sat down and began to feel her pulse.
"Doctor Ahmad, can we change her medication? My sister is not responding to this one."
"Changing the medication won't help. The patient is in a state of deep trauma. The best therapy is to keep talking to her. We need to find out what she's thinking about."
"Yeah. If her servant had not fetched me, I wouldn't have known if she was alive or dead."
"He should've brought you sooner. I'm afraid, she is dying."
"She forbade him to contact me. She was angry with me for taking her daughter's side."
"You must notify the family," said the doctor, picking up his brief case. "Her condition is critical."
"Chandra Mukhi," urged Sunder Mukhi, holding her hand. "Can you tell me what you want?"
Chandra Mukhi moved her lips slightly.
"She's responding. Go ahead and engage her into opening up to you? I'll come back later."
"Chandra Mukhi, please tell me what you want?" asked Sunder Mukhi.
"Saya, Pearly, Matthew, Ashley."
"Do you want to see them?"
"Forgive me. Forgive me. Forgive me."
"Do you want me to write to them to come and see you?"
Chandra Mukhi nodded.
Sunder Mukhi quickly scribbled a few lines to Saya and sent the servant to mail the letter.

06/06/1906

Dear Saya:
Your mother is lying on her death bed. Her last wish is to seek forgiveness from you, Pearly, Matthew, and Ashley, in person. Please come immediately before she dies, carrying the burden of guilt on her soul. She has very little time left.
Waiting for you,
Aunt Sunder Mukhi

Sunder Mukhi opened the big curtains, flooding the sunlight into the room. Chander Mukhi opened her eyes. Shankar walked in with a bowl of hot water and sponge. Sunder Mukhi washed her body, combed her hair, and changed her. The servant came back with a bowl of hot cereal.

"Good news! Saya's coming home tonight," she said. "She has forgiven you. You must eat."

Chandra Mukhi opened her mouth.

"Saya's is going to have another baby."

Chander Mukhi's face became alive with a smile.

Her hands began to shiver with excitement.

"Pearly, Matthew, and Ashley are coming with her, too." Sunder Mukhi kept talking to her.

"Brave girl! Now I want you to rest, and wait for Saya," said Sunder Mukhi, wiping her mouth.

Chandra Mukhi fluttered her eyelids.

She kept eying the door until she fell asleep.

"They've arrived ... arrived ..." the servant yelled, running for the suitcases.

Sunder Mukhi ran to meet them at the door. They embraced each other and whispered for a while before entering Chandra Mukhi's bedroom. Chandra Mukhi lay motionless with her eyes closed.

"Masa," whispered Saya, sitting beside her bed and touching her hand.

Chandra Mukhi opened her eyes. Her face lit up.

"Masa, it's me ... Saya."

Tears started trickling down Chander Mukhi's eyes.

"I—1—1 was waiting to see you ... before dying. Can you ever forgive me?"

"I'm here because I've forgiven you, Masa. Pearly, Matthew, and Ashley are here to see you."

"I—I wronged you, Pearly," she uttered. "Your angry face haunted me. It shattered me inside."

"I forgive you, nana," said Pearly crying bitterly, reaching out for her hand.

"I'm sorry. I—I couldn't die . . . without your forgiveness," whispered Chander Mukhi, holding her hand. She then looked at Matthew and Ashley and said, "Matthew and Ashley, please . . . forgive me."

Matthew and Ashley cried, squeezing her hand.

"Ashley," said Chander Mukhi, pulling an envelope from under her pillow. "This is for you . . . my peace offering. Please accept it and do not say no. Please think kindly . . . of me."

Ashley hesitated. Saya and Pearly nodded, putting their arms around Ashley.

"I've divided my . . . estate in two parts—Ashley and Saya," she continued. "This house goes to Sunder Mukhi and thirty thousand rupees go to Shankar, my servant. Please accept my gifts."

"Oh, oh, Matthew . . . the baby is . . . coming," Saya screamed, holding her stomach.

"Follow me," screamed Sunder Mukhi. "I'm glad I made the arrangements in advance."

Matthew quickly swept Saya into his arms and followed Sunder Mukhi. Ashley grabbed her bag and the servant started boiling water. Matthew stayed by Saya's side throughout the delivery. Everyone exclaimed when the shrill cries of the newborn filled the room.

"Thank you, darling. We've another beautiful girl," said Matthew, kissing Saya's forehead.

The entire family gathered around Chander Mukhi; Pearly holding the baby and Matthew carrying Saya in his arms.

"Thank God," whispered Chander Mukhi, breathing heavily.

"Pearly, Promise me . . . that you will bring Ashley's niece back. Promise me—?"

"I promise you, nana," cried Pearly, holding her hand.

"I will bring Aunt Symoune's and Aunt Ashley's Pearly

back to her."

'I die . . . in peace," murmured Chandra Mukhi, closing her eyes forever.

SYMOUNE FAMILY CURSE
LEGACY OF DEMONS

We are playing hide and seek; sometimes she is there, sometimes she is here.
I feel her presence, I hear her whisper; I reach out to her and she disappears.

The magic of spring was in the air. Baby Priyanka had turned one-year-old and the mansion was filled with children, celebrating her birthday. Hundreds of balloons were let into the air as soon as Pearly cut the cake, holding little Priyanka's hand. Priyanka clapped her hands with joy. A little boy from the *Krishna Sanctuary* approached Priyanka and placed a butterfly on her palm.

Priyanka stood motionless watching the butterfly until she wriggled her fingers and the butterfly flew away. Priyanka ran after the butterfly, giggling. The children roared with laughter. Saya ran after Priyanka and slipped; Matthew quickly swept her up in his arms. Saya blushed, shaking her head.

Everyone clapped.

"This is a perfect time to share our good news with you," said Matthew, holding Saya's hand.

"We're expecting our third child who will be playing with you very soon."

"Hooray," the children jumped.

Congratulations poured in from all sides. Swami Krishna and Father Elliot smiled. Pearly rushed to embrace her parents. Ashley broke into tears. She whispered to Annie, "I wish I had—"

"Finish the sentence, Dr. Ashley."

"Forget it."

"I know what's on your mind. I've seen the look."

"What look?"

"You wish you had what Saya has. You care for Matthew . . . very much."

"So do you," Ashley became defensive. "Matthew is a great friend."

"If you say so."

The boys finished their cake and started flying kites and the girls went chasing after the butterflies. Ashley and Saya followed Pearly and Priyanka to the swings.

Saya stopped hearing a whisper . . .

"Susana . . . Susana . . . Susana!"

"Ashley, did you hear anything?"

"No. Oh, the girls look adorable on the swing holding on to each other with their eyes shut?"

"Susana . . . Susana . . . Susana!"

Saya heard the whisper again. A shiver ran down her spine.

"What's the matter, Saya?"

"Look over there. She — she — she's standing behind the girls?"

"Who, where? I don't see anyone behind the girls."

"Pearly, honey," Saya screamed, pulling her hand.

"Mom?" Pearly opened her eyes. "What's wrong?"

"Get off the swing. Get away from her—"

"What? Get way from whom?" Pearly shot Ashley a bewildered look.

"Ignore it, honey. Let's go. You mom is not feeling well."

Pearly followed with a puzzled look.

Ashley sat quietly sipping tea and watching the paintings of Symoune and Priya, hung side by side in the drawing room. Watching the paintings had become a daily ritual for Ashley.

"*Why haven't I heard from Menaka?*" wondered Ashley. "*She did promise Matthew that she'll tell Priya the truth. Why hasn't she told her yet?*"

"*What if she never tells Priya? What options do I have? Saya is so close to delivering the baby that Matthew can't leave her in this condition. I must wait until the baby is born.*"

"Ashley," Saya, walked in looking distraught. "I'm afraid, it's happening again—"

"What's happening again?"
"The visions—"
"What kind of visions?"
"Like seeing things ... beyond sight. I'm seeing a ghost."
"You saw her ... yesterday. Didn't you?"
"Yes. She wants to tell me something but I get so scared that I lose her."
"What does she look like?"
"I know her intimately when I see her. She calls me Susana. The visions started with my first pregnancy. They stopped after my second pregnancy and have started again."
"Honey, women are ultra-sensitive when they are pregnant," said Ashley, holding her hand.
"The fact that you still blame yourself for the unfortunate turn of events that took place after you left your baby could be causing these visions. Your hormones are interacting with your guilt; thus producing these visions. You must get rid of the guilt and accept the *Karma as I've* accepted it. I forgave you a long ago. But you must forgive yourself."
"No. Ashley, it's something more than guilt—like some unfinished business from the past life. I seem to have a deep connection with the ghost and I intend to find out what it is."
"How do you intend to do that?"
"Swami Krishna has given me a *mantra*. The daily *japa* of the mantra will give me the strength to face my visions without fear."
"You've already talked to the Swami?"
"Yes. Please don't mention this to Matthew and Pearly. I feel lucky to have been given another chance to bear Matthew's children and be close to Pearly and be happy for a few more years."
"A few more years?"
"Yes. I intend to enjoy every minute with them because every minute with them is like eternity. "
"You sound like Symoune. I'm beginning to see striking similarities..."
"There's much more to the similarities than you and I know," Saya whispered, putting an arm around her. "I take comfort in knowing that it is you who will take over my role one day and become the most loving part of my Matthew and my children's lives."

A look of surprise rose in Ashley's eyes.

Saya was sitting in front of the mirror, brushing her long, wavy hair. Matthew was watching her.

'There's something mystical about your beauty that intrigues me..."

"I wish these moments forever stay; nestling softly in a tender way," she whispered.

"I wish the moments never end," said Matthew, running his fingers through her hair.

"They won't, because..."

"We'll turn each moment into eternity," he finished the sentence.

"Darling, I can't wait to see our third child. I wish I had one hundred children with you."

"I wish I had an eternal life with you, but I'll settle for a short heaven."

"You are my soul, Saya," said Matthew, disappearing into the bathroom.

"And you are mine," Saya smiled, closing her eyes momentarily and picking up her brush.

"Susana... Susana... Susana!"

Saya's eyes flew open and froze on the reflection of Symoune's ghost in the mirror.

The brush slipped from her hands to the floor.

Saya closed her eyes and started reciting the Mantra.

"Om Bhui Bhava Savaha. Om Tapaha..."

The *Priya Mansion* shook with commotion. Matthew, Ashley, Pearly, Father Elliot, and the servants were frantically looking for Saya. She had left Pryanka with Ashley, shortly after the breakfast and no one had seen her since then. They had checked all the places and she had not been there. Ashley, Father Elliot, and Swami stood whispering quietly in the corner.

"Matthew, come with me," said Swami. "Father, can you stay with the girls?"

"I'm coming with you," said Ashley, slipping Pryanka into Pearly's arms.

With torches in their hands, Swami, Matthew, and Ashley kept going over every inch of the ground followed by the servants until they saw a figure of a woman sitting near the swings, cradling someone in her arms.

"It looks like someone over there," said Swami Krishna. "Follow me."

They rushed to the spot and found Saya lying on her back, bleeding. She winced with pain.

"Hurry!" yelled Ashley. "Saya's in labour. Get her to the clinic quickly."

Matthew lost no time in carrying her to the clinic. The baby came out crying within minutes.

"Meet *Arman Ashley Scott,*" said Matthew, holding Pearly's hand. "A symbol of unity and strength between two magnificent cultures; two intriguing religions; two devoted parents; two beautiful sisters; two strong mothers and two awesome Godfathers, Father Elliot and Swami Krishna."

They walked to the drawing room together to seek blessings from the Swami and the Father.

"You gave us quite a scare, Saya," said Ashley, wiping the beads of sweat on Saya's face.

"I slipped into the ditch and couldn't get up . . ." Saya smiled.

"Who pulled you out?"

"Ashley it was her—Symoune. I've been seeing Symoune. She pulled me out of the ditch. She took care of me and stayed with me until I was found. I'm not afraid of her any more. Symoune was the angel who saved me and Arman Ashley Scott," she whispered, falling asleep.

"Arman Ashley Scott . . . Arman Ashley Scott."

The words echoed in Ashley's head.

"I saw someone cradling Saya in her arm and she disappeared. Could that be Symoune?"

Ashley sat still.

Chapter Nine
The End of the Aristocrats

MYSTICAL WEDDING
CURSE OF THE BLACKBUCK

I feel so torn inside by strife; strife between the wrong and right.
Each day I try to reason with it; each day I become more uptight.

Ashley was nervously pacing the floor. Saya was feeding the baby and little Priyanka was playing beside her. Matthew had been gone for days and there was no word from him. He had gone to visit *Fort Priya*. Major Partap Singh had graciously invited him to stay with him when Matthew wrote to ask him, if he could introduce him to some of the local artists to facilitate his research into the Indian art of wood carving with ivory. Matthew needed an excuse to get back into the mansion. He was determined to hold Menaka to her promise.

"Mom, Aunt Ashley's digging a hole into the floor," whispered Pearly, entering the room.

"Honey, she's anxious to find out if Menaka has fulfilled her promise to tell the truth."

"Mom, I'm as anxious as Aunt Ashley, if not more. A day doesn't go by when I don't think about Priya. I want her to come back to Aunt Ashley and restart her life."

"It's a delicate situation, honey. It cannot be rushed. We don't know how Priya would react to the truth. She adores her parents and may not want to part with them. Besides she's the pillar that's holding the family together. Matthew told me that her brother, Pooran, is a compulsive gambler. He shudders to think what would happen to the family if that pillar is pulled from under them. Did you hear the door? I think it's your dad."

"It is dad. He has arrived! " Pearly jumped. "Daddy," she rushed into his arms.

"Dada . . . Dada," Priyanka clung to his legs.

"Ashley, why don't I wash up and change before I join you?" said Matthew, picking up Priyanka and embracing Saya and Arman. Pearly and Ashley waited in silence until he came down, looking tense.

"Matthew, I'm afraid to ask." Ashley felt apprehensive, studying the lines on his face.

Matthew took a deep breath. The tension mounted in the room.

"Matthew? Did Menaka honour her promise or not?"

"Yes, she did," he replied softly. "It took her enormous strength to spill the truth."

"That's good."

"Not really."

"How did the Major react?"

"He had a stroke."

"Oh, no! He did survive. Didn't he?"

"Yes, except he doesn't remember the incident before the stroke. He thinks he had a dreadful nightmare concerning Priya that caused the stroke. He doesn't remember the details."

"We're back to where we started," replied Ashley, burying her face in her hands.

"Not really. There's someone else in the family who found out about the secret."

"Who?"

"Pooran Partap Singh. He overheard the conversation."

"How did he react?"

"He walked out of the door with an unpredictable look."

"Menaka took too long to bring the truth to light?"

"Between Pooran Partap's daily episodes of drinking and gambling, Menaka had to find the right time to spring the truth on her husband."

"How do you think Pooran Partap will handle the secret?"

"He is deep into alcohol and gambling. I'm afraid; he'll use this information to destroy Menaka."

"Priya doesn't know anything yet?"

"No. Menaka intended to tell her but backed out after the stroke. She's afraid that Pooran will force her out of the house for the treachery and Priya could end up into a state of shock, like her father."

"Pooran Partap holds the cards now." Ashley began to cry.

"Everything depends on how he plays his cards," Matthew replied, placing an arm around her.

"How will he play his cards is the big question?"

"Who knows? One thing is clear—there's a time bomb ticking in that house, ready to explode."

"Pooran, why are you sitting here in the dark?"

"I'm trying to unravel a mystery that eludes me, mother."

"What kind of a mystery?" Menaka shuddered.

"The one that drives Pooran to the bottle and Menaka to lies? I think it's worth exploring. Don't you?"

"Yes," replied Menaka, dreading the drift of the conversation.

"Why don't we start with Pooran before we figure out Menaka? Do you mind?"

Menaka shook her head.

"Tell me, if Pooran's mother had not died, who would have been the legal heir of Major Singh?"

"It would've been Pooran Partap."

"Right! But she did die and when she did, do you know how the little Pooran felt?"

"Not really—"

"Pooran felt empty inside. His father re-married to fill the void but between his busy schedule and his step-mother's continuous child bearing episodes; Pooran became an invisible entity. The only place he could find solace was his ancestral home—*Fort Partap*, because it reminded him of his mother. He felt her soul in the mansion. He felt her love through her paintings."

Menaka let out a deep sigh.

"Then one day, his step-mother was blessed with a baby girl. Pooran's father became so joyous that he took away the one and the only thing that Pooran had loved the most, next to his mother—*Fort Partap*. Slowly, one by one, all the reminders of his mother were removed to usher in the new era. Little Pooran felt abandoned and displaced. He took to the bottle to numb his pain. His step-mother became too busy with the newborn to notice the step-son, who was stifling for love. Pooran was labeled as lazy and worthless. He became unwanted and unloved."

Menaka started to sob.

"The question is—does that unwanted, lonely son have the

right to ask his step-mother why didn't she ever reach out to that child? Why did she allow differential treatment in the same house?"

"You're right . . . I should've tried," she said, crying into her veil.

"Why did you keep the truth from my father about the fact that you gave birth to a stillborn?"

"Because I—I didn't know the truth myself."

"But when you did find out, you still kept my father in the dark. Why?"

"Because I thought that it would . . . destroy him."

"No. You kept him in the dark because you didn't trust Pooran. You thought that he would destroy you. Guess what, I've known the truth for weeks now. You've been wondering what I will do now that I've found out the truth. Right?"

"Yes," sobbed Menaka.

"Would I destroy you or would I bargain with you for my silence?"

"Yes."

"What if I told you that I will do neither? I would rather find out what will you do knowing what I know."

"Now that I know the pain I've caused you," Menaka hesitated. "I will restore *Fort Priya* to you."

"Just like that? Out of your sense of goodwill. Right?"

"On one condition that you will never drink and gamble again."

"Bravo! Menaka has finally revealed herself," remarked Pooran, clapping his hands. "We got the answer to the motivation behind the actions of Pooran and Menaka."

"What do you mean?"

"The answer is—pain drives Pooran to the bottle and fear drives Menaka to lies," he added. "The same fear that forced her to drive a wedge between a father and son; miscarry multiple times; alienate friends and keep the family in the dark. Am I right?"

"Yes. I'm glad to find out the answer because maybe now I can do what's right. It feels as though, I've never lived those years; merely managed to survive through the life of fears."

"The problem is that your offer comes from fear not from love. Pooran wants your love, trust, and acceptance. You can't give those to him because you're too afraid to love; too afraid to trust, and too afraid to accept Pooran as he is—the product of your own upbringing."

"If you give me a second chance . . . I would like to make amends?"

"If you ask me to stop drinking and gambling out of love, I will do that in a heartbeat. Don't ask me that question out of fear. Even though I hate you and your lies passionately; I do have compassion for you and will never knowingly blackmail you or destroy you. Can you say that about yourself?"

"I would like to change and trust you to change. Now may I ask the same question again--this time out of love?"

"Yes, and I promise to stop drinking as of today. As for gambling—I've previously accepted the challenge from Nareshwer Singh to defeat him at the tables on the night of *Diwali*. As a *Rajput*, I'll have to honour my word. I promise to play only once and never again. I don't know what the outcome will be. But can you promise to love, trust and accept me even if the outcome is wrong?"

"Yes, I accept you as you are and will restore *Fort Priya* to you not out of fear but out of love and deep respect for the way you've handled this situation with me."

"It's your call. Remember, you are free to change your mind."

Priya was sitting in front of the mirror combing her long hair. She was getting ready for one of the most sacred festivals of the *Hindus*, called the *worship of Durga*—a beautiful ten-armed warrior goddess, seated upon a tiger. The festival was celebrated annually by the masses with rituals, feasts, and fasts in honour of the supreme goddess who was invoked to remove obstacles, create miracles and bring harmony to the people.

The festival opened nine days ago with colorful *Pandals*, fully furnished with *Durga* statues, lights, sounds, and food stalls. The village was filled to the brim with tribesmen and women from the outlying communities. They had been camping outside the main temple of *Durga* and floating around the village from *pandal* to *pandal* to participate in the open house ceremonies organized by the different groups. The Images of the goddess were created anew every year with clay; painted gorgeously and decorated with jewellery and immersed into the river bank on the tenth day. The houses of the rich people were splendidly illuminated and thrown open to beggars. Following the ritual of breaking the fast and the ceremonial aarti *at home*, Menaka and Menakshi took to the streets to feed the beggars.

"Pooran, your mother, and I are leaving for *Dehra Dun* tonight for a couple of weeks to recuperate," said Major Partap Singh, anointing his forehead with red-tilka. "I want you to behave responsibly in my absence. And you must escort your sister to the Durga temple tonight to make her offerings."

Pooran Partap walked to the carriage with a bored look. One thing he had hated more than his stepmother was the tradition of going to the temple. He leaned back on the seat and never uttered a word until the carriage stopped. The temple was swarming with the devotees carrying offerings. Pooran looked at the crowd with disdain as Priya got off, adjusting her long veil, and holding the basket full of offerings and a little statue of the goddess.

"Go ahead and make your offerings to the goddess. I'll join you," said Pooran, lighting his cigar. With the sound of the drum echoing in her ears, Priya headed towards the twelve foot long statute of *Durga* set on a raised platform in the middle of the open air compound of the temple. Some of the devotees were dancing in front of the goddess in perfect unison with the beat of the drum, while the others were waiting in line for their turn, to hand in their offerings to the priest.

As Priya reached the altar, her eyes fell over a tall, dark stranger standing beside her with his eyes closed, holding a garland and the offerings on a silver tray. Suddenly a gust of wind hit across the room and blew the garland away from his hands, landing it neatly around Priya's neck. The stranger opened his eyes and turned his head, settling a steady gaze on Priya.

Startled Priya stepped back, wide eyed.

"May the blessing of *Durga* be on the couple," muttered the priest.

"We . . . aren't . . . married," said Priya, reaching for the garland.

"If you aren't, you are destined to be. It's an omen," replied the priest.

"The garland was meant for the goddess. It accidentally blew in my direction," said Priya.

"There's nothing accidental about destiny. Things happen for a reason," replied the priest.

"May I have the garland?" the stranger extended his hand.

"Yes, of course."

As she bent her head to remove the garland, her elbow struck his tray, knocking down the container of *sindoor*, spilling it neatly in the middle of her head, face, and hands.

A hush fell across the hall. The devotees stopped dancing.

Priya stood aghast staring at the garland and *sindoor* over her hands.

"Jai *Durga;* Jai mystical couple," the priest broke the silence by sprinkling holy water over them.

The crowd cheered and began to throw rose petals over their heads. Priya quickly removed the garland and rushed outside, handing the garland back to the stranger. She slowed down at the sound of footsteps.

"You forgot your goddess at the altar," said the stranger, following her.

"Thank you."

"I'm Nareshwar Singh from the adjoining village *Naresh Garh*."

"I—I'm ... Priya Partap Singh."

"Priya Partap Singh? Are you ... the one, who I think you are?"

"If you are referring to the *Fort Priya*, yes, I am."

"Then you've heard the exaggerated accounts of the bad blood between your clan and mine."

"I feel no enmity towards you."

"I visited the *Fort* once when I was a child. I still remember how beautiful the structure is. It pales in comparison to your beauty. I've never seen anyone more beautiful."

"Please, I'm enough embarrassed as it is."

"May I join you in immersing the goddess into the water?"

"I don't mind."

They walked quietly to the river *Ghat*, filled with devotees, immersing their statues into the water.

"Please forget the incident earlier. It was merely an accident."

"If you so believe."

"You forgot to immerse the garland," said Priya, observing the garland wrapped around his wrist.

"I've saved it for the right time," the stranger said, disappearing into the crowd.

Priya shivered at the sound of the rifle shots as she walked back to her carriage.

"Where is my brother, Pooran?" she asked the coachman.

"He followed a bunch of deer into the bush."

"Oh, no!"

Priya rushed frantically towards the bush. There was no sign of Pooran. She was about to turn back when she heard the firing shots again. The blood drained from her face as she followed the sound. She kept running deep into the bush until she heard three quick shots, fired at a close range. She jumped in the direction of the sounds and stumbled on the wounded black deer lying on the ground, shaking like a leaf, with her stomach slit open by the bullets. Pooran was kneeling beside her. A stream of blood sprouted through her wounds and fell across Pooran's face as a wounded baby deer popped out of her belly and fell a few yards away into a pool of blood. The mother began to crawl in slow motion towards her newborn in excruciating pain. Twisting and moaning, amid horrid screams, she dragged herself until she collapsed, placing her face over the baby's. The mother and the baby clung to each other, making ghastly sounds. Pooran lifted his hand to wipe his forehead, smearing blood all over his face and clothes. Priya froze with fear.

"Pooran, what have you done?" Priya screamed, going down on her knees and pulling the mother deer and the baby in her lap. They lay shivering and rolling tears in her lap, until they died.

"You've killed the blackbucks!" sobbed Priya, putting her arms around them. "They're revered by the Bishnoe tribe. The curse of blackbucks will now follow us."

Suddenly a bunch of Bishnoe gypsies appeared on the scene with spears and arrows and began to shout in their dialect. A couple of them removed their turbans and disappeared; the were wrapping and carrying the blackbucks on their backs, while the others stood glaring at Pooran and Priya.

At the nod of their leader, two of the gypsies advanced towards Pooran and pushed him to the ground. They stripped him and forced him to lie on the hot sand, face down while kicking him and pouring hot sand over his body.

"We worship blackbucks," shouted the leader, grabbing Priya by the arm. "We'll kill our children before we let anyone kill our blackbucks."

"Please . . . forgive my brother," pleaded Priya, trying to free herself from his grip.

"Tie his hands behind his back and drag him to the tree," said the leader.

They dragged Pooran by the hair and tied him to the tree, while Priya helplessly looked on.

"Look, what you've done. Watch, what we'll do," said the leader, picking up the rifle with his free hand and hitting Pooran in the stomach. Pooran doubled up in pain, vomiting blood.

"Teach him a lesson," shouted the leader, pointing to his spear. "Wound him deeply."

The gypsies started piercing Pooran's arms and hands with spears, giving him a blood bath.

The forest began to echo with the screams of Pooran.

"Enough!" shouted the leader, pushing Priya towards the men.

"Tie her up and give her a blood bath. Show no mercy!"

"Help! Help! Help!" Priya began to scream, as the men dragged her ruthlessly to the tree.

Suddenly two men rode in with guns blazing. The gypsies ran helter skelter.

One of horsemen swept Priya off the ground and the other one freed Pooran and rode off with him.

"You and your brother are safe . . . safe . . . safe."

The words echoed in Priya's head as she fainted in his arms.

FALL OF FORT PRIYA
STUNNING PROPOSAL

I feel disappointed without regrets or pain;
And still playing with cool my losing game.

Priya tossed and turned all night in bed. Her mind kept flashing the images of Pooran's blood smeared body, the dead blackbucks, and the gypsies dragging her by the hair.

"Help! Help!" she shrieked, opening her eyes. "What a dreadful dream!" Priya sat up.

"A real nightmare for the family perhaps," replied Menakshi, watching her from her chair.

"Oh, grandma . . . something dreadful—dreadful occurred last night."

"I figured that. Your brother was dripping with blood and you were smeared with *Sindoor*. A couple of horsemen escorted you home at midnight. Can you imagine the shock—?"

"Who were they? What did they look like?"

"They rode off before I could take a good look at their faces. The only thing that stands out in my memory is the garland wrapped around the wrist of the one who carried you in."

"Oh, my God . . . it was him," thought Priya.

"Where's Pooran? How is he?"

"He has been delirious all night. The doctor has tended to his wounds. What the hell happened?"

"We were attacked . . . by the gypsies."

"Why would the gypsies attack you?"

"Pooran shot and killed the blackbuck and the baby buck."

"What? He took the rifle with him? How stupid can he be?"

"I didn't realize that . . . until it was too late."

"No wonder you were attacked. Everyone knows that the

blackbucks are worshipped by the *Bishnoe* tribe. Pooran has earned the wrath of the gypsies and there will be hell to pay. Where did you get the *sindoor* in your hair?"

"I had an encounter with a stranger. His garland blew in my direction; spilling *sindoor* all over me."

"Who was the stranger?"

"Someone named, Nareshwer Singh."

"You mean the Nareshwer Singh of the Narersh Garh?"

"Yes. I guess he was the one who found us and brought us home."

"Your guess is right. I saw the garland around his wrist. I've a bad feeling about this. You mustn't step outside even for a second. I'm going to wire your parents."

"Why grandma?"

"Because something tells me that hell is about to break loose. The people in this area are primitive. They believe in superstitions and rituals. The curse of the blackbuck and the temple incident will come back to haunt our family for generations to come. Go and check on Pooran," shouted Menakshi, leaving the room.

"Oh, my God, Pooran," cried Priya holding his hand.

"Can you forgive me . . . Priya?" whispered Pooran, opening his eyes. "I let you down big time. I'll never hunt again. I'll change my ways if you promise to stand by me."

"I will—I will. You are my brother and I love you," Priya sobbed, patting his shoulder.

Nareshwer Singh was so deeply struck by the beauty of Priya that he kept seeing her face wherever he turned. The more he tried to forget her; the more she haunted him. He fell asleep thinking of her and woke up with her on his mind. He kept reading her note until it burned in his memory.

Nareshwer Singh:
Thank you for rescuing my brother and me. We are forever in your debt.
Priya Partap Singh

"I'm under the spell of the goddess," he whispered.

"Then why haven't you approached the goddess's father to seek her hand?" asked his friend.

"Because something tells me that they will not accept my proposal unless they have to."

"You mean, unless you've something to hold over their head?"

"Exactly."

"How badly do you want her?"

"I want Priya at any cost."

"Go ahead and march to her house."

"What if they refuse?"

"Leave it to me. I'll set it up. They won't be able to refuse."

The news of the *mystical wedding* at the *Durga Temple* spread through the village like wildfire. The people developed an insatiable hunger for the details. The village priest found himself swarmed with invitations from the villagers wanting to hear a firsthand account of the story. The witnesses of the incident began to relish in storytelling. The Partap family held their breath as a big procession marched inside their residence echoing the sound of trumpets and drums. Dressed in a ceremonial outfit, Nareshwer Singh walked in proudly with his relatives and friends followed by villagers carrying huge baskets of fruits, sweets, and ornaments. The priest stepped forward to make the introductions.

"The Nareshwer family has come to seek the hand of your daughter, Priya, for their son," said the priest.

"Fort Priya welcomes you," said Partap Singh. "Since we were ill prepared for the surprise, may we have some time to consider the proposal?"

"What's there to consider?" asked the priest. "The match was made and blessed by the goddess."

"Still we need some time to discuss the proposal with our daughter," replied, Partap Singh.

"You mustn't minimise the importance of the profound incident that happened at the temple," replied the priest. "It was divine intervention by the goddess to heal the rift between the two clans that have been at one another's throats for twenty years. You must act upon the proposal of the Nareshwer family and solemnise the wedding as soon as possible."

"It's rather a sudden move," said Partap Singh.

"Somebody had to make a move," replied the priest. "The people of the village are counting on it. Your daughter is now being revered as a goddess. The people of both townships are rejoicing in the blessing of *Durga* and so should you. There are people waiting outside your residence as we speak to catch a glimpse of the goddess-bride. They're rolling dice and making bets to predict the wedding date."

"May we discuss the details in private?" asked Partap Singh.

A silence fell across the room. The guests looked at each other as the Nareshwer family began to confer with the priest. Everyone turned silent when the priest began to speak again.

"The Nareshwer family begs your permission to depart," he announced, straightening his shoulders. "They will come back on the day after *Diwali* to claim their bride. They, like the people of the town believe that the wedding has already been solemnised by the *Goddess Durga*, so it need not be solemnised again. Should you refuse to give away the bride, the wrath of the goddess and the people of this village will be upon you."

Major Partap Singh decided to stand up to Nareshwer Singh and face the wrath of the goddess and the people. His lawyer assured them that the incident at the temple could not be held legal and binding. So he sent a curt note, refusing to give the hand of his daughter to Nareshwer Singh.

"I've news for you," wrote Nareshwer Singh to Priya. "Your brother Pooran is in my custody. He lost *Fort Priya to* me at a game of chess last night. I'm prepared to return him and *Fort Priya* in exchange for the wedding."

Priya wrote back to him.

Nareshwer Singh:
Bring my brother safely back. Revert the ownership
of Fort Priya back to my father and I will marry you.
Priya Partap Singh

END OF THE ARISTOCRATS
MARRIAGE OF PRIYA

I see my demon digging my grave.
I hear a whisper; I shall be saved.

As the news of the blackbuck hunting spread through *Naresh Garh*, a big procession of Bisnoe gypsies marched through the streets to protest the killings. The posters went up on the walls condemning the killings. The gypsies prayed in large numbers at the temples, urging the goddess to avenge the killings.

"You must call off the wedding," said the mother of Nareshwer Singh. "We cannot allow you to marry into a family under a curse."

"Mother . . . I'll have hell to pay if you utter one word about this story," replied Nareshwer.

"Nobody can ever find out who killed the black bucks — end of the story."

"You can seal my lips but you cannot make the curse go away."

"Why are you talking about the curse? This match was made by the goddess."

"Until Priya's father defied the goddess by going over her head to the lawyers. Now his family will face the wrath of the goddess and the curse of the blackbucks. I don't want to be associated with them."

"Mother, I'm going ahead with this wedding at any cost. There's nothing you can say to stop me. If you utter one word about the blackbuck or cancelling the wedding, you will lose me forever. Now I want you to make preparations to welcome the bride or you will lose me forever. I mean it!"

Priya let out heart-wrenching screams as she departed from the house of her parents with her bridegroom. Major Partap

Singh, Menaka, and Pooran shed buckets of tears, escorting Priya to the carriage drawn by beautiful horses. The people poured into streets to see the spectacular wedding party depart. The bridegroom left on a big decorated elephant, wearing a shimmering *sherwani* and *turban*. The father and the family of the groom hurled gold coins into the air.

The beggars rushed to collect the coins.

The rich and colourful procession finally made its way home through the streets; blowing trumpets, dazzling dancers and fireworks. As soon as the procession stopped in front of the residence, a series of fireworks lit up the sky, making earth shattering noises. The elephant got spooked and ran wildly, throwing Nareshwer Singh on the ground, trampling him under his feet and knocking him unconscious. The people screamed; running out in all directions. The bridegroom was rushed inside the house, soaking in blood. A number of doctors were rushed in and out of the house to deal with the emergency, leaving the bride alone and abandoned in the bridal carriage standing on the doorstep. "We've been able to save his life but there could be complications," the doctor said.

"What kind of complications?"

"Serious ones. Unfortunately Nareshwer Singh has been paralysed waist down."

The festivities turned into mourning.

"Oh, God, No one brought the poor bride in? She's is still outside in the carriage."

"No one has lifted her veil yet," said Nareshwer's sister. "Let's go."

"Wait," yelled Maya, Nareshwer's mother. "No one will lift her veil or see her face until my son recovers."

Everyone listened in stunned disbelief.

"Furthermore the bride would not be allowed to set one foot in the main house or allowed near my son. Take her to the spare chamber adjoining this building. That will be her place of residence. She will be sent meals twice a day and wear white clothes. No one will be allowed to converse with the cursed one until my son recovers," she shouted, retiring to her bedchamber.

Too afraid to challenge Maya, the family members submitted

to her will. In a matter of minutes, the status of Priya was reduced from a goddess bride to the cursed one. Alone and abandoned, Priya woke up from the longest night of her life to find a box on her bed containing a white *Sari*, a statue of *Lord Krishna*, a copy of the holy Geeta and a list of instructions to follow from her mother-in-law:

To dress in white; speak quietly and walk quietly.
To keep her face hidden behind the veil.
To fast every second day on milk and rice.
To pray five times a day for her husband.
To remain in seclusion until her husband recovers from the paralysis.

With shivering hands, Priya picked up the white *sari* and draped it around her body, pulling the cover over her head. A maid servant appeared with a tray. She placed the tray on the table and left without a backward glance.

The news of the accident hit *Fort Priya* overnight. Major Partap Singh was rushed to the hospital where he died, the next morning. A deeply remorseful Pooran Partap lit the funeral pyre of his father, vowing to atone for his sins. He immersed the ashes of his father in the holy river, Ganges, and completed the ritual of a purifying bath, feeling closer to his father in death than he had ever been in his life.

"I'm responsible for the family downfall," he admitted. "I must seek atonement."

"No! The wedding plans were in motion long before the fall of *Fort Priya*," Menaka replied.

"You were set up. May God forgive me for wronging you, Priya, your father, and Ashley and bring you peace."

Following the tearful farewell, Pooran Partap shaved her head and left *Fort Priya* forever to join the *Bhakti Ashram* in *Vrindavan*. Two weeks later Menaka had a stroke.

"Now that I'm dying, mother," said Menaka, closing her eyes. "Promise me that you will fulfill my promise to tell Priya the truth and unite her with Ashley."

Menaka never opened her eyes again.

Chapter Ten
The Death and Rebirth of Pearly

OBSESSION OF PEARLY
MYSTERY OF SUZANA

The rolling years revived no new hopes except again revived
the hope for release;
one last hope surviving out of millions has like madness now
my whole being seized.

One year had passed and there was no word from Menaka. The lines of anguish began to grow deeper on Ashley's face as the hope of seeing Priya began to fade away into a distant future. An overwhelming depression engulfed her and she yearned for Priya. She began to search for her in Pearly's face.

"Auntie, do you need more tea?" asked Pearly.

"Tea?" Ashley kept staring deep into Pearly's eyes.

Pearly's heart broke into pieces.

"Aunty, you're doing that again; looking for Priya in my face. How do I assure you that I intend to bring Priya back even if I've to die for her?" snapped Pearly.

"Oh, Pearly, forgive me," cried Ashley, grabbing her by the shoulders. "If I was searching for Priya it was because she's so far away. If you were far away, I would pine for you. I love and need you both."

"Don't say anything because you've no idea how painful it is for me . . . to live with the fact that I was the reason you lost her. Let go of me. I need to be alone," screamed Pearly, freeing herself.

Ashley stood aghast watching Pearly step out into the pouring rain and disappear out of sight.

"Matthew, Matthew?" Ashley screamed. "Pearly ran out on me. We had a misunderstanding."

"Oh, no!" burst out Saya, "I'll go with you to find her."

"No! Darling, you're pregnant and it's slippery outside. Ashley and I will go," shouted Matthew, heading out.

They searched for Pearly for hours until they found her lying on a rock, deep inside the bush, shivering from head to foot with a high temperature.

"Doctor White, what's the prognosis on Pearly?" asked Matthew.

"Although Pearly has survived the stroke, her condition has deteriorated rapidly. The fact that she was born with valvular heart disease and the condition of the valves has worsened over time has complicated the situation," replied the doctor. "The recent stroke and the rheumatic fever have caused a heavy inflammation in the inner lining of her heart. The flow of the blood is being blocked by the infection and clots. The damage to valves is so severe that the infection is not responding to the antibiotic therapy. To make the matters worse, she's deeply traumatised."

"What's your advice?"

"Other than praying for a miracle—acceptance. The doctors may not be able to do much for Pearly any more. I regret to say that your daughter is slipping fast into the other world and the only thing that's holding her back is her determination to bring Priya back."

Saya was sitting with a worried look when she heard the whisper...

"Suzana... Suzana... Suzana...!"

She opened the window and saw a shadow moving across the garden.

"My mind is playing tricks on me. It always does when I'm pregnant," she thought.

"Suzana... Suzana... Suzana...!"

"It's happening again. I'm seeing... things," she rubbed her eyes. "Wherever I go, wherever I walk, shadows of gloom walk with me. Behind the shimmering, shining sky, deep dark clouds my eyes see. I wish I knew what the matter is with me and what's happening to me? Things that are there, matter not; things that aren't there my eyes see."

She began to follow the shadow. It stopped at the swings. Fear gripped Saya and she closed her eyes. When she opened her eyes she saw two little girls: one girl was sitting on the swing and the other one was pushing her. She also saw two women sitting close together on the grass, watching them and arguing. They were the spit images of Saya and Symoune.

"Oh, my God . . . that's me arguing with Symoune. How could that be?" wondered Saya.

"Savanna, tell your daughter to stop pushing so hard. My daughter will get hurt."

"Suzana, you worry too much. The girls are having fun."

"Savanna, tell her to stop pushing so hard. My baby will get hurt."

"Suzana, nobody's going to get hurt—"

"Savanna, either you listen to me or you will earn my curse for your recurring indolence."

"And your curse will bounce back on you with full force because I'm being unjustly accused."

The argument ended abruptly.

The baby girl slipped from the swing, hitting the rock and dying instantly. Savanna and her daughter froze in shock as Suzana clutched the dead child to her chest; her anger turned into a demonic rage. She waved her finger in the air and pronounced the curse.

"*Your daughter will be separated from you as was mine. Every one you love will be separated from you. My curse will follow you . . . follow you . . . till hell freezes over.*"

Bewildered Saya blinked her eyes and found herself on the swing. It began to go up higher and higher. Saya slipped off the swing; crashing her head on the rock and becoming unconscious. "Oh, my God, I've lost my baby." she cried, opening her eyes to find her head in Symoune's lap.

"Don't be afraid, I've saved your baby," replied Symoune quietly. "Lie still. You're wounded in the head."

"Symoune . . . why do you always save me and my children?"

"So that you could save mine . . ."

"I just saw us arguing. How could you be both Symoune and Savanna?"

"Just like you could be both, Suzana and Saya."

"I don't understand?"

"We were sisters, Savanna and Suzana before we came as Symoune and Saya. Your curse followed my daughter and killed her in a fire incident at her school. The same curse is bouncing back on your children with full force. The curse that separated Ashley and me from my daughter also separated you from your daughter. The curse will continue to haunt our children until you call it off."

"How do I call off the curse?"

"By forgiving me and you as I've forgiven you and myself. I've been safeguarding your children from the curse. Now you must safeguard mine. I was the one who turned Pearly's nightmares into mystical adventures by bringing her the magic crystal. I was the one who brought Matthew back to you. Now you must give Pearly the permission to bring my daughter back to Ashley."

"You said that the curse is bouncing back on my children. Is my Pearly going . . . to die?" sobbed Saya.

"Momentarily, because I will revive her. Let Pearly go and make things right. This time she will come back as Priya and Priya will come back as Pearly as they should have come in the first place. Are you with me?"

"All the way! My head is throbbing with pain. I think my time is running out on me."

"You were given six years of uninterrupted bliss with Matthew in exchange for the six years of total devotion you gave each other in the past life. Now, you must set Matthew free. If you don't, you will lose him."

"Why would I lose him?"

"Because you left him alone in a tortured state after your daughter died in the accident. Ashley was the only person who helped him get his sanity back. He fell in love with her and they were going to be married when you stole him back. Ashley died with him on her mind. Now you must free him and your children to be with Ashley to pay for the suffering you caused both of them in the past and the present life."

"But I'm afraid of dying."

"Your soul will not die. It will transition into a new beginning. Your ability to accept, forgive, and detach yourself from this world of the *Maya* (illusion) will free your soul from the cycle of life and death and lead you to the state of Nirvana. I'll stand by you through your transition into the state of Nirvana..."

"What is Nirvana?"

"It's the state of achieving the ultimate peace; a transformation from being a mortal to an angel."

"Symoune, I do forgive you and myself. I promise to set Matthew free and give permission to Pearly to bring Priya back," said Saya, closing her eyes. "I do look forward to ending this painful journey into the state of Nirvana and be an angel like you to watch over our children."

Saya was still whispering the words over and over when Matthew and Ashley found her.

"Darling, how are you?" asked Matthew, as soon as she opened her eyes.

"How did I get to the hospital?" she asked, touching the bandage around her head.

"We found you at the swings. How did you get hurt?"

"The only thing that matters is that an angel saved me and my baby again."

"We saw a light around you and found you whispering..." said Ashley. "Did you see Symoune?'"

"Yes. She told me that a curse from the past is following us. We must forgive each other and ourselves to break the spell of the curse that has haunted our children for generations."

"What else did she say?"

"We must give Pearly the permission to bring Priya back because she's the only one who can."

MYSTERY OF PRIYA
LEGEND OF SUTTEE

Shall I jump through the fire to make amends?
Or just burn slowly like a candle on both ends.

The release of Pearly and Saya from the hospital brought the smiles back on the faces of everyone. The *Priya Mansion* began to pulsate with excitement again as the children of the *Krishna Sanctuary* began to decorate the *Sanctuary Garden* (named after them) with balloons and banners for the homecoming reception. Even Pryanka and little Arman memorised a special poem to welcome their mother and sister back home.

"I think the tyre's gone," said Matthew stopping the car. "I must change it," he added, opening the trunk and kneeling down. Saya walked out of the car and knelt beside him. Pearly began to read her book.

"What's taking them so long?" she wondered, putting the book down. *"Where have they disappeared?"* she frowned, circling around the car. *"What could've happened?"*

She began to walk straight and narrow until she hit the *"Dead End"* sign. She turned right and began to walk, stumbling on the *"Road Closed"* sign. She turned left, shaking her head and hit the *"Road Ends Here"* sign.

Unable to move forward she began to go backwards. She kept going backwards until she came upon a dead body. She knelt down beside the body; pulling the cover. A look of surprise crossed her eyes and she began to cry, holding his head in her arms. Suddenly she felt the movement in his body and he opened his eyes, making her tingle from head to foot.

"Goddess, you found me," he said, closing his eyes. "I was waiting to see you . . . before I died."

She raised her head at the sound of drums and saw a group of men and women approaching, carrying a bride on an open chariot. She was wearing exquisite jewellery and standing face down. Pearly quickly jumped behind the bush. As the bride descended from the chariot, the men and women began to kneel down in front of her. Every one of them touched her feet and shouted ...

"*Jai Suttee!* ... *Jai Suttee!* ... *Jai Suttee!*"

Suttee kept standing, looking dazed until she was forced to sit in a lotus position over the funeral pyre, holding the dead body of her husband in her arms.

Within minutes the *Suttee* was surrounded by pieces of wood and the funeral pyre was lit up. The *suttee* woke up from her trance and stood up, flashing her terrified face, caged in the scorching flames. She saw Pearly hiding behind the bush and screamed.

"Pearly, save me ... I'm being Sautéed."

"Oh, God, that's Priya being Sautéed," realized Pearly, jumping into the fire to save her.

"Fire! Fire! Fire!" screamed Pearly, moving her arms frantically to put out the flames.

"Honey, wake up! Wake up, honey!" yelled Saya and Matthew, wrapping their arms around her.

Pearly opened her eyes, hearing their voices, as if those came from a far off place.

"I just saw Priya being forced to commit *Suttee* and burn alive on a funeral Pyre," shrieked Pearly.

"She's in danger. I'm going to Ram Garh to save her. I don't care whether you call it my obsession or my dying wish."

The *words of Symoune hit Saya.*

"The *curse that killed my daughter in the fire is bouncing back on your children with full force. You must give Pearly the permission to bring my daughter back to Ashley.*"

"Yes, Pearly. You must go to save Priya, because you're only one who can," said Saya, as the car stopped.

The children welcomed Pearly and Saya with garlands.

"Matthew, what's the matter. You look troubled?" asked Father Elliot.

"Father, Pearly had a dream about a *Suttee*. What is *Suttee*?"

"A practice that prevails in India of a widow burning herself on the funeral pyre either with the body of her husband or if he died at distance, separately," replied Father. "Suttee or *Sati* means a true wife. Though the practice has been abolished, it still prevails in the remote parts of India. The act started out as voluntary but in orthodox communities women are still being forced to commit *Suttee*. The instances of *Suttee* are marked by inscribed memorial stones — the shrines to the dead women who are worshipped as goddesses."

"Pearly believes that Priya is in danger. She insists on going to *Ram Garh* to bring Priya. I can't leave Saya at a time like this. Ashley's hands are full with children. I don't know what to do?"

"Yes, she told me. Her mind is made up. If it makes you feel better, I offer to go with her."

"Mom, dad and Aunt Ashley," said Pearly, bidding a tearful farewell. "I've had my happiest moments with you, Pryanka and Arman. It's not that I love you less or love Priya more; it's just that Priya is my focus now. I've to do this for Aunt Ashley, because I can't live with myself if I don't."

"Honey, put this magical crystal on," said Saya, hugging her. "We'll pray for your safe return."

"Yes, the magical crystal that transforms my nightmares into unexplainable adventures. Here it is to another adventure quite unlike any I had before," thought Pearly, gazing deep inside the crystal, before putting it on.

"I had lost all hope of saving Priya," cried Menakshi, welcoming Father Elliot, and Pearly.

"Priya's life is in danger," she said, relating the tragic incidents leading up to her marriage and the end of the family. "Nareshwer's dying. Priya is terrified and must be rescued before the unthinkable happens," she added.

"By the unthinkable, do you mean Priya could be forced to commit *Suttee*?" asked Father Elliot.

"There have been incidents of *Suttee* in that village, although some of them have been voluntary, and in the cases of women who had no children," replied Menakshi. "It's a heinous act. I know how it feels to be trapped in the fire. We must come up with a plan to get Priya out of that house tonight."

They put their heads together and kept whispering to each other until they came up with a plan.

As they approached the Nareshwer residence, Menakshi shot a nervous glance at Pearly. She was sitting disguised as her maid, draped in a cheap *sari*, *with* the cover pulled below her chin and plastic bracelets going from her wrists to the elbows. They walked in on the scene of commotion. Nareshwer was hemorrhaging from an open wound inside his chest. He was drifting in and out of consciousness.

"Nareshwer's bride should be allowed to be with him during his last moments," advised the doctor. Maya, the mother-in-law, reluctantly gave in. Menakshi's heart sank when she was told to bring in Priya.

Alone and terrified, Priya quickly hid her face behind the veil at the sound of the footsteps.

"Priya it's me, Pearly," she whispered in her ear, closing the door. "We've come to rescue you. The only way we can get you out of this place is if we exchanged our clothes. There's no time to lose. You must slip out with grandma, wearing my disguise and I'll cover for you, wearing yours."

"No, I can't leave you here alone," Priya began to cry. "These people are primitive and dangerous."

"Don't worry Priya. My escape is pre-planned," said Pearly. "There's a secret door behind the Annexe that leads to the tunnel outside. Father Elliot is camping there, disguised as a gypsy. Your grandma has told me everything I need to know. Now hurry up and change."

Within a blink of an eye, they were transformed into different disguises.

"Priya, I left you a letter on the dresser. Be sure to read it," said Pearly, giving her a hug.

"*Help me, beautiful woman,*" *she wished on the crystal, before stepping outside with them.*

The Nareshwer residence was drenched in darkness as a symbol of the mourning. Maya and her family members stood on the top of the steps, waiting to receive the bride. Menakshi bid them goodbye at the foot of the steps, before walking out with a terrified Priya, following her. Hiding her face behind the veil, Pearly climbed up the steps, one by one, until she reached at the top. A series of strange and unexplainable things occurred as soon as her feet touched the threshold: A powerful sensation passed through her fingers to Maya's feet, astonishing her when she touched her feet in a traditional Indian ritual of respect; all doors flung open; all diyas and candles lit up and all the bells in the temple inside the house began to chime. In a trance like state, Pearly crossed the threshold to find herself standing face to face in front of the big statue of *Goddess Durga* with the totally mesmerised family members following her. Bowing gracefully before the goddess, Pearly moved across to the little mute girl sleeping on the floor. She touched her softly on the head. The little girl got up and began to dance, singing. "*Jai Goddess! Jai Goddess! Jai Goddess!*"

In stunned disbelief, the family and friends watched the miracles unfold.

In a dazed state, Pearly found herself sitting in front of Nareshwer; lying with an open wound, bleeding in his chest. Pearly closed her eyes and touched the crystal before putting her hand over his chest. The bleeding stopped immediately and the blood began to evaporate into the air, closing the wound.

"It's a miracle. The wound has disappeared, "announced the doctor after checking the spot.

"Jai Goddess Priya! Jai Goddess Priya! Jai Goddess Priya!" shouted everyone.

"Goddess, have you come . . . to fulfill my dying wish?" asked Nareshwer, opening his eyes.

"There's no such thing as death. It's only a transition. What's your transitional wish?"

"To be whole again and have a few days of total bliss with my bride."

"How many days are a few days?"

"Full seven days!"

"*Tathastu* — so be it. Seven days from now, it is. You will be a whole person for full seven days," she said, getting up. "I'm tired now and going to my chamber to sleep. No one is to follow me."

The crowd stood silent; watching her glide out of the room.

Pearly was sitting across the mirror combing her hair. Maya walked in followed by several women carrying boxes of dresses and jewellery.

"Please forgive me for calling you the cursed one," pleaded Maya, kneeling beside her and seeking her forgiveness. "You are a goddess. You made so many miracles in our house yesterday. My son, Nareshwer woke up in perfect health this morning. My limp is gone and my mute niece can speak again."

"Did I do all those things? I don't remember anything except being very tired," wondered Pearly.

"You are a goddess with a power to heal. My son wants to see you. The girls have come to help you into your bridal outfit. Please let them help you dress, goddess," pleaded Maya.

Before Pearly could say anything, they had dressed her into the bridal clothes and carried her on a chair inside the house shouting, "Jai Goddess Bride! Jai Goddess Bride!"

"Nareshwer, here comes the bride," they knocked on the door and left.

"Come in."

Pearly began to glide down the stairs, catching his reflection in the opposite mirror; sitting still like a statue of an Indian mythological God, with chiseled features, sculpted body, wavy hair and deeply arresting eyes.

"Oh God, he's the same man I saw in my dream. He has got the kind of eyes that will destroy my composure and force the truth out of me," dreaded Pearly, taking a deep breath. "I can't do it – " she stopped abruptly, half-way through the stairs.

"Won't you come down, please? I'm dying . . . to catch a glimpse of you?"

As Pearly walked past him; deciding to sit as far away as possible, the corner of her veil brushed across his chest, sticking to the button on his vest. Pearly knelt down beside him, extending her hand across his chest to free the veil. He clutched her hand, holding it over his heart with his mesmerising eyes penetrating the veil.

Pearly felt her body on fire.

"I'm sorry . . . my veil got stuck."

"Maybe if you sat close to me, we'll find out if I could free you?"

Pearly rose to her feet and sat down beside him with

downcast eyes, watching him free her veil.

"Don't you feel the mysterious force which brings you closer to me each time you turn away?" he whispered beneath his breath. "You almost turned away at the stairs and almost . . . slipped past me."

"I didn't mean to."

"I was just thinking about the mystery of Priya," he spoke softly. "There's more to Priya than meets the eye. The strange happenings that have led her to me have made me wonder if there're more than one Priya."

"More than one Priya?"

"Yes. One Priya is an illusion; the other Priya is my soul. One Priya breaks me into pieces and the other Priya wakes me up at nights and makes me vibrant and alive. One Priya brings me disasters and the other Priya brings me healing. I'm almost afraid . . . to lift that veil. I don't know which Priya is hiding there. Is it the one who will turn me cold as ice or the one who healed me last night?" he asked.

"May I dare to find out?" he asked, pulling at the veil.

They sat motionless; gazing into each other's eyes as the veil came sliding down revealing the stunningly beautiful face. Pearly kept looking; holding his gaze and failing to look away.

"I felt my heart stop for a moment," he whispered. "There's something breathtakingly different about your looks tonight. I remember you hair being darker and your eyes being slightly greener around the corners. Who are you? You're not the Priya I remember—"

Pearly had barely opened her mouth to say something when she found his hand covering her mouth.

"Don't say a word or the spell will be broken," he said. "Let me feast my eyes on the beauty of the mysterious Priya who has transformed right in front of my eyes into a goddess of love and touched my soul in an indescribable way," he said, pulling Pearly's head gently to his chest and stroking her hair.

"You don't have to say a word. Your eyes tell it all. I've felt your soul through your eyes," he whispered.

Pearly felt like she had known him and been with him for ages.

"I know now why we were joined at the temple; why we were separated at my doorstep; why you were forced into seclusion; why you found me again; why you healed me. We were destined to meet. I'm not afraid to die now."

"I remember why I saw you in my dream. We were destined to meet," said Pearly, gazing deep into his eyes and ruffling the garland around his wrist. "I know now why I'm here tonight and why you had to save the garland."

"I was saving it for the right time and right Priya. It is the right time. Would you do me the honour?" he asked, removing the garland from his wrist.

Pearly placed the garland around his head.

"Now we are really married and now you are really mine," he said, holding her close to his heart.

Nareshwer and the Goddess Priya enjoyed the full seven days of marital bliss. On the eighth day, they visited the *Durga* temple together. They were found dead with their arms together and heads bowed in front of the deity.

The last words of the goddess to the people were:

"There will be prosperity and happy marriages in this village. No woman will be ever sautéed again."

Following their deaths the legend of Nareshwer and the Goddess was born in the town of Naresh Garh. The people shunned the practice of *Suttee* to honour the words of the Goddess Priya.

DEATH OF PEARLY
REBIRTH OF PEARLY

As if by magic someone moulded you;
in whichever form I dreamed of you.

A dramatic change took over Saya after Pearly's departure. She became noticeably quiet and distant and began to spend a great deal of time at the *Krishna Ashram,* leaving the children in Matthew and Ashley's care. She took a great fascination to the black and white roses; the kinds that were Symoune's favourite and began the fill every corner of the house with them. She was often found sitting on the floor in the lotus *asana* and chanting . . .
OMMMMMMMMMMMMMMMM
Ommmm Nama Vasudeva. Ommmm
"What do those words mean to you," asked Ashley.
"I surrender to the divine in me and accept things as they are," replied Saya.
"That's what Symoune used to say," said Ashley. "She was acting like you before she died."
"It's called *Metamorphosis* because there's no such thing as death, Ashley. Symoune is still around in a different form and I see her all the time. I told you everything that transpired between us except the two major changes that are in the works as we speak."
"What kind of changes?"
"I want to prepare you, because the welfare of my children and Matthew depends on that."
"Oh, Saya, you're scaring me."
"My time's running out. Be prepared to take my place as the mother of my children and as Matthew's wife."
"That's absurd. Don't say that," shouted Ashley.

"Symoune asked me to set Matthew free because he now belongs with you. Symoune is never wrong. She promised me that Priya will come back as Pearly and Pearly will come back as Priya."

They were interrupted by the knock on the door. The postman stood at the door with a telegram, which said:

*Priya has been successfully saved by Pearly. I'm bringing her back.
Father Elliot*

They had just begun to feel relieved when an hour later, another telegram arrived.

*I regret to inform you that Pearly expired today at 5:00 PM
Father Elliot*

A cloud of darkness enveloped Saya and she fell to the floor, dripping blood.

"She's in labour," screamed Ashley and Matthew, carrying her. Priya picked up the letter from her dresser and began to read it:

Dear Priya — Soon to be Pearly:

I have battled long and hard to give you back what is rightfully yours — your rightful name.

Your rightful name is Pearly Ruby Boone and you belong with Aunt Ashley. I found out the secret on the night of the fire at the Annexe.

There was an abandoned newborn waiting to be adopted at Aunt Ashley's clinic the night Aunt Menaka gave birth to her fourth stillborn. The baby was handed to Aunt Menaka. The babies got switched accidentally. Aunt Symoune's baby ended up with Aunt Menaka. I ended up with Aunt Ashley.

Matthew and Saya Scott are my real parents. The Angel who united me with them is restlessly waiting to see you united with Aunt Ashley and take on your real name. The name of the Angel is — Symoune Ruby Boone. I call her — the "Beautiful Woman" who saved my life time and time again in a hope that I will save yours.

My task is done. I will have to die, although only momentarily, both as Pearly and as Priya so that you can go back as Pearly and I can come back as Priya. The time has come to bring peace to the wounded souls of your mother, Aunt Ashley, and mine who are eagerly awaiting your arrival. It's the time to rejoice in the new beginnings — yours and mine.

You will find me waiting for you at the Priya Mansion.
Pearly – Soon to be Priya.

"My suspicions were right," screamed Priya. "Granny, is it true that Aunt Symoune was my real mother?"

"Yes. Your mother tried to tell you many times but the circumstances didn't allow her," said Menakshi. "We are guilty of being possessive. We've been punished severely for our mistakes. Please don't turn on us."

"I knew that my mother was keeping something from me. How could she do that to me? Look, what she has done. Now I've lost my friend forever. She has died for me. Did you know this, Father?"

"Yes. Matthew tried very hard to bring the truth out but it didn't work. Now we must leave for Simla. Ashley has been waiting for your arrival for the last six years. Forgive your mother and grandma. They've repented more than you can imagine."

Priya nodded her head, crying.

"You must look forward and start your life as Pearly," said Menakshi. "Don't look back. That part of your life is over forever. You are not Priya anymore. You are Pearly Ruby Boone and belong with Ashley."

After an agonised labour of twelve hours, Saya gave birth to a beautiful baby girl. A look of shock settled in Ashley's eyes as the baby started to turn blue and within a matter of minutes, she lost her heartbeat.

"Ashley, what's wrong with the baby?" cried Matthew.

"Matthew, I'm afraid, the baby has died."

"How could that happen? She was alive when she was born. I felt her heart beat."

"I did, too. She was alive but—"

"No. Symoune promised to save my children. Ashley, can you bring me my baby, please?" asked Saya.

As soon as Saya held the baby, she began to kick her arms and legs, astonishing everyone.

"The baby is back," smiled Saya. "Priya is back. Matthew, welcome your daughter—Priya Ashley Scott. Symoune has fulfilled her promise and now I must fulfill mine before my time runs out."

"Dev Das, where is everybody?" asked Father Elliot, stopping at the staircase.

"Everyone is upstairs. Madam Saya just had a baby girl named, Priya Ashley Scott."

"Ashley, where are you? I've brought your girl back," said Father Elliot, jumping up stairs.

"Aunt Ashley?"

"Thank God, my Pearly is finally back for good," replied Ashley, clinging to Pearly.

"Symoune and I are happy now," said Saya. "Pearly, this is Priya — waiting to see you,"

"Just like she had promised in the letter — I would be waiting for you at the *Priya Mansion*."

"Father Elliot, can you pray for me?" asked Saya, breathing deeply.

Father Elliot pulled the chair by the bed and started praying.

"Ashley, I want to return everything that belongs to you before my time runs out," said Saya, placing the newborn in her arms. "I return to you Priya and Pearly and all my children. It's time to rejoice."

"Oh, Saya," sobbed Ashley, holding baby Priya.

"Ashley and Matthew, may I ask you to join hands, please?" said Saya.

"Saya?" cried Matthew.

"Please Matthew, grant me my last request," Saya paused, breathing deeply.

"Matthew, I free you to be the soul mate to Ashley. You belong with her now. I'm going far, far away with my sister, Symoune. We've accomplished our tasks and are at peace now. There should be no mourning for me. I've had the most blissful six years with you. Now Ashley and you must look after all our children. Symoune is waiting to lead me into the other world, where there is no sorrow, no pain — only everlasting joy, and peace."

Saya closed her eyes, taking her last deep breath.

Chapter Eleven
The Return of the Prince, 1910

UNFOLDING OF THE DIVINE
THE RESTORATION

Heavens have opened their doors for me.
I'm surrounded by angels, wherever I see.

"So the four of you—Pearly, Priya, Pryanka, and Arman are my amazingly beautiful flowers. Just like the little flowers, you need to close your eyes and rest so that I can see your smiling faces in the morning," said Ashley, tucking Pryanka and Arman in the bed.

"Where do the people go when they die?" asked Pryanka.

"God turns some of them into angels and some into stars so that they can watch over their children."

"Where's our mom?" asked Arman.

"Come here and I will show you," said Ashley, opening the curtain. "Look at the beautiful big star in the middle of the sky, that's your mom—Saya, shimmering in the sky."

"What does it means when she shimmers?" asked Arman.

"It means that she's smiling at us. Whenever you gaze at that star you will feel the joy."

"I feel the joy gazing at my mom. Do you feel that too, Arman?"

"Yeah, I do! What about our sister, Priya? Can she feel her smile?"

"Yes, she does! That's why baby Priya is always bubbly and smiling. She feels the joy. The babies are little angels from paradise and they can feel our emotions. Now you must sleep so that I can check on Priya and Pearly. They need me as you do. Goodnight."

"Matthew, can I come in," asked Ashley, softly opening his door. As usual, she found him sitting in the dark. Matthew had kept to his room since the day Saya had died.

"Matthew, you haven't touched your meals."

"Ashley, I can't eat; I can't sleep and sometimes I can't even breathe," he replied. "I cannot reconcile with the fact that the two most beautiful women, who were my heart and soul, just vanished out of my life. Now I feel empty inside, a man without a heart and soul."

"Matthew, they are still with you in a different form. The spirit of Saya is still alive in your beautiful children. And your beautiful Pearly has come back with a stronger body and spirit in little Priya. You've been given another chance to see her grow and watch her baby steps—all those moments you had missed."

"Ashley, I held baby Priya in my arms yesterday and felt the missing moments with Pearly. I feel grateful for the gift of Priya and shall cherish her forever but I'm still mourning for Saya and Pearly—the life, the moments, and the memories we had together. The images haunt me."

"Saya had asked that there be no mourning for her because she is in a place of eternal bliss. Now you must pull yourself together and pay attention to the children who are in a state of bewilderment. They've lost their mother and they desperately need their father."

"I intend to be with them body, mind and soul, but I need to go away for some time to come to terms with this tragedy. It may be a lot to ask, but can you look after the children while I'm away?"

"When do you intend to leave?"

"Tomorrow I will go to Banaras—the place where I met Saya and fell in love with her and married her."

"How long will you be gone?"

"I don't know, Ashley. I'll come back when the turmoil inside me subsides."

"I understand. Goodnight, Matthew!" said Ashley, walking to the door.

"Ashley--"

"Yes, Matthew?"

"Would you wait for me?"

"Yes, I will. I will wait for you." Ashley smiled.

"I will wait forever if I have to, Matthew, because you may not

love me yet, but I've loved you since the moment I saw you the first time. If Saya was your soul; you are mine," muttered Ashley, closing the door.

Pearly stood watching the Painting of Symoune, loving every line, every curve with her eyes until she memorised the tiniest detail. Then she moved over to her own painting, hung besides Symoune's and began watching every detail, getting struck by the remarkable resemblance.

"No wonder, I had always fantasised about being Pearly and was drawn towards that painting. Little did I know that she was my mother and I was her daughter — Pearly Ruby Boone," she murmured. "For the first time in my life, I feel totally peaceful. The restlessness I always felt is gone."

"Is that the picture of my mom when she was pregnant with me?" Pearly asked, looking at the family album.

"Yes, honey. Your mom treasured the pictures she took every month during her pregnancy," replied Ashley. "Here's the picture taken a few days before your birth. She talked to you on a daily basis; she sang for you and painted imaginary portraits of you. I must look for the portraits she had done."

"What did she talk to me about?"

"She knew that she was going to be saved but, she was worried about the family curse that she thought would follow you. She said that she had breathed into your soul a special gift — the gift of being reborn. She wanted you to turn inwards whenever you are at a crossroad. Your soul will awaken the angel in you — who will reveal to you the secret of being reborn."

"What does that mean, auntie?"

"I'm not sure except that she had some kind of a telepathic connection with you and Daniel. I remember her telling you to never give into despair, no matter how miserable the family curse makes you feel. She wanted you to stay connected with the angel in you; because he will help you deliver the ghosts of our past."

"How do I find my angel?" asked Pearly, holding the picture of her mom in her hands and closing her eyes. "I would like to move into my mom's room. That door should be opened and the room should be lived in."

"Here's the key to your mom's room, honey," said Ashley,

pulling the key from the drawer and placing it on the table beside Pearly. "No one has ever slept in Symoune's bedroom since the day she died. We always lock it after we clean it. Now I must go and tend to Priya."

Pearly felt a strange sensation unlocking the door of her mother's bedroom and walking in. *"I'm surprised. The room looks lived in and the windows are open. I must close the big window,"* thought Pearly, walking towards the big window.

"Please leave the window open, Pearly. I like the fresh air," said someone, startling her.

Pearly turned sharply to find her breathtakingly beautiful mother sitting in the chair, smiling.

"Mom, is that you?" asked Pearly, standing still.

"Come here, my baby," smiled Symoune, opening her arms. "I've longed to hold you in my arms."

"Mom . . . I'm surprised," exclaimed Pearly, running into her arms.

"Welcome back home," said Symoune, holding her tight.

"Mom, you are much more beautiful than your portrait," said Pearly, touching her face.

"So are you, my baby. You're the spitting image of me. Your dad painted that beautiful portrait of me."

"Mom, I love his paintings. I've looked at every one of them a thousand times and have memorised every line and every detail. I wish I had seen my dad."

"Well, there he is," said Symoune, walking to the window, holding her hand.

They saw a tall, handsome man with a shining head of curly locks standing in front of an easel and painting.

"Dad?" Pearly yelled.

Daniel lifted his head momentarily and smiled, waving at her.

"That's one of my favourite paintings Daniel did before taking the last trip of his life with the Maharaja. Let's go backwards and see my life with your dad," said Symoune, sweeping her hand into the air.

Pearly stood spellbound, watching the entire life of her mother and father unroll in front of her eyes.

"You're back where you belong; it's the time to rejoice. Your dad is an angel now and we're together."

"Mom, I'm so glad that Priya is back but where's Nareshwer?"

"He's as close to Priya as Swami Krishna is," smiled Symoune.

"Mom, I love Ryan and a day never goes by when I don't think of him a million times?"

"And he loves you back. He's on his way to be with you."

"Oh, really mom? Mom, I've a few more questions . . ."

"The beauty of life is hidden in its mysteries. Let it be. I'll only answer one more question."

"Mom, can you show me my *Angel Divine*?"

"Perhaps it's time to unfold one more mystery before I go back to the *Sanctuary of Angels*. Your angel will reveal himself to you. Lie down on my bed," said Symoune, sweeping her hands across Pearly's forehead.

"Close your eyes and you will see things you could never see before with your eyes open. There's about to open within you . . . The Third Eye."

As if mesmerised, Pearly gazed at the flowing hair, the deep set eyes and the cool disposition of the stranger who looked every inch human and yet an angel.

"What does the Third Eye mean?" Pearly heard her voice; just a whisper.

"It's the eye of the God that resides inside us and makes us see things beyond sight. I'm here to unfold the mystique of the third eye and guide you through your search for the most secret of all eternal gifts—THE GIFT OF BEING REBORN, each time you are dead."

Like the soft rustle of the leaves his voice fell on Pearly's ears, sinking her into the deep tranquility of the manner that shocked her as much as it elevated her.

"Each time I'm dead? I thought a mortal lives and dies only once," asked Pearly, closing her eyes.

"Living one life and dying only once is a myth. A person lives and dies many lives within a one life span. Many times the death comes only as a mockery to steal the body that has been dead for a long time."

"I'm intrigued," she murmured, not knowing if she was in a trance, a dream, or a reality.

"Just like the human body grows slowly in parts, so does

the body die slowly in parts. Even an otherwise healthy person could be half-dead inside. Some of the forms the death takes are the death of emotions, death of the spirit, death of the reasoning, death of the intellect and finally — the physical death. A person fights the cycle of life and death each moment a person breathes. The cycle of slow death is called suffering."

"How do we deal with the suffering caused by death?"

"The suffering in this instance results from the mind's resistance to accept the phenomena of change, also from the general belief that if we can't see something with our eyes and physically touch it, it's not there. Love and affection are born from the spirit and are meant to be felt in the spirit and seen with the mind's eye. Death cannot destroy the spirit. The power of death may be super but the power of the spirit is supreme. Seeing and touching something and believing it's there is as much a truth as sensing and feeling its existence in the spirit. I'm here now and you can see me, yet your eyes are closed. Were you to not open your eyes and not see me, would you say I was never here?"

"Why is the death so painful?"

"The pain is the curing ointment which heals the body and mind through the process of time. We're released from the pain the moment we accept what we cannot change and realize that those whom we love are only as far and as close as our spirit is. It is just a matter of belief."

"How should we deal with the hatred and love?" asked Pearly.

"These emotions change from one to the other very quickly because these are flames that burn quickly. One burns to light up and sustain life; the other burns to consume and destroy life. Each time we choose one over the other, we choose to build or to destroy the people around us."

"What's the secret to tame these emotions?"

"Make no friends, no foes when you mingle with others. Treat this life as a journey. Be friendly, yet be aloof. Never lose yourself completely because no one can be a better friend and guide than you. Look within for direction, for energy, for wisdom and strength. Believe, accept, and respect the phenomena of change. The five basic elements which create all forms — earth, water, fire, sky and air — don't die; they only change forms. Just like the childhood changes its colour into youth, so does the brightness of youth turn into the bluntness of age. Yesterday can never be today and today shall never be tomorrow. Respect and move with the changes."

"How do we deal with the loneliness that comes with the changes?"

"A person is never alone. There are always two persons inside us. A visible person that operates outside, an invisible person that directs, and guides from inside. It tells us—don't go there or go ahead. The inner self is the second you—the sacred one that signals the right direction and tells no lies. This is the one that maintains the balance and harmony in our lives. It's only when conflict occurs between the two selves that disharmony, imbalance and spiritual decline follow; forcing the person to lead a split life—a healthy as well as an ailing life, causing confusion, pain, loss of direction and tragedies."

"What is the key then?"

"The key lies in finding our estranged, lost, weak or dead inner self. If you were to find it, befriend it and nurture it back to health, you will be able to breathe life back into it and through it into yourself."

"This is when you will be REBORN and you will be whole again, in balance and fully alive. You will gain the ability to see things beyond sight, conquer time and space, become unbreakable and indestructible. This is the Mystique of the Third Eye; the secret of being REBORN."

Pearly fell asleep thinking about the magical powers of the inner self—the constructive force that maintains health, happiness and balance in life – the mystique of the third eye and the secret of... being reborn.

"Oh, Pearly, did you fall asleep? I thought you were moving into your Mom's room?" asked Ashley.

"Didn't I? I thought I did," thought Pearly, rubbing her eyes.

"I'll do that now," said Pearly, picking up the key.

She unlocked the door and looked around in amazement.

"I was here," she murmured. "I saw my mom and dad and their entire life. I saw my Angel."

She was startled by the doorbell. She opened the door and found a single red rose, wrapped with a note:

Pearly:
I'm on my way to be with you.
Ryan

Pearly clutched the rose and danced her way out of the porch; colliding with a stranger.

"We've to stop colliding like that . . . Princessa," said the stranger, taking his cap off, and tossing it in the air.

"My goodness, is that you, Ryan? How did you appear so fast?" jumped Pearly, with stars in her eyes.

"It's called magic. I'm here like I was never gone because I love you, my lady," said Ryan, picking her up in his arms and circling her round and round.

"Put me down, Ryan. Someone might walk in on us."

"Not until you say that you love me and only me, now and forever."

"I love you, Ryan, in this life, life hereafter and forever and ever," shouted Pearly, bursting into laughter.

"The Princessa with the Rose," asked Ryan putting her down and kneeling beside her.

"Yes?"

"Miss Pearly Ruby Boone, will you marry me, Ryan Hugh Prince?"

"Yes! Yes! Yes!" said Pearly, putting her arms around him.

"Did you hear this, God? The Princessa said yes, yes, yes — three times," shouted Ryan, picking her up in his arms and waltzing her around, until both of them crashed on the ground, laughing out loud like two little kids.

FESTIVAL OF COLOURS (HOLI)
RETURN OF THE PRINCE

I bloom up like a rose when my love and I meet.
I sweep him in my arms; he sweeps me off my feet.

"Annie, come quickly. Do you know the gentleman Pearly is with?" asked Ashley, pulling at the curtain.

"What gentleman?" asked Annie. "My goodness—Ryan is back!" replied Annie with a big smile.

"Who's Ryan?"

"Matthew had introduced that gentleman to you at his reception at the coronation in Delhi. His name is Ryan Hugh Prince. He's the one who escorted Pearly to the fantasy fundraiser and wrote the beautiful poem—English Rose, which won the first prize?"

"I remember. He's Matthew's nephew. I read the write-up on him in the *Fantasy Book*. What's he doing here?"

"What does it look like? He's proposing to Pearly."

"Did you know that they were in love?"

"No, but it's clear now that they are. I'm going out to meet him."

"Well, if it isn't Mr. Ryan Hugh Prince?" coughed Annie.

"I was trying to catch with Miss Boone."

"A little more than a catch-up, I should say," interrupted Ashley, holding Priya in her arms.

"Dr. Ashley, I'm Ryan Hugh Prince. We met at my uncle—General Scott's reception in Delhi," replied Ryan, shaking hands with Ashley.

"Yes, I remember. Please call me auntie. We are all in the family now."

"I didn't know my uncle Matthew was your uncle as well? I thought your uncle was—" said Pearly.

"Brigadier Edward Hugh Prince and Matthew are cousin brothers. Uncle Ed has served as a General in Delhi," replied Ryan. "Is that yours and Uncle Matthew's baby girl?"

"This is Matthew's and Saya's baby girl—Priya. Saya passed away three months ago. I'm looking after Priya while he's away."

"I met Uncle Matthew briefly in Banaras last week. We didn't have a chance to talk at length. I had met Saya briefly at the reception in 1903. I had no idea they were married," said Ryan. "I've returned from England after graduating from the Willington College and Military Academy at Sandhurst. I've been seconded to the 62nd Punjab Regiment as the Commissioned Lieutenant and have come to seek the hand of your fair niece, Pearly, in marriage."

"A proposal hard to refuse, considering the fact that it has already been accepted," laughed Ashley.

"The question of the ring is still outstanding," laughed Ryan, producing a tiny box from his pocket.

"I can't wait," burst out Pearly, giggling with excitement.

"Aunt Ashley, with your permission, may I?"

"By all means!"

"Miss Pearly Ruby Boone," asked Ryan, going down on one knee. "Would you accept my ring as the token of our engagement?"

"Yes, I will," said Pearly, extending her hand. Ryan slipped the ring on her finger.

"Oh, Ryan what a lovely heart-shaped ring, just like the one you gave me at the pavilion," exclaimed Pearly.

"So that's where you had slipped," remarked Annie.

"Pearly, open the lid and see."

"Oh, it's engraved—R and P," exclaimed Pearly, shivering from head to foot.

"Yes, it is! Welcome to our family," said Ashley and Annie, hugging Ryan and Pearly.

"Pearly will you show Ryan around and we'll fix the tea. Would you like to have tea in the garden?"

"Wherever Pearly orders," he laughed. "Who are those two kids peeking at us?"

"Arman and Pryanka come here," said Pearly, holding their hands. "Say hello to your uncle, Ryan."

"Hello, uncle," replied Pryanka and Arman.

"Ryan, your arrival is very timely. We're celebrating *holi* — the festival of colours with the children of the Krishna Sanctuary tomorrow on the grounds," said Ashley, pouring tea. "The tables will be full with all kinds of dry and liquid colours. I'm sure Pearly would love to play *holi* with her fiancée."

"Yes, thanks, auntie. Pearly has already invited me. I wouldn't miss playing *holi* with my fiancée," replied Ryan, holding Pearly's hand. Pearly turned red in the face.

The *Priya Mansion* turned into a huge rainbow with Pearly and her friends dancing to the beat of the *holi* music and sprinkling everyone with all kinds of colours. The children of the Krishna Sanctuary danced around the garden chasing each other with hands filled with colours. Arman and Pryanka had so many colours on them by the afternoon that they were unrecognizable. Even Ashley and baby Priya became multi-coloured.

"The sight of Pearly playing *holi* with her friends will remain as the most beautiful sight of my life," murmured Ryan to Ashley, plucking a red rose from the garden.

"To my Princessa," he said, presenting her the rose.

"And this is for my prince," said Pearly, picking a handful of red colour from the table.

"No, no," shrieked Ryan, running away.

"Yes . . . Yes!" said Pearly running after him, breathlessly.

They kept running in circles until Pearly caught up with him and smeared his face and clothes with bright red and pink colours.

"*I've never seen her look happier than she is today. There's a mystical glow around her. I had no idea that Pearly and Ryan had loved so deeply. What an intriguing secret? How wonderful it is to find love. Nothing compares with love. It is the essence of life,*" thought Ashley, watching them.

"Pearly and Ryan remind me of Symoune and Daniel, Matthew and Saya, and Nareshwer and Priya. Finding love is like finding God. God is love and love is God. I wish that Matthew was here playing holi with me."

"*Wishful thinking . . . but wouldn't it be so romantic if he came through the cloud of mist and sprinkled the rainbow of colours on me . . . like Ryan did on Pearly.*"

"*Oh, Matthew, I love you so deeply and you're not even aware of* it. You only had eyes for Saya."

"Symoune and Saya were the two most beautiful women. They could have any man eating out of their palms. How can a plain Ashley compete with the likes of Saya and Symoune?" mused Ashley.

"Ashley . . ." someone whispered in her ear, bringing her down to earth.

"Yes," she replied turning around.

There stood in front of her Matthew with hands full of red and pink colours. A wide-eyed Ashley stood still with surprise.

"Happy *holi* to you, Ashley," he smiled, holding her in his arms and sprinkling the colour all over her.

"Just wait, Matthew," laughed Ashley, grabbing handfuls of colours and chasing after him. She kept chasing him until he slipped and landed on the ground. Ashley caught him by the shoulders and pelted him with colours, laughing out loud. Pearly, Ryan and the children came running to the site, surrounding them. They began smearing the two with all kinds of colours until they begged for mercy.

"Ryan, help me," pleaded Matthew.

"May I have your attention, everyone," said Matthew gasping for breath. "Children I want you to say a big hello to my nephew—Ryan. I met him briefly in Banaras last week before he headed for Simla. He's going to be a closer family member now. I'm proud to announce the engagement of Ryan with Pearly."

"Hello, Ryan," shouted the children, clapping their hands.

"Thank you, uncle," said Ryan, holding Pearly's hand. "Both Pearly and I want to let you know that this is the unforgettable day of our lives. Please think of me as your friend."

Everyone clapped.

"I've another announcement," said Matthew, holding Arman and Pryanka's hand and looking at Ashley.

"Dr. Ashley Rose," he said, going down on his knee and pulling a ring from a box, "Will you marry me?"

Ashley froze with disbelief.

"Miss Ashley Rose, will you marry me and be the mother of my children—Pryanka, Arman and Priya?"

"Say yes! Say yes! Say yes!" shouted everyone.

"Say yes, Ashley," said Swami Krishna, walking in with a baby in his arms. "Next announcement is mine."

"Yes, auntie," shouted Pearly. "Grab the ring."

"Yes, Matthew I will be honoured to be your wife and mother to these beautiful children whom I love more than my life," replied Ashley, shedding tears of joy.

Matthew placed the ring on her finger. Ashley looked through the misty air into Matthew's eyes reflecting the rainbow of colours around them.

"You and Ryan have made me and my niece the two most envied women on the face of the earth," said Ashley, opening her arms to all the children around her.

"Now it's my turn," said Swami Krishna. "First I want to congratulate Ryan and Pearly and Matthew and Ashley. I wish them a lifetime of joy," he paused. "I'm deeply honoured to announce that I have become a father of this beautiful baby, named Nareshwer Swami."

"Hooray!" jumped everyone.

"Now go back to whatever you were doing before," said Swami, placing the baby in the crib with Priya.

"Swami, that's wonderful news!" said Father Elliot, walking in. "I heard the rumours. Evidentially, they are true. Where did you find this baby?"

"My sister and her husband were killed shortly after the baby was born. I adopted him as my son."

"When was he born?"

"Incidentally, the same day Priya was born."

"Where did you get the name — Nareshwer?"

"He was named after my grandfather — Nareshwer Swami. Why?"

"The lord walks in mysterious ways. There might be more to the incident that he was born the same day, Priya was born and was named Nareshwer," replied Father Elliot, nodding his head.

"What do you mean?" asked Swami Krishna.

"Someday I will let you know."

MARRIAGE WITH PRINCE
DOUBLE WEDDING

My eyes are dreaming day and night a million beautiful dreams.
You're the angel of my dreams; I'm never going to let you leave

"I'm sorry the clinic is closed," said Annie, picking up the receiver. "We're not taking any appointments because Dr. Ashley and her niece are getting married this month. Can you hold on one second?"

"Annie, where do you want me to put the box of invitation cards," interrupted Dev Das.

"Place them on the table. Do you know if caterers have arrived yet?"

"Yes; Sir, Matthew and Dr. Ashley are attending to them," Meera cut in.

Annie nodded, resuming the phone call.

"Yes, I've been asked to be the maid of honour and Sir Matthew's brother will be the best man. It's a double wedding, a semi-military wedding. The grooms, best man, and the ushers will appear in military uniforms and the couples will pass through the *Arch of Swords*. I will convey your sentiments to them."

"Where's Miss Pearly?"

"She's with the lieutenant, talking to the florists."

"Oh, Annie, meet General Ed, Matthew's cousin," said Ashley. "He has arrived for the wedding."

"The best man looks forward to working with the maid of honour in ironing out the wedding details."

"Thank you. Your first order of the business is to review the invitations and work with me on the big list."

"Of course. Let's look at the invitations," he said.

Everyone flocked around the table to look at the invitations.

> General Edward Hugh Prince Requests the honour of your presence at the Double Wedding of
> his nephew Lieutenant Ryan Hugh Prince (British Indian Army)
> to
> Pearly Ruby Boone
> his cousin brother General Matthew Gerald Scott (Rtd. British Indian Army)
> to
> Dr. Ashley Rose
> On May 15, 1910 at half past ten at Simla Bible Chapel
> Reception at half past five at Priya Mansion

"Thanks, Annie, for all your help. What's going on outside?" asked Pearly,

"The grooms and the party have arrived in sparkling uniforms. Sir Matthew's wearing all his medals."

"I can't wait to see them in uniform," remarked Pearly. "Auntie, tell me the truth. Do I look as beautiful as you do? I can't take my eyes off you."

"Ryan won't be able to take his eyes off you," replied Ashley, straightening the hem of her veil.

"You, my beauty, look as beautiful as Symoune did on her wedding day. I feel like I'm intruding on your special day."

"Nonsense! Ryan and I are absolutely honoured to share our special day with you and Uncle Matthew. Our special day will become unforgettable because of you two tying the knot at the same time."

"Annie, are you guys ready?" Edward knocked on the door.

"Just a minute," replied Annie, opening the door and handing the flower baskets to Pryanka and Arman.

"Now Pryanka and Arman, you know what you've to do, right?" asked Ashley, emerging out of the room, carrying Priya in her arms.

"We have to walk ahead of you, sprinkling flowers," said Pryanka.

"And then we will go and stand beside dad," added Arman.

"Meera, will you take care of Priya? Keep her closer to us at all times."

"My two favourite girls," *said* Edward, positioning himself in the centre of the brides. "Before you embark on your enchanting journey, I want you to know that I feel proud to walk you down the aisle."

Everyone gasped for breath when the two stunningly beautiful brides glided down the aisle followed by *Pryanka* and Arman, sprinkling flowers on the way. Matthew and Ryan smiled, looking distinguished in their uniforms. The audience looked on, enchanted by the perfection of their profiles and the well-rehearsed ceremony, right from the beginning to the end, until Father Elliot pronounced the magical words:

"Ladies and gentlemen, welcome — General and Mrs. Sir Matthew Scott and Mrs. Ryan Hugh Princessa."

A big round of applause greeted them when the couples passed through the Arch of Swords, kissing each other. The rest of the day turned into a fairy tale evening, filled with enchanting music, dance and the feast. Ashley slipped out of bed at midnight and grabbed her diary. She wrote:

He attracts me like a magnet; like stars he makes me shine.
His touch is intoxicating enough; I need not touch the wine.

Pearly woke up as well and grabbed her diary. She wrote:

I held my breath and he held my stare;
he kissed me through my tangled hair.

Chapter Twelve
Final Episode – India, 1945

THE GREAT WAR, 1914 - 1918
PROMISE OF SWARAJ

Tilak's slogan – Swaraj is my birthright and I shall have it; set the entire British Empire on fire with a single matchstick.

The Political scene of India in the beginning of the nineteenth century was filled with the growing spirit of Indian nationalism. Even though the British successfully had crushed the great mutiny of 1857, they were unable to uproot the spirit of anti-colonialism which emerged out of the mutiny. A number of revolutionary groups sprang up in India. The three main leaders of the radical movement were Lala Lajpat Raj in Punjab, Bal Gangadhar Tilak in Maharashtra, and Bipin Chandra Pal in Bengal. They were popularly known as Bal, Pal, and Lal. These leaders toured the country, made fiery speeches, and worked tirelessly in building a strong national structure of local branches to mobilise demonstrations, public meetings, and agitations in favour of Indian self-rule. The provinces of Bengal, Maharashtra, and Punjab became hotbeds of anti-colonial activities; nearly paralysing the regional administration and causing permanent dents in the British Empire.

Bal Gangadhar Tilak was the first Indian nationalist to embrace the idea of Swaraj (self-rule) as the destiny of the nation. Tilak criticised the British government for suppressing the freedom of the press; the lack of Indian participation in the affairs of their nation and for rejecting the bill, which would have allowed Indians and Britons to be tried on an equal footing in court. He opposed British education, which he felt robbed the people of their cultural heritage and values. For these reasons, he considered Swaraj as the only solution to British imperialism. His declaration, *the right of self-determination – Swaraj is my birthright, and I shall have it*, became an eye opener for the Indian masses, igniting patriotism like wildfire and uniting Indians from coast to coast.

The British utilised the policy of divide and rule against the anti-colonial uprisings in Bengal. They partitioned Bengal in 1905 on communal boundaries, thus creating a permanent rift between Hindus and Muslims. Tilak defended the revolutionaries in his Newspaper Kesari, and came out swinging against the British government for its brutality in suppressing the protests against the division of Bengal. He was charged with sedition and arrested. Tilak's arrest sparked a nationwide protest against British rule. The Indian intellectuals were united and formed the Indian National Congress to fight for equal rights and equal treatment. The British encouraged the Muslims to form *the Muslim League* to fight for a separate Muslim state within India.

In August 1914, the First World War broke out in Europe in the midst of a deep political turmoil in India, fanning the flames of growing Indian nationalism. Britain needed the support of its empire in the fight against Germany and Central Powers, and therefore seemed inclined to make any concessions in exchange for the support of the British Indian Army in the Great War.

Indian leaders raised their voices in favour of *Swaraj and Swadeshi* (Indian goods). Annie Besant, the supporter of the *Irish Home Rule League* and editor of a newspaper called *New India*, supported the slogan of Tilak by attacking the British government and calling for clear and decisive moves towards self-rule.

Tilak was released. The British government made promises to take steps towards Indian self-government after the war. The Indians leaders welcomed the promises and began to support the war efforts of King George V. India contributed heavily to the British war effort by providing men and resources. About 1.3 million Indian soldiers and volunteers put on military uniforms and left their homes to serve in Europe, Africa, and the Middle East. The Indian government and the princely states opened their purses and contributed large supplies of food, money, and ammunition. A regiment of the Indian soldiers was immediately dispatched to Turkey to secure the Suez Canal. Indian women put on a united front and sent their men to war.

Feeling exhausted by the strain of sending Ryan to the Great

War, Pearly fell asleep quickly.

"Ryan?" she murmured, extending her arm across the bed. "Darling, where are you?" She opened her eyes, feeling the empty bed.

"Oh, God," she woke up. "Ryan has gone to fight the Great War—"

Ashley rushed to her side, hearing the crying sound.

"Princessa, are you all right, honey?" she asked, tying the sash around her gown.

"No. I'm not all right," replied Pearly, resting her head on her arms and crying.

"Honey, you've got to be brave," said Ashley, patting her arm. "It is the duty of the soldiers to defend their country and the duty of the wives to pray for their safe return. This is the time to remember the love you two have shared and pray for the safety of our soldiers."

"I know. Go back to bed," replied Pearly, wiping her tears.

"Can I stay and talk to you?" asked Ashley, walking reluctantly to the door.

"Go back to bed," said Pearly, eying the rose neatly tucked in the vase.

"Take this rose as a symbol of my everlasting love for you," she remembered Ryan's words.

"Ryan, how will I live without you?"

"With the faith in the return of your prince. You must have faith that I will come back."

"I promise to have faith," she whispered, remembering the touch of his kiss on her forehead.

She remembered the long lineup of people in the streets, clapping and waving farewell to the soldiers—hurling garlands in the air; women, children and elderly crying openly, the dust and the smoke rising as the trucks rolled out of the streets, disappearing into the thick fog.

During war, music played a great inspirational role in homes, schools and the battlefields. Wartime songs became a powerful medium for the British for recruiting soldiers, instilling patriotism, raising funds and making false promises. The Indian leaders used music to ignite the vision of Indian self-rule.

"Fight for the king; fight for the empire and bring glory," became a popular western song on the radio. "Vande Matram," written by a Bengali poet, Bankim Chandra Chattopadhyay gripped the imagination of millions of Indians and became the theme song of the Indian Swaraj movement.

The song, Vande Mataram, which translates as *"Hail to the mother India"* became the rallying cry for Indian soldiers who marched to the battlefields, chanting, *"Vande Matram"* and many died with *"Vande Matram"* on their lips. The song became a vision of an independent motherland for millions of Indian masses who threw themselves, body, mind, and soul, into the Swaraj movement.

In 1916, Tilak and Annie Besant formed the Home Rule League, drawing wide support from Indians. In June 1917, Annie was arrested and interned at a hill station for show of defiance. Mohan Das K. Gandhi, who had become a national figure with his mild manners and nonviolence movement, took a stand to launch nationwide strikes if she were not set free. Annie Besant was released and she was elected as the President of the Indian National Congress in 1917. Gandhi started touring with Annie Besant to spread the message of Swaraj and to recruit Indians in the British war.

"We are gathered here tonight to celebrate the freedom of Dr. Annie Besant from jail,"

said Swami Krishna, clapping his hands, "and to make the announcement that Mrs. Besant will be arriving in Simla tomorrow to inspect our War Relief Centre at the Krishna Ashram and to bring her message of *Swaraj – Indian Self-Rule.*"

The hall echoed with the sound of applause.

"I would like to appeal to everyone to welcome Mrs. Besant with "Vande Matram" slogans. We will welcome her with garlands — so start preparing the garlands. We will make a vow at her reception to buy Indian goods and wear Indian clothes, Indian shoes, and converse in Indian dialects."

A round of big applause broke out again.

"We would like the people to line up outside the Ashram exactly at 3:00 p.m. I've heard from a reliable source that Mrs. Besant could be accompanied by a surprise guest speaker and that guest speaker could be none other than Mr. Mohandas K. Gandhi. This brings us to the end of our proceedings today. *Namaskar, Jai Sri Krishna and Vande Matram* everyone!" he said, folding his hands in front of his chest.

"*Vande Matram,*" chanted the crowd at the end of the meeting.

Life size portraits of Annie Besant and her mentor, Sri Aurobindo Ghosh, Gopal Krishna Gokhley, Netaji Subhash Chander Bose and Gandhi adorned the walls of a large outdoor stage. Hundreds of people came out in the streets to catch a glimpse of Dr. Annie Beseant as her motorcade passed through the lower Mall to the Krishna Ashram. People shrieked with joy when they noticed Mahatma Gandhi sitting beside her.

Jai Gandhi! Jai Annie Besant!
Vande Matram! Vande Matram!

Wearing Indian dhotis and shawls, Annie Besant and Gandhi took to the stage, addressing the audience in a pin drop silence, punctuated by the sound of roaring applause.

"I'm not against the British, I'm against British imperialism," spoke Gandhi, standing tall in his home-made wooden sandals. "Swaraj is our birth right and we shall have it; not with violence but with Ahimsa—Non-Violence Movement called, Satyagraha."

"Nonviolence is the greatest force at the disposal of mankind. It is mightier than the mightiest weapon of destruction devised by the ingenuity of man," he added.

The people cheered and gave him a standing ovation.

"Our cause is just and we are prepared to make any sacrifice to free mother India. Half of our population has marched to the battlefield to fight the Great War for the Empire. The others are prepared to go to jails to realize Swaraj. We will fight but we will fight a non-violent fight—an honourable fight for the just cause and teach the entire world the higher principles of humanity. Are you willing to stand up and join the fight at the home and war front and be counted?" challenged Gandhi.

"I will."
"I will."
"I will."
"I will."

The people began to stand up row after row.

"I will," said Annie, standing up tall and surprising Matthew,

Ashley, and Pearly.

"I will," shouted Father Elliot, chanting *Vande Matram*.

Suddenly the entire hall began to echo with the sound of *Vande Matram*.

The next day the BBC announced the proceedings of Gandhi-Besant visit to Simla as:

The most powerful and awe inspiring spectacle in the British Indian history.

The following headlines hit the newspapers:

"*Last night in Simla, the man, named Gandhi gripped the Imagination of the masses with his AHIMSA – the non-violence movement . . .*"

"The tea smells great, Ashley," remarked Swami Krishna, walking in with a newspaper rolled under his arm.

"Great timing, Swami," laughed Ashley, pouring tea. "Why didn't you bring Nareshwer with you?"

"Nareshwer is getting ready for the trip. Make sure that the children are ready by 8:00 a.m."

'Good Morning?" Matthew greeted Swami. "The children will be ready by 8:00 a.m. They're looking forward to meeting the yogis of the Vrindavan and learn their well-kept yoga secrets. Though I – 1 wish that you could."

"You wish what, Matthew?"

"I wish you could persuade Pearly to accompany you. It would divert her attention from the war."

"Where's Princessa?" Swami asked, sipping tea.

"Cooped up in her room listening to the radio," said Matthew. "I'll go and get her."

"Swami, Swami, we can't wait to be on the bus to Vrindavan," yelled the children, running to the porch.

"Pryanka, Arman and Priya, go wash your hands before touching the cookies," interrupted Ashley.

"Ashley and Matthew, what did you think of the meeting yesterday?"

"The energy around Gandhi and Dr. Annie Beseant was phenomenal," said Matthew.

"We were stunned to see Annie and Father Elliot join the movement," replied Ashley.

"Why? There are so many Europeans joining the movement

every day. Each time Mahatma Gandhi speaks, hundreds of followers spring up. Here comes Pearly," remarked Swami.

"Good Morning, Swami," said Pearly, grabbing the cup of tea from Ashley.
"Pearly, I've come to invite you to accompany us to Vrindavan tomorrow. The Ashram has chartered a bus for this trip. It will be very healing for you."
"Actually I was thinking along the same lines. I need to get away for a change."
"We interrupt the regular program to bring you a special news bulletin," announced the radio broadcast.
Pearly quickly turned up the volume, spilling tea all over her dress.

"Yesterday, on August 25th 1917, the British Army endured the bloodiest day, suffering heavy casualties. 19,000 soldiers were reported dead during the first hours of the enemy attack. The entire counter offensive cost the British Army almost half a million men . . ."

"Oh, my God! Where's the paper?" shrieked Pearly grabbing the paper from the table. She quickly opened the casualties' column and began to finger the names while crying all over the paper.
"Here, let me check, honey," said Matthew, grabbing the paper.
A complete hush fell over the room.
"Relax, honey. Ryan's not on any list. I've checked the wounded, missing and causality lists," replied Matthew, folding the paper and noticing the telegraph delivery boy entering the premises on his bicycle.
"Telegram," he shouted, ringing the bell.
Pearly ran down the steps, almost tripping.
With shaking hands, she tore open the yellow envelop and read the telegram:

Arrived safely in Bombay this morning for supplies. Going back in two weeks. Possibility of war ending soon. I will be home soon. Keep up the faith.
Ryan.

"Thank you, God, for keeping Ryan safe," said Pearly,

breathing a sigh of relief.

"Does that mean you will accompany us to Vrindavan, Pearly?" asked Priya.

"That's exactly what it means. Now if you'll excuse me, I've some packing to do," she said.

"Pundit Vasudeva is Vrindavan in Delhi?" asked Priya, getting on the bus.

"No. Vrindavan is situated in north India about 151 km south of Delhi," said Pundit Vasudeva.

"It is the place where Lord Krishna spent his early childhood and is one of the holiest cities of India. There are over 5000 temples in Vrindavan and we've seen as many temples as we could last week. Now we are headed for Ram Ashram, a place of learning, where we will do something different."

"What will we do in the Ram Ashram?" asked Nareshwer.

"We will visit the ashram and the cave, where the founder of the ashram spent two years meditating. You may be very young but your mind will absorb its healing qualities and trigger the learning that is about to take place."

"Are we going to stay in the ashram?" asked Arman.

"Yes. We will stay in the ashram for the entire week. The accommodation is free and they serve home-cooked vegetarian food on banana leaves. The food is cooked in the community kitchen by the volunteers and disciples of the ashram. You will learn classical yoga techniques from several experienced and qualified teachers who live in the ashram and teach yoga and meditation techniques all year round. Now I want you to get into a single line and follow me quietly into the ashram. Can you do that?"

"Welcome to the Ram Ashram. My name is Swami Pooran Ananda," said the yogi with a composed smile. "Today I will teach you the key five principals of yoga. Do you know what they are?"

The boys and girls stared at each other.

"The five yoga principles are: proper breathing, proper exercise, proper relaxation, proper diet and proper meditation," he said, picking up a chalk and writing on the blackboard.

The boys and girls became attentive.

"We will find out what happens to the body, mind, and

spirit when we combine these principles with four paths of yoga called the *Karma Yoga, Bhakti Yoga, Raja Yoga and Jhana Yoga*. The first lesson is to sit down cross legged on the floor and try to strike this pose called the Kamal Asana," he added, sitting down on the floor and striking the lotus position.

The boys and girls quickly went down on the floor and struck the lotus position.

"Excellent! Now we will learn the proper technique of inhaling and exhaling our breath. Just watch me," he said, placing one finger over his right nostril and exhaling from the left nostril.

"Do this five times."

The kids began to copy the techniques.

"Now, we will conclude the session with the chanting of Om Mantra," he said, closing his eyes.

"Close your eyes and chant Ommmmmm; feeling the energy flowing through your veins."

"OMmmmmmmmmmmmmmm."
"OMmmmmmmmmmmmmmm."

Pearly walked into the room over the chanting of Om, feeling the peaceful vibrations. As she moved across the room, stopping directly in front of the yoga instructor, her eyes grew large with surprise.

Swami Pooran Ananda opened his eyes, catching sight of Pearly, standing still in the corner staring at him. He closed his eyes momentarily and opened them again. This time his eyes lingered on her face, unblinking. The two kept staring at each other totally oblivious of all eyes on them, until Pundit Vasudeva broke the silence.

"Is something wrong, Swami Pooran Ananda?" he asked, rising awkwardly from the floor.

"No. Let's call it a wrap," Swami Pooran Ananda replied quietly, standing up.

He waited until Pundit Vasudeva led the kids out of the room, then walked towards Pearly with a smile.

"What a surprise?" he said, opening his arms.

"A wonderful surprise for me to find my long lost brother, Pooran?" said Pearly, slipping into his arms. "I had come to Vrindavan hoping to find you. I looked for you in every temple.

I asked every one if they had known you. God answered my prayers and brought us face to face."

"I have dreamt about you many times and prayed that you will find me and give me a chance to seek your forgiveness. I wronged you and my parents. I've atoned for my sins and sought forgiveness from God, but I didn't have the courage to face you."

'There's nothing to forgive . . . nothing at all. My life turned out all right. I'm back with Aunt Ashley, right where I belong. I'm happily married to the love of my life."

"I know all about it. I went back home and sought forgiveness from grandma shortly after you were freed. I couldn't stay at the Priya Mansion. I came back and found peace here."

"You've done your atonement and now you must go back to where you belong and help grandma find peace. She has been living with a terrible burden. She can't die peacefully knowing that the entire Partap estate will go into ruins. You must take charge of the estate and continue your charitable work at home," said Pearly.

"I will go . . . if you will accompany me," replied Pooran Partap.

"When do we leave? I can't wait to see the look in grandma's eyes when we walk in together," said Pearly.

"If you will support me, I will vow to restore the family name."

"As always, you have my unconditional support, brother Pooran."

"Maybe it's time to utilise my skills and experience to create awakening in my home town. Wouldn't it be wonderful if I converted the entire west wing of the mansion into Partap Ashram for the sick, young and old and make it the biggest yoga and meditation centre in Punjab?"

"Wake up Pearly, there's good news! There was an announcement on the radio. The war has ended as surprisingly as it had begun," shouted Ashley, patting Pearly on the shoulder.

"Are you sure?" replied Pearly, blinking her eyes in surprise.

"Yes, honey. Matthew and I heard the news together."

"Look outside," shouted Priya and Arman. "The people are dancing in the streets. The war has ended."

"It's true, honey," remarked Matthew, turning on the radio. Everyone tuned in to the announcement.

"*On November 11, 1918, the eleventh hour of the eleventh day of the eleventh month, a ceasefire has come into effect and an armistice with Germany has been signed at 11 a.m. The opposing armies on the Western Front have begun to withdraw from their positions. All over the world the people are celebrating the end of the war by dancing in the streets, drinking and hailing the armistice.*"

"*On a sad note, George Lawrence Price is reported as the last soldier killed in the Great War. He was shot by a German sniper at 10:57 and died at 10:58 while his family was celebrating the end of the War. We salute the great soldier hero.*"

A hush fell across the room.

A knock on the door at midnight created a stir in the house. Everyone rushed downstairs.

"Is that you, Ryan?" Pearly stammered with a hand on the door latch.

"Open the door. I'm home, Princessa."

"Ryan, you're back! You're back home from the Great War," Pearly jumped into his arms.

"I keep my promises," replied Ryan, spinning her around.

"Uncle's back from the Great war," the children shouted.

Ryan opened his arms wide to include everyone in his embrace.

The steady beat of time worked its magic back into Pearly's life, bringing her closer to her Prince than she had ever been before. For the first time in her life, Pearly felt totally peaceful. Ryan's eyes lit up each time she walked into the room.

"Ryan, what do think about my flower arrangement?" she asked, fixing the roses in the vase.

"Breathtaking!"

"I was talking about the roses," she laughed. "You're staring at my face."

"I was watching the glow around your face. It becomes you."

"It's the magic of a new life that's breathing inside my womb, a symbol of our love, a part of you and me. This baby will be the testament to our devotion and love."

"Have you picked a name for the magical baby?" asked Ashley, walking in with Priya.

"We will call him Narayan Hugh Prince," replied Ryan, placing his hand over her belly.

"Or Aryan Ruby Princessa, if it's a girl," Pearly finished his sentence.

"Aunty, can I feel my brother, Narayan, or sister Aryan?" asked Priya, jumping up and down.

Everyone burst into laughter.

Narayan Hugh Prince, an image of his father, Ryan, was born on December 31, 1919, sharing his birthday with his mother, thirty years later. Pryanka, Arman, and Priya were ecstatic to see their little brother. The children of the Ashram were ecstatic with the new playmate. The Priya Mansion began to pulsate again with the feet of happy children running around. In sharp contrast to the happy atmosphere at the Priya Mansion, the lives of the millions beyond the mansion began to deteriorate fast. The high casualty rates of Indian soldiers, soaring inflation, compounded by heavy taxation, a widespread influenza epidemic, the decline of trade in the post war period, began to escalate the human suffering in India to a dangerous level.

The unfulfilled promise of Swaraj began to cause disillusionment among Indian soldiers. The political leaders began to feel betrayed by the false promises of Swaraj when in lieu of Swaraj, the British offered the 1919 Government Act of Reforms; a dual system of government, Diarchy, which Annie Besant called: *Unworthy of England to offer and India to accept.*

The people began to rally behind the radical leaders who had been building revolutionary networks in foreign countries to end colonialism. A large number of Indian soldiers had smuggled arms into India during the First World War to overthrow the British rule. The government suppressed the revolution by the passing of the *Rowlett Act*, known as the *Black Act*. This act vested the Viceroy's government with extraordinary powers to quell sedition by silencing the press, detaining the political activists without trial, and arresting any suspect without a warrant.

In protest of the Black Act, the leaders called a nationwide cessation of work agitation.

Unfortunately the non-violent agitation culminated on 13 April 1919, in the notorious *Jallianwala Garden Massacre* of Amritsar in Punjab.

A thoughtless British military commander, General Reginald Dyer, blocked the main entrance of the garden and ordered his soldiers to fire into an unarmed and unsuspecting crowd; killing 5,000 men, women, and children and wounding 1100, who had assembled at *Jallianwala Bagh*, in defiance of the ban. The tragedy shattered all hopes of goodwill towards the British; paving the way towards full blown *Purana Swaraj, and Full Indian Independence Movement*, led by multiple revolutionary leaders like Lala Lajpat Rai, Shahid Bhagat Singh, Shahid Udham Singh in Punjab, Subhash Chander Bose in Bengal and moderates like Nehru and Gandhi in Maharashtra. It led to an unending chain of Stayagraha and mass internments.

At the same time, a big political revolution along the lines of Indian Independence Movement broke out in Burma, a British Colony in 1920. A group of Burmese students and intellectuals began to organize against colonial rule; *giving birth to the rise* of Burmese nationalism along the ideals of Gandhi, Nehru, and Marx.

Burma's educated elite began to demand a greater say in the running of the governmental machinery. Huge public protests by students broke out at the Rangoon University. An increasing discontent spread through the countryside. The impoverished farmers began to prepare for a massive peasant revolt. The rice crops had failed, and there was growing resentment against Indians. The British rulers rushed to quell the uprising by recruiting soldiers from the marginalised ethnic groups in Burma and transferring officers from India.

Colonel Ryan Hugh Prince was immediately dispatched to Burma where he served for nine years (1920 -1930). He was allowed to come home every three years for three months.

"Wait for me. Your love will bring me back. I will return," he promised each time he left.

As promised he always returned safely. Pearly and Narayan heaved the sigh of relief, each time he came back. And when he departed, they looked forward to the next homecoming in three years. This went on until Ryan returned home for good in

December 1929; taking early retirement from the British Indian Army in 1930.

He spent the magical next two years with Pearly and his thirteen year old son, Narayan until the fateful day when someone knocked on their door and changed everything.

DISAPPEARANCE OF THE PRINCE, 1932
THE ACCIDENT

I'm going away to a place where angels go; I shall be doing what angels do.
Should you, darling, ever lose your way; you'll find my soul surrounding you.

"The house is awfully quiet today. Where's everyone," asked Matthew, placing the box on the table.

"Princessa, Ryan, and Narayan have gone to the fair," replied Ashley. "What's in that box?"

"I bought some rare artifacts from the royal auction," replied Matthew, unwrapping the items in the box.

"Matthew, these are exquisite pieces of jewellery! Who did they belong to?"

"These pieces of jewellery once belonged to the legendary Rani Jhansi of India, the brave queen, who fought alone against one hundred British soldiers to protect her honour. These were auctioned today among many other items. We will display these at the 10th Anniversary of the Princessa and Scott Art Centre next month."

"With your collection of the rare colonial artifacts and priceless paintings of Daniel and Pearly, our art centre has become one of the most sought after centers in India. Why don't we open the store in England? Ever since the children left with Uncle Ed, the house does not feel the same and Narayan feels terribly lonely, too. I think we should seriously consider moving to England."

"Yes, the political climate is getting more and more volatile here every day. It would be wise to leave the country before the civil war breaks out. Now that Ryan has retired, what's holding us? I will talk to Ryan and you talk to Pearly. I'm going to put this box in the safe. We will surprise Ryan and Pearly at the anniversary of the art centre."

"Grandma, look what I got on my arm?" Narayan came jumping into the room, all excited.
"The bright red rose on your arm. Looks great!"
"Look at my arm," laughed Ryan, displaying the rose on his arm.
"And mine," said Pearly, pulling up her sleeve.
"Identical tattoos! Just like Symoune; you love Indian festivals and tattoos."
"What kind of posters are those?"
"Narayan bought some posters of Gandhi. He's a Gandhi fan," said Ryan.
"Aunty, can you pour some tea?" asked Pearly, picking up at the letters. "Whose letters are those?"
"Those are from Father Elliot and Annie."
"What did they write?"
"They are in an ashram in Gujarat, working with hundreds of Gandhi volunteers. They're undertaking a massive educational campaign to protect the interests of Hindu widows and the untouchables."
"Sounds exciting! What else did Father Elliot say?"
"Father writes about the dreadful plight of Hindu widows in Gujarat. The widows are abandoned by their families as soon as their husbands die; their heads are shaved and all their possessions are confiscated. They are forced to survive on charity. Many are reduced to begging on the streets and are not allowed to remarry. Gandhi has initiated the widow remarriage and untouchable integration campaign."
"Those are much needed reforms," remarked Matthew. "The British viceroys did try to push for social reforms at the turn of the century, but they faced so much opposition against the abolishing of Suttee that they gave up the idea of meddling into the social and religious practices of the Hindus. You know that Suttee, the immolation of women on their husband's funeral pyre, is still being practiced in India," he added.
"I think the British were successful in ending the Cult of Thugge, which was such a menace," said Ryan. "I've read hair-raising tales of the evil deeds that were committed by the twisted

devotees in the name of the Goddess Kali."

"What did Annie write, aunty?" inquired Pearly.

"Annie is busy with her newspaper *'Awakening.'* She is educating the public against child marriages (Bal Vivah), the practices of living with more than one wife, honour killings, and the rigid caste system—denying the untouchables the right to vote."

"Those practices must be abandoned. Saya was a victim of some of those practices. I read the other day that the British asked Gandhi how they can extend untouchables the right to vote when the Hindus refuse to consider them as an element of the nation's life," commented Ryan.

"How did Gandhi answer?" asked Pearly.

"He replied by adopting an untouchable girl as his daughter and she's living with his family in the ashram. With his initiative, the Indian National Congress has passed the resolution renaming the untouchables as Harijans, or the people of God, and recognising them as part of the nation," said Ryan.

"Well, if anyone can change hearts, Gandhi can," said Matthew. "Remember how he changed the British ruling on the salt tax through the mass Civil Disobedience Movement last year, in 1931. He marched to Dandi with 100,000 followers and broke the British law by teaching people how to make their own salt."

"And now he's teaching them how to start their own industries by spinning the Charkha–wheel," said Ryan.

"Too bad he has been arrested for that and sentenced to six years of imprisonment," said Pearly.

"No. He has been released and invited to participate in the First Round Table Conference in England. The British government has promised to listen to his demand of Swaraj," replied Ashley.

"I'm not surprised," replied Matthew. "Each time the British government imprisons Gandhi, thousands of Indians offer non-violent arrests. The prisons aren't big enough to handle massive arrests. They can't punish Gandhi, because the guy is non-violent. They end up letting him go and he starts another Stayagraha—the civil disobedience movement. The British are baffled."

"What a Guy!" laughed Ashley. "The British have more

problems dealing with Gandhi than with the entire British Empire. They dare not underestimate this well-mannered, polite man who commands so much respect from all over the world and transcends all barriers."

"The British can't underestimate the strength of the revolutionaries either," remarked Ryan, looking at Devdas waiting to speak with him. "They hang one revolutionary and a hundred more spring up. Look how Bhagat Singh, Rajguru and Sukhdev threw the bomb in the legislative assembly to protest the Labour Act in broad daylight and have become the famous Indian Martyrs of 1932 and are being respected as much as Gandhi. Mark my words that one of the revolutionaries is going to take down General Dyer for gunning down hundreds of innocent Indians in the Jallianwala Garden Massacre. It's only a matter of time."

"What do you want, Devdas? Why are you standing there?" asked Ryan, standing up.

"A man is here to see you, Colonel Sahib" coughed Devdas, interrupting the intellectual discourse.

"Who?" Ryan raised his eyebrows.

"He said that he met you in Burma. Shall I show him in Sahib?"

"It must be, my friend, Bali. He has relocated to Kulu. I'll greet him myself," smiled Ryan walking out.

"Ryan, why don't you and Pearly accompany me to Kulu?" asked Bali at the breakfast table.

"It's a place worth visiting. Kulu is called the valley of hundred temples and thousand deities."

"I don't know about Princessa, but I would love to go," smiled Ryan.

"I wish I could go, honey," replied Pearly. "But I have to help Narayan with his art festival."

"Would you mind if I go with Bali? I've been cooped up here ever since I came back from Burma. I want to do something adventurous."

"Then come with me to Kulu," encouraged Bali. "We've so much catching up do, man to man. Besides, Kulu is breathtaking at this time of the year. We will visit Manali, Lahul, Spiti, and the Rohtang Pass at the foot of the Himalayas, the place of the glaciers. Is that adventurous enough for you?"

"It depends on Princessa. Can I go for one week, honey?" pleaded Ryan.

"I don't mind your going, but the idea of you driving back alone through the zig zag valley spooks me."

"Honey, if I made it through the first world war and some of the most dangerous places in Burma, I will make it out of the Kulu valley. I'm an expert driver. Don't worry?"

"Pearly, let him go," said Matthew. "The man needs an adventure. Go pack his bags, sweetie."

"On one condition—you'll send me a telegram as soon as you reach Kulu and before your departure."

"Agreed," smiled Ryan. "Where's my son, Narayan? I need his permission before I go."

"Narayan, can I talk to you about something?"

"Daddy, ever since Pryanka, Arman, and Priya left for England to live with Uncle Ed, I feel terribly lonely here. Swami told me that he's sending Nareshwer to England in the fall. I'm seriously thinking of going to England and live with my brothers and sisters. Uncle Matthew and Aunt Ashley think it's a good idea. Dad, can I go to England with Nareshwer this fall?"

"I've already discussed this matter with Uncle Matthew and your mom. If you really want to be with your brothers and sisters, then we will all move to England together. There's nothing holding us here. Why don't you hold the thought and we will discuss it further when I come back? In the meantime hold on to this symbol of my love for you," said Ryan, placing a gold coin on Narayan's palm.

"Thank you, dad. I'll look forward to moving to England," said Narayan with a hug.

"Princessa, hold on to this rose as a symbol of my love," he said planting a kiss on her forehead. "Take care of your mom for me, Narayan," Ryan winked at Narayan.

"Promise to come back in one week, daddy?" reminded Narayan.

"I'll come back like I never left. All you've to do is wait for me," assured Ryan, driving off.

"Ryan, I think you should wait until the rain stops," insisted Bali, looking at the sky. "The roads can be quite treacherous around here."

"No. The rain might not stop for another week. I'll be stranded," replied Ryan.

"But the weather does not look promising. I insist."

"No. I promised Pearly and Narayan to be back home in one week. I can't let them down," replied Ryan, packing his bags. "I've been through worse weather than this. If I get out now, I could be in Pathankot by 9.00 p.m. I intend to stay at the hotel tonight and head for Simla tomorrow morning. I've already sent the telegram and if I'm not there by tomorrow evening they will send a search party out."

"But I'm afraid the snowflakes have started and the snow here . . ."

"No buts, please! My mind is made up. I'll manage. I miss home. Thanks for the terrific trip!"

"I don't feel comfortable in letting you go in this weather."

"Don't forget that you're talking to a soldier. Now, where's my salute?"

"So long soldier," Bali laughed, kicking his heels together and raising his arm in a salute.

"So long, soldier!" smiled Ryan, taking to the wheels and raising his thumb.

Ryan drove through the pounding rain for several hours before it dawned on him that he had made a dreadful mistake. The steady rain followed by the early snowfall made the roads disappear so quickly that suddenly Ryan found himself in the middle of nowhere. He glanced uncomfortably at the huge valley on one side and the Vyas River on the other side. With a wink of an eye, his van skidded and rolled off the road, landing on the top of the deep ditch, bruising him all over. With his heart racing, he managed to get out of the jeep and began to work his way up the steep hill.

There was no one in sight.

He began to walk on the highway; soaking wet, from head to toe.

"I should've listened to Bali," he thought, shivering.

Hoping to find a shelter, he kept on walking until it turned dark.

Suddenly out of nowhere a vehicle emerged on the scene

and stopped right in front of him.

"*Thank you, God.*"

"Where are you headed?" the gentleman, pulled his head out of the window and asked.

"I was on my way to Simla when my van rolled off the road."

"You can't go that way. The highway has been closed. I'm heading back to Manali. C'mon, Jump in."

"Thank you."

"My name is Brian Carl Hugh," the man introduced himself. "I own a tourist resort in Manali."

"I'm Colonel Ryan Hugh Prince and I live in Simla. I was going home from a vacation trip to Kulu."

"I was headed to Delhi to receive my wife and daughter. They're arriving from England tomorrow. I left my daughter when she was five years old. She is ten now."

"So who will receive them?" asked Ryan.

"I managed to wire someone to escort them to Manali after the snowstorm. Why don't you stay with me in Manali until the weather clears?"

"Thank you. I'll take you up on that."

"There's a bottle of whisky under the seat. It will warm you up."

Ryan opened the bottle and gulped it down his throat.

"Don't close the bottle yet," said Brian, reaching for the bottle. "Here let me a have a few gulps. There is my jacket and a shirt in the back seat. Why don't you change quickly before you catch cold?"

"Thank you," said Ryan, changing into the dry clothes. "So what's the name of your daughter?"

"Emily," he said, drinking from the bottle.

"A beautiful name!"

"She's a piece of my heart, the only reason I'm getting back with her mother, Natalie. Emily has become a bridge between us."

"Sounds like a special bond."

"Yeah, a special bond indeed. There's nothing I wouldn't do for Emily. I've named my tourist resort after Emily," he said with a beautiful smile.

"Where do you come from?"

"I come from a very poor background. I was practically raised in the orphanages of Ireland, until I was nine. Natalie's father took me under his shelter and educated me. Natalie and I fell in love but the differences in our grooming and life styles tore us apart. I left Natalie and came to India. I made a lot of money and went back to England and she became pregnant. I fell in love with my daughter as soon as I laid eyes on her. I had the most wonderful five years with her before I came back to India to make more money. I built a chain of tourist resorts and sold them. I moved to Manali at the beginning of this month because my manager had to head back home to Ireland. Tell me about yourself."

"I retired from the British Indian army two years ago. I served in First World War and Burma. I live in Simla with my wife, Pearly, and son Narayan. My uncle Matthew and his wife Ashley live with us. Their three children have gone to live with my uncle in England and now we are planning to move there as well."

They kept on chatting until Ryan closed his eyes.

He woke at the sound of a big bang.

The vehicle they were traveling in smashed in front of his eyes into the hill bursting into flames. Brian's body was pushed out of the van with such force that it landed on the ground making an earth shattering sound. Ryan's body rolled out of the van on the dead cold pavement, catching fire.

Oozing with blood, Ryan kicked at the fire, feeling torn from limb to limb. He managed to crawl a few feet towards Brian but the tearing pain inside his body and mind knocked him out. He fell a few yards away from Brian internalising the dead silence, broken occasionally by the smouldering fire engulfing the vehicle.

The two lay motionless in the blanket of darkness.

The freezing rain kept burying their bodies deeper and deeper under the snow with the each passing hour.

No one arrived and no one moved . . .

"There's a telegram from daddy," yelled Narayan, tipping the delivery man. "He's arriving tomorrow."

"The news we've been waiting for," said Matthew, closing the book. "Let's call it a night, Ashley?"

"Yes, I'm tired," Ashley yawned.

"Wait, where's the telegram, aunty?" asked Pearly.

"I think Narayan took it to his room," said Ashley, getting up.

"Narayan, where's the telegram?" asked Pearly, knocking on his door.

"Under my pillow, mom," said Narayan. "I want to keep it there."

"I'll bring it back. I want to read it," said Pearly pulling the telegram from under his pillow and walking to her room. As she opened the door, a look of surprise emerged on her face.

"I don't believe my eyes," she exclaimed. "Ryan, weren't you supposed to arrive tomorrow?"

Ryan kept on writing as if he never heard anything.

"Ryan, what are you writing that's more important than answering me?"

"I thought you would be pleased to see me, Princessa?" replied Ryan, putting the pen down.

"I'm, but it is physically impossible for a person to be in two places at the same time."

"I had to keep my promise to return before going away again. Come here, I don't have much time."

"What do you mean," asked Pearly, sitting on the edge of the bed. "Where are you going?"

"I'm going to a place far, far away," spoke Ryan, putting his hand under her chin.

"Ryan, what kind of a joke is this?" demanded Pearly, bewildered.

"It is not a joke, Princessa," said Ryan tensely.

"Then what would you call it?"

"I will call it a mystery."

"Why would you call it a mystery?"

"Because you, my Princessa, are going to lose your Prince again."

"Will I be able to find my Prince?"

"The answer lies in whether you will have faith in the return of the prince."

"Can you tell me where my prince is going?"

"The clues are on that paper," said Ryan, pointing to the writing pad.

Pearly picked up the writing pad and read:
I'm going away to a place where angels go; I shall be doing what angels

do.
Should you, darling, ever lose your way; you'll find my soul surrounding you.

"What kind of a mystery is it, Ryan?" screamed Pearly, waking up, wide eyed.

"Oh, my God, Ryan wasn't there. It was a dream. A dreadful dream —"

A week passed and there was no sign of Ryan. The family contacted the police. The police searched the highway from one end to the other. Bali became concerned and organized a private search party with volunteers, but they came up with nothing until one day the police van stopped at their front door.

"Sir Matthew has Colonel returned home yet?" asked Inspector Anand, shaking hands.

"No. We were hoping you would have some news?"

"I'm afraid I'm a bearer of bad news," said Inspector Anand, taking a long pause. "We have located the vehicle registered to your nephew but we have not been able to find him."

"Where did you find the vehicle?"

"Off the road on highway number ten," the inspector replied. "It appears that his vehicle rolled off the road and landed upon a ditch on the brink of River Vyas. We've searched the entire area. The divers have combed through the river. There's no sign of him. There's no place to take shelter within thirty miles around that area. He has simply disappeared. It is a mystery."

Colour drained from everyone's face.

Narayan rushed upstairs crying and Pearly fainted.

Matthew and Ashley rushed to comfort her.

"How far is Kulu from here, Sir?" asked Emily, moving impatiently in her seat.

"This is the fifth time you've asked him within the last ten minutes," said Natalie.

The escort smiled.

"I can't wait to see dad," replied Emily. "I wonder what my dad looks like. I wish we had a picture of him."

"Your dad hated to have his picture taken," said Natalie. "We don't have any pictures of him, honey."

"Mom, can you describe my dad to me again?"

"I've described him to you a million times before, honey."

"Do you mind if we described him together?"

"Slim and tall, curly blonde hair; blue eyes and a straight nose and he calls me Tinkle," they said together.

"Mrs. Hugh, welcome home, Madam," said the servant, showing them in.

"My name is Natalie and this is my daughter, Emily and what's your name?"

"You can call me Madho, Madam."

"Madho, where's my daddy? Why is he not here to receive us?" asked Emily, looking cross.

"Your dad is in the hospital, resting comfortably, Miss Emily," replied the servant.

"What hospital; why?"

"He met with an accident last week when he was on his way to Delhi to receive you."

"Is my daddy all right?"

"Yes, he is. Even though, I've never met him, Miss Emily."

"How come he employed you?"

"He didn't employ me. A friend who worked here before me employed me after your dad was admitted to the hospital. My friend had to quit to look after his ailing mother. He told me before he left that the master was resting comfortably. The doctor is waiting to see you."

"Dr. Gupta, my husband is bandaged from head to foot," said Natalie. "He never opened his eyes once when we visited him. I believe his condition is more critical than you would have us believe."

"No, Mrs. Hugh. Your husband's condition is stable," replied the doctor, removing his glasses.

"He has no life threatening wounds. No broken bones. He's responding well to the medication and is resting comfortably. The bandages will come off within two weeks. As soon as the effect of the medicine wears off, he will start communicating and we will discharge him from the hospital."

"Why do I feel that you haven't told me everything?"

"You are very perceptive, Mrs. Hugh."

"Please call me Natalie."

"Very well, Natalie. I should make you aware of one thing," said the doctor, taking a long pause. "Brian is still in a state of shock. Based on my observations, I believe that he might suffer from a temporary, and I emphasise the word temporary loss of memory which is quite normal in an accident like this."

"You mean he may not recognise me and Emily?"

"As I said before it may only be temporary," said the doctor, handing her a bag.

"I want you to have this bag of the clothing he was wearing. If you and your daughter are patient with him, he will return to his normal self much sooner. He was very lucky to have survived the accident. The poor guy who was travelling with him didn't make it."

"Was there someone else travelling with him?"

"Yes. He was a white man. Since there was no identification on him, we had to bury him yesterday."

"How could you bury him without trying to find out who he was?"

"We took pictures of him, from different angles. I've placed the pictures in this bag in a hope that you would advertise in your white community and locate his family. Now if you'll excuse me, I've other patients to see."

Emily spent every waking hour looking after her dad at the hospital. The staff at the hospital was struck by the devotion of a ten-year old daughter for her father. Emily was deeply excited on the day Brian's bandages were to come off and couldn't stop chatting about it with everyone at the hospital.

"Mom, the doctor said that dad's going to be fully awake today and he will definitely notice me. What should I wear? I want to look my best today," she asked with stars in her eyes.

"Everything looks good on you, sweetie," replied Natalie.

"What's dad's favorite colour, mom?"

"It is white, sweetie."

"I'll wear the white dress with frills on the sleeves. Does daddy like frills, mom?"

"Yes, sweetie. He likes frills on you."

"Mom, since dad can't remember anything, I think I should remind him that he used to call me Tinkle?"

Natalie nodded.

"Sweetie, what are those baskets of sweets and blankets doing in the living room?"

"Madho told me that we should take baskets of sweets to the hospital to celebrate dad's recovery," said Emily. "So I'm going to distribute the sweets right after the bandages are opened. Madho promised to take me to the temple of the Manali Goddess to distribute the blankets to the poor. You could stay with daddy till I come back."

"Sure," smiled Natalie.

Emily stationed herself directly in front of Brian, overshadowing Natalie when the bandages came off.

"Daddy, you look exactly as mom had described you," screamed Emily, clapping her hands and ignoring his confused look. "Slim and tall with curly blonde hair, blue eyes, and a straight nose. Please call me Tinkle, daddy. Please call me Tinkle."

Everyone burst into laughter except Natalie.

She felt like someone had splashed a thousand pails of icy water on her.

The man who sat before her was not Brian.

He was a total stranger.

"If that man in the hospital is not Brian, then where's Brian?" thought Natalie, rushing home. She opened the bag which doctor Gupta had given her and began to examine the pictures. A look of horror rose to her eyes when she examined the pictures.

"Oh, my God, these are the pictures of Brian," wailed Natalie. "It was my Brian who died that night."

"How shall I tell Emily that her loving daddy is dead?"

"Emily's world will fall apart."

"What should I do? We are in a strange country. How will we survive?" Natalie became frantic with horror.

She cried her eyes out until an idea popped up in her head.

"I'm not going to tell Emily and break her heart," resolved Natalie. "I'll grieve privately for Brian. The stranger in the hospital does not remember who he is. I will go to the hospital tomorrow and bring the stranger home. He will have to fill in for Brian."

Natalie pulled herself together and hid the bag in the suitcase, carefully locking the closet.

She washed her face, combed her hair, and put on a cheerful look for her Emily.

Despite the mental confusion, Brian's condition started to improve quickly. Emily kept hanging around him day and night. She read stories to him and practically danced to his every move. Natalie had never seen her daughter happier than when she was with Brian. Brian began to respond warmly to her hugs and listen to her stories with a glimmer in his eyes. He looked forward to being with them and even laughed when Emily told him that she had been going to the temple of the Goddess Manali, every day with Madho for his speedy recovery.

Though Brian remained aloof with Natalie; the connection and chemistry between the father and the daughter bloomed and became subliminal.

"Natalie, I hope you don't mind if I can't share the bedroom with you until my memory returns," asked Brian timidly. "I don't feel comfortable because you are a complete stranger to me at the moment."

"I'm so sorry, you can't remember anything or anyone, Brian, but we are here now and we will do everything in our power to help you get your memory back," said Natalie, holding his hand.

"Daddy, you can't forget me because I won't let you," laughed Emily, putting her head on his shoulder. "I'm your Tinkle and I've more love in my heart for you than any daughter has for her dad on this earth."

Brian smiled through his eyes before confusion took over.

RETURN OF THE PRINCE, 1945
MYSTERY OF THE ROSE

A ruby and a pearl, a bright red rose and a face is driving me crazy. Those are the only real things in my life, everything else seems hazy.

Ten years passed and there was no news of Ryan. He simply vanished without a trace. Every search party organized by Matthew came out empty handed, but Pearly and Narayan remained steadfast in their faith in the return of their prince. They kept on waiting for his return each day.

"I will come back. I always do. Wait for me," the words of Ryan echoed in their ears.

In the meantime, the political climate for the British in India turned hostile after the end of the Second World War. The fact that the British government had declared the war without consulting the Indian leaders had created hard feelings. The disillusionment of the 250,000 British Indian soldiers whose contributions were totally ignored after the war, coupled with the broken promise of Swaraj enraged the Indians masses. They took up arms and rose in revolt against the British Empire, chanting the slogan of "Do or Die." A wave of riots spread through the country and the British began to lose their grip on India rapidly. The Indian National Congress reacted by passing the Quit India Resolution at the Bombay session on August 8, 1942 which acted as oil on the fire. Gandhi challenged the British government by organizing the Civil Disobedience Movement known as the historical "Quit India Movement."

"I want you to act as an independent nation and do not follow the orders of the British," said Gandhi, leading the movement. "I want every Indian to participate in the non-violent civil disobedience movement and show the British that we will settle for nothing short of full Independence of India. I want you to march through the streets of India chanting the slogan—Quit India, Quit India now," he added.

The British retaliated by arresting Gandhi and the entire Indian National Congress. They banned the party. The British move angered the people and the movement turned violent. People banded together and held large-scale protests and demonstrations all over the country. Strikes were called. The people marched through the streets chanting:

Quit India, Quit India now! Jai India, Jai Gandhi!

The revolutionaries turned violent and sabotaged the country. The Indian underground organisations carried out bomb attacks on allied supply convoys. Government buildings were set on fire; electricity lines were disconnected and transport and communication lines were severed. A total over 100,000 arrests were made nationwide. Mass fines were levied, bombs were airdropped, and the demonstrators were subjected to public flogging. Suddenly, the British woke up to the fact that it was not possible to rule India anymore and they must pack up their bags and leave the country.

"Brian, we must leave the country before a civil war breaks out," pleaded Natalie. "We can't continue to stay here. Life is getting dangerous."

"I'm afraid, you and Tinkle would have to go without me," replied Brian, completing his drawing. "I can't leave now when I'm beginning to get the flashbacks."

"We won't go without you, Brian," said Natalie, with a touch of frustration. "You are not remembering anything that's relevant to you. You keep sketching a mysterious woman with a rose and a boy who resembles you. It could be nothing more than a repressed childhood memory syndrome."

"No. The boy in my dream has a name, Narayan."

"But Narayan and Brian are similar names."

"Except for the fact that Narayan is an Indian name."

"There's no connection of this name with you, if you ask me," argued Natalie. "Narayan means God in the Indian language. You hear Madho chanting the prayer Swami Narayan, Swami Narayan all the time. Your subconscious has somehow picked up the name and transferred it to the imaginary boy."

"It's true that the name Narayan triggered the image of the

boy, but the boy in my dream is real. I talk to him and we connect well in my dream."

"And how does this boy communicate with you in your dreams?"

"He tries. I can see his lips move but I can't make out what he says."

"It's the trauma of the accident that's generating these images with no relevance whatsoever. You should forget about these images and concentrate on finishing the packing. We are leaving this week."

"No. The boy is not the only one I see. I also dream about a woman holding a bright red rose. She's wearing rubies and pearls. The rose, the rubies, and pearls mean something. The woman and the boy are more real to me than anything else."

"Do you communicate with her in your dream?"

"Yes! I tell her that I'll come back. I always do. Wait for me. I know you think it is irrelevant. But why don't I dream about anything relevant? Why don't I dream about Ireland or you and your father who took me in? Why do I dream about being a soldier in the First World War instead?"

"I don't know," hesitated Natalie. "What do the woman and the boy look like?"

Like this drawing," said Brian, finishing the drawing. "Come and see for yourself."

Natalie stood before the canvas wide eyed.

"Where did I see that woman?" she thought hard.

She turned and tossed all night until she remembered where she had seen the mystery woman. She sneaked out of her bed and pulled the hidden bag from the suitcase. She unfolded the pants and a photo dropped from the pocket on her lap.

She felt like she was struck by lightning.

With shaking hands she picked up the picture and saw the face of the mystery woman sitting snug with Brian, holding a rose. A teenager, bearing a striking resemblance to Brian, stood behind them, smiling.

"Dear God, Brian is remembering his past. What should I do?" prayed Natalie, feeling weak in her knees." I've committed a sin by hiding this picture. I was supposed to advertise the picture but I didn't want to lose him. I did it for Emily. I can't tell him now. He never will

forgive me. It's too late now. We will leave for Ireland this week. He will forget about these images sooner or later."

"Pearly, I must talk to you, honey," said Matthew, holding her hand.

"If it's about leaving the country, my answer is no," replied Pearly. "Narayan and I will not go without Ryan. Our minds are made up. If you want us to accompany you, find Ryan."

"I've looked everywhere for him. He is not to be found," replied Matthew. "You must face the fact that there is a good chance that he might be . . ."

"He's not dead," shrieked Pearly, picking up her purse and running out of the door.

"I didn't mean that, honey. Come back." Matthew ran after Pearly.

"Leave her alone, Matthew," said Ashley, stopping him from following Pearly. "Give her some space. She can see the writing on the wall and knows that she must accompany us to England this week. She is a mother and won't put her son's life in jeopardy. She will come around."

"I'm afraid, Ashley, that if we don't leave now, we won't be able to leave at all; at least not alive. India is going to be partitioned soon and the civil war between Hindus and Muslims is about to break. According to the prediction, it is going to be the bloodiest civil war in the history of the world. Millions and millions of people are going to be butchered by the angry mobs. We don't want to get caught up in the bloodbath."

"Why don't we concentrate on finishing the packing, hoping that Pearly and Narayan will join us?"

Matthew nodded his head.

Burning with agony, Pearly wandered down the hill into the streets of the Mall. She kept on pacing the footpaths aimlessly in the pouring rain until she saw a small sign in the window — Luxmi, The Psychic. Pearly walked timidly inside the shop and sat down in front of the gypsy girl.

"Still looking for the lost one?" asked the gypsy girl.

"Why don't you tell me?" replied Pearly.

"Why don't you put your hands over this crystal ball?"

"Both hands?" asked Pearly, wiping her hands on her dress.

The girl nodded, closing her eyes and placing her hands over Pearly's.

"The people who think he's dead are wrong," she said slowly, opening her eyes.

"What do you mean?" asked Pearly, looking surprised.

"The man you're looking for is alive and well."

"Tell me more." Pearly sounded breathless. "How do I find him?"

"He will find you?"

"I don't understand."

"He's about to walk back into your life as mysteriously as he walked out."

"When? I'm running out of time."

"He will be on board on the biggest journey of your life. And —"

"What?"

"You must do one thing and you will never be apart again. Come closer."

"Why did you whisper the message in my ear?" asked Pearly.

"The message is to be transmitted quietly for it to come out true."

"What do I owe you?"

"Just thanks. Your suffering is going to come to an end."

"Thank you from the bottom of my heart."

"Your devotion has defeated your demon. Go home and rejoice!" the gypsy girl smiled.

"Why are you sitting in the dark and crying as if someone has died," asked Pearly, walking in.

"Someone has died," replied Ashley. "Father Elliot and Annie were shot in the head today."

"No. Why?" Pearly felt like the earth shattered beneath her feet.

"Sometimes the things we create are the ones that destroy us," said Matthew.

"Is that what happened with Father Elliot and Annie? Who could've killed them?"

"The people who opposed their widow remarriage and untouchable reforms. They killed them in broad daylight to end their campaign."

"Pearly, we must leave India together this week. Father Elliot and Annie's sacrifice must not go in vain. We must learn from it. They would've wanted us to go together. It's getting dangerous outside."

"I'm prepared to go on one condition," sobbed Pearly, putting her arms around Ashley and Matthew. "If you would do this one last favour for me," Pearly whispered into Matthew's ear.

"Consider it done, honey," replied Matthew, releasing a sigh of relief.

"Emily, have you packed everything?" asked Natalie, putting labels on the suitcases.

"Yes, everything is packed except the sketch of the mystery woman and the boy. Daddy, can you hand me the picture, please?" asked Emily, going down on her knees on the floor, holding the scissors and the tape.

Brian did not answer. He kept staring at the sketch on the wall.

"Daddy—?"

"Tinkle, I will accompany you and your mom to Ireland on one condition."

"I accept any condition as long as you accompany us to Ireland."

"I'll take you to your grandpa's house and come back to India alone. I must look for that woman and the boy and find out the connection I have with them. I can't be expected to live in a place I don't remember," replied Brian, taking the picture off the wall and handing it to Emily.

"Agreed daddy," said Emily, picking up the newspaper from the table and spreading it on the floor to place the picture. As she bent forward to wrap the picture, her eyes grew large with surprise and she began to read the article.

"What's the matter, Tinkle?" asked Ryan and Natalie.

"Daddy, look here. There's a picture of you with the mystery woman and the boy matching your sketch. They exist. The headline says: A British Woman Desperately Looking for her Husband."

"What do you mean?" asked Brian, grabbing the newspaper and reading the article:

British Woman Desperately Searching for her Husband

Pearly Ruby Princessa, a British woman, belonging to Simla, is searching for her husband, Colonel Ryan Hugh Prince, who went missing on Sept. 10, 1932 during his trip back from Kulu. Dr. Narayan Hugh Prince, their only son, who was thirteen at the time when his father went missing, is now twenty-six years of age.

Dr. Narayan, who is the exact image of his father, is a co-owner of the Princessa and Scott Art Centre in Simla. His Uncle Retired General Matthew Scott and his wife Dr. Ashley Scott had organized several search teams to locate Colonel Ryan Hugh Prince and they did find the vehicle he was travelling in on the highway number ten, but were not successful in finding him. If anyone has any information about Colonel Prince, please contact us at the following address and telephone number.

"Daddy, you looked exactly like the guy in that picture when I saw you the first time."

The colour drained from Natalie's face. She stood staring blankly at Brian.

"Daddy, why don't you say anything?" asked Emily, looking distraught.

"I've to leave for Simla at once," said Ryan, folding the newspaper and putting it into his bag.

"Wait, daddy, we'll go with you."

The picture and the article had a profound effect on Brian. His mind began to unfold the images of his past life with Pearly and Narayan and he sat still at times; trying to put together the pieces of the puzzle.

"I remember," he exclaimed, breaking into tears. "I remember the explosion. Someone was with me."

"Who was with you, daddy?"

"I see two accidents. I see my vehicle rolling off the road and landing at the edge of a ditch," he murmured, wiping the sweat off his cheek. "I see myself walking in deep snow and a vehicle approaching."

"Daddy, think slowly," said Emily, comforting him. "It will come to you."

"I remember the face of the gentleman in the other vehicle," burst out Brian, breaking into tears, as they approached Simla. "He was tall and slim with curly blond hair and a straight nose.

He told me his name. It's on the brink of my tongue. Oh—"

"We've approached the Mall, Sahib," said the driver, slowing down.

"Stop the car in front of the Princessa and Scott Art Centre," said Brian, hurrying out of the vehicle and walking to the shop followed by Emily and Natalie.

"I remember this place," he whispered looking around. "There used to be that painting on the wall. Oh, there it is," he added, walking towards the painting and standing still."

He kept staring at the painting until someone said, "May I help you, sir?"

Ryan turned around sharply, colliding with the woman. They both got back on their feet, feeling awkward.

"I'm sorry," said Brian.

The words froze on his lips as their eyes met. They stood still staring at each other.

"Can I help you with something, Sir?" interrupted Narayan breaking the silence. "This is my mother, Pearly Ruby Princessa and I am Dr. Narayan Hugh Prince . . ."

Their eyes locked into an intense gaze.

"Do I know you from somewhere, Sir? You look so . . . familiar . . . Sir," Narayan said.

"You look exactly like I did when I was your age," said Brian.

"That's because you are his father," said Pearly, looking dazed. "Don't you recognize your dad, Narayan? Your daddy has come back!"

"Yes, that's daddy! You came back," Narayan opened his arms.

In a split second, Ryan's memory came back and he screamed with joy.

"Yes, I remember who I am. I'm colonel Ryan Hugh Prince and you are Princessa and my son, Narayan. I've been dreaming about you since eternity," he said, wrapping his arms around them.

"Daddy! Daddy! Daddy!"

"Ryan, you are back . . ."

"I think there is some mistake here," interrupted Natalie, pushing her tears back. "His name is Brain Carl Hugh and he is my husband, not yours."

"No. He's Ryan Hugh Prince," said Pearly, vehemently. "He is my husband and my son, Narayan's father. Don't you see the unmistakable resemblance between the two?"

"No. That resemblance is coincidental. You can't prove it that he is not Brian Carl Hugh. Let's go Brian," said Natalie, holding Ryan's arm.

"Wait!" yelled Pearly. "I can prove it beyond the shadow of a doubt that he is Ryan."

"How can you do that?" asked Natalie, looking tense.

"The three of us have a bright red rose tattoo on our right arms. C'mon Narayan, show her the rose? I bet Ryan has the same tattoo on his arm," added Pearly, pulling up her sleeve and displaying the rose.

"Yes, I do," said Ryan, baring his arm.

"We got these tattoos in a fair shortly before Ryan went missing," said Pearly. "I hope you're satisfied."

"I'm beginning to remember everything," said Ryan. "I just remembered taking a ride from a man. He told me that his name was Brian Carl Hugh and that he had daughter, he adored. He told me that her name was Emily. I remember the explosion and saw Brian's body pushed out of the vehicle with such force that he didn't raise his head again. I crawled towards him but fainted and lost my memory."

"I—I—I'm guilty of deceiving you," said Natalie, shivering. "You—you—you had lost your memory and I—I had no choice but to pretend that you were Brian. I—I did this to save Emily because she loved Brian so much that her whole world would've crashed without him."

"How could you do that, mom? It was so cruel on your part not to let me mourn for my daddy even for one second. I'll never forgive you," cried Emily, dashing out into the crowded street.

Natalie ran after her, colliding with the car. She fell to the ground instantly, smeared with blood.

"Please God, don't let her die," Emily dashed back throwing herself over her crushed body and crying.

Ryan, Pearly and Narayan rushed to the scene, horrified.

"Call the ambulance, someone," yelled Ryan, pulling Natalie's blood-soaked head on his lap.

"Forgive me," whispered Natalie, holding tightly to Ryan's

hand. "I did this for my daughter, Emily. Even though you could never be a husband . . . to me. You . . . were a perfect father to Emily."

"You're not going to die. We've called the ambulance," said Ryan.

"Please tell me that you've . . . forgiven me."

"I forgive you," cried Ryan.

"Promise me that you'll not abandon . . . Brian's precious, Tinkle. Promise me . . ."

"I promise you that Tinkle will never lose her dad."

"We'll all take care of her," said Narayan, putting an arm around Emily.

Natalie closed her eyes and succumbed to her injuries. Narayan, Pearly and Ryan put their arms around Emily and cried.

"The time has come to say farewell," said Matthew, looking tearfully at the room full of friends. "We are gathered here this morning to mark the end of an era and to celebrate the new beginning, because every end is a new beginning."

The room echoed with the sound of applause.

"Let us mark the end of the era of colonialism and the birth of a new and free India."

"To a new and free India!" said the crowd.

"Tonight we remember our friends, Father Elliot and Annie who sacrificed their lives for the Indian freedom movement and the social reforms. Please give a big hand of applause to Father Elliot and Annie!"

"To Father Elliot and Annie," cheered the crowd.

"Tonight we honour the freedom fighters -- Annie Besant, Sri Auro Bindo Ghosh, Mother Mira Richard, Mahatama Gandhi and people like Swami Krishna who kindled into the members of our family the spark of freeing India. I want to thank all our Indian friends who allowed us to work with you in promoting the cause of Swaraj. I speak on behalf of every member of my family when I say that we are as proud of India and Gandhi as you are."

The sound of applause.

"This is the time to celebrate another new beginning as a family. Let's raise our glasses to Emily — the new addition to our family and to the Return of the Prince."

"To Emily and to the Return of the Prince!" shouted everyone.

"As we leave for the airport, we take with us the memory of the wonderful times we shared with you. Before I hand over the keys of the Priya Mansion to Swami Krishna, I would like to take one last look at this magical place, which will soon be transformed into Princessa and Matthew Ashram—an ashram for the children -- who will be called Children of Princessa and Matthew. Let's raise our glasses one more time to the hundreds of new Children of Princessa and Matthew."

"Let's drink to the Children of Princessa and Matthew," said the crowd.

The Scott and Princessa family members sat proudly as their van made its way to the international airport in Delhi, encountering the scenes of sabotage, burning buildings and countless marchers chanting on the roads:

Jai Mother India! Jai Gandhi! Jai Mother India! Jai Gandhi!
Vande Matram! Vande Matram! Vande Matram!

"Look, India is burning, Narayan," said Emily, pointing to the chaotic scenes outside. "There is disorder and chaos everywhere."

"Tinkle, India is not burning; India is glowing with the spirit of freedom—the spirit of Swatantra," corrected Narayan, patting her hand. "India is going through its metamorphosis. Out of the disorder and chaos, a new, free, and strong India is being born."

Ryan smiled, putting an arm around Pearly and continued reading her journal:

A tale of two nations, entering an era of new beginnings, coinciding with the love story of Pearly Ruby Princessa . . .

"You're writing our love story, Princessa?"

"And the story of our struggle and joy in the rebirth of India," she replied, placing her head on his shoulder.

A SPECIAL THANKS TO:

Shiellah Jay Todio, who monitored the development of my book from the beginning to the end, and became a powerful motivating force in the completion of this project.

Marcia Carroll, who edited the original manuscript and became my mentor, and my Guru.

Ryan Lynds, who worked hard with me on this daunting project.

Liz Bennett, who reviewed my first draft and loved it.

Swarup Nanda, Omkar Thakur and Oswald Pereira, Mishta Roy and Sirawon Khathing who welcomed me into the family of 'Leadstart Publishing' and their excellment teamwork.

My son, who provided valuable insights in writing this book.

My mother, father and grandfather, who believed that I could do no wrong, and taught me to love unconditionally.

My Angel Divine, who blessed me with the gift of creatively and art and helped me transition through my metamorphosis into a new beginning.

I'm slipping out of my oblivion and I'm feeling dazed.
Thanks for leading me out of my overwhelming maze.

Sukh D. H. Khokhar
June 15, 2012

SUKH D. H. KHOKHAR is a Canadian writer, poet and multi-dimensional artist. She is the author of *The Mystery of the Rose: The Return of the Prince* and illustrated mystical adventure, *Dark Mystery -- I'm a Demon. I'm a Ghost...*
E-books available at: amazon.com & BarnesandNoble.com

REFERENCES:

Eyewitness/oral history account of the British era by my Great-Grandfather, Captain Ram Singh, a freedom fighter, who served as A.D.C. to Lord Curzon and to Maharaja Bhupindra.

Wikipedia, the free encyclopedia articles on a) Indian Independence Movement b) World War 1, c) British Rule in Burma.

Wahididdin's Web - Living from the Heart: Gayatri Mantra-Upnishad (1, 13-14).

HISTORICAL BACKGROUND
THE CORONATION OF KING EDWARD VII, 1902

A.D.C. to Viceroy Lord Curzon   A.D.C. to Maharaja Bhupindra

The inspiration and historical background for the novel came from the life and times of my Great-Grandfather, Captain Ram Singh, who served as the aide-de-camp (A.D.C.) of Viceroy Lord Curzon. He commanded a contingent of 100 Sikh army men to England in 1902, to participate in the Coronation of King Edward VII. He had the distinct honour of being a royal guest for twenty-two days and was awarded the Order of the British Empire (O.B.E). The proceedings of the event are recorded in the Victoria & Albert Museum in England.

His contributions to India were in bringing fame to the Indian army by fighting meritoriously in the Sudan Campaigns of 1884-85 and 1897-98 on the North – West Frontiers of India in the 15th Sikh Battalion. He was awarded the title of Sardar Bahadur, meaning Brave Heart, for his bravery and awarded 125 acres of land. Following his retirement as A.D.C. of Lord Curzon in 1908, he was appointed as his aide-de-camp by His Highness, Maharaja Bhupindra of the Patiala State. He joined the Alkali Agitations of 1920's to fight for the freedom of India and relinquished the title of O.B.E. He was jailed with fellow freedom fighters from 1923 to 1926. He displayed enormous courage in standing up for the cause of recovering the *"Keys of the Golden Temple Treasury"* from the British in 1920, following the Jallianwala Garden massacre in 1919.